SUPER
NOVA

The Author would like to thank;

My awesome editor and friend:
James R. Woestman

My brilliant support tech and friend:
Robert J. Hornickel

My sweet friend and Beta reader:
Ginell McLean

Molly at We Got You Covered Book Design who always does an amazing job on my book covers and formatting. I'm so lucky to have found you!

My Caleb and Cammie who have been my biggest cheerleaders and the true joy of my life. I thank God everyday for giving you both to me. I love you more than you can ever know.

SKY WALKER

SUPER
NOVA

Cynthia L. McDaniel

SUPER NOVA

ISBN- 978-1-7325796-2-0

This book is lovingly dedicated to my lifelong friends,

who were a big inspiration to this series. You filled my childhood and teenage years with so much laughter and unforgettable memories, while helping me stay out of trouble and keeping me from becoming another statistic to my surroundings.

I love you, Amy, Kasi, Alicea, Kim, Tracy, Pam and Tina.

"...perhaps you were born for such a time as this."

- Esther 4:14 -

PREFACE

"YOU KNOW, YOU don't have to do this Claire," Johnny whispered, as we stood face to face, my hands holding tightly to his. I squeezed extra hard, hoping my grip would stop my body from trembling and somehow calm my nerves. Johnny was already stressed enough and if he knew how scared I was inside, he would immediately shut the whole press conference down.

"Johnny, I have...I have to," I stammered.

"No you don't," he said firmly. "You don't Claire. We can walk right out that door and you can quietly fade into the past. People forget. They move on and forget as soon as the next big thing comes along. They'll forget about you and your flying power and you'll become a folk tale or...or some kind of a myth." He pulled me closer. "We can move to some place where no one knows us and start our lives over."

My heart broke at the desperation in his voice. The thought of being with Johnny anywhere and spending my life with him made me catch my breath. I felt so loved and protected by him in this moment and wanted to give in to his plan, but I knew that was not possible. I had to give this press conference. I had no choice but to share my super power with the world. I was tired of hiding who I was and refused to live my life scared and afraid of the unknown.

"Johnny, I love you and I value your opinion so much," I said. "But I think you and I both know this has to be done. I don't want to hide anymore."

Johnny's eyes fell. I knew he loved me enough to trust my intuition and support whatever decision I made.

He kissed my forehead softly. "Let's go," he simply said. He gently took my hand and led me to the elevator that would take us down to the main lobby of the headquarters building at Ft. Campbell, where news reporters were awaiting our arrival.

I took a deep breath as the elevator door dinged. My life would never be the same again.

ONE

ONE OF MY favorite stories ever is the Biblical story of Queen Esther. Do you know that one? Simply put, she was miraculously chosen to be Queen of a land called Persia. An unlikely choice in that she was a commoner who eventually, because of her royal position, saved her people from a crazy man who plotted to wipe them off the face of the earth.

My mom would read that story to me and my sisters a lot when we were growing up, always emphasizing the last part of Esther 4:14 "...and who knows but that you have come to your royal position for such a time as this."

"There's a reason this has happened to you Claire," my mom said to me not long after she found out about my flying super power, as we sat on our back deck on a warm fall night. "You just have to find it."

"Does everything have to happen for a reason Mom?" I teased her. "Could it be that I'm just clumsy and fell onto an old crate that just *so happened* to be holding a secret government flying potion?"

Mom shot me an amused look. "So you're just clumsy Claire? Is that how you see it?"

I shrugged my shoulders as I looked up at the black, glittery sky. "I'm trying to find the positives in it, mom. I really am."

"They are there, positives and purpose and you will find them," she reassured me.

I smiled back at her as she quoted the Esther verse to me for probably the thousandth time. Above us the sky began to rumble and lightning cracked across the darkness. My body shivered uncontrollably as I rocked back and forth, the warm air around us, being sucked away and replaced by a frigid stinging rain.

"Gram!" I heard a male voice yell, pulling me away from my dream and my mom's kind smile and plunging me back into present reality. The wet metal boat I was laying in the bottom of, stung cold against my bare arms. As I slowly moved them off the floor, a clanking metal sound echoed on the bottom of the boat. I opened my eyes and looked down at my wrists that were zip tied together behind my back.

"Seriously Gram?" A man's voice asked in a thick New Jersey accent. "Ya forgot her ankle! Did ya forget that this chick can fly?"

I squinted my eyes at Gram giving him the meanest

stare I could, as he slammed an ankle cuff on me that was already attached to the side of the boat. Ok, so apparently they knew I could fly.

I watched the guys intently, trying to figure out what was happening and who they were. Just moments ago they had kidnapped me off my small island, in the dead of night while I slept. My first thought was drug smugglers, but they were well trained and too precise in what they were doing for that. I hadn't even heard them approach my island and I always slept with one eye open.

Then Commander Whitley's voice echoed through my mind. *"Claire, other countries are always spying on us... we worry you will become a target for them...a real life superwoman is something any government would love to add to their arsenal of knowledge."*

"Could that be a possibility?" I thought. *"Maybe this had something to do with the guys who had tried to kidnap me before."* But they didn't sound foreign, I argued with myself and their choice of vocabulary, though they were mostly quiet, was very Americanish.

"Alright, let's go! We're almost out of time!" I heard someone in the distance yell.

I shivered again in the bottom of the boat, my teeth chattering uncontrollably. All I had on was some sweats and a cami, but no one seemed to care. The rain fell even harder, cold and fast, drenching my body and turning my lips blue. My long curly brown hair was sopping wet and stuck to my shoulders and back.

The wind picked up speed considerably and I felt the

boat shudder as it pushed through the storm. No wonder why I hadn't heard it approaching. It barely made a sound, but now the rain beating against the ocean was deafening, as the waves grew bigger. We fought against them for a good twenty minutes before finally slowing down. All at once, everyone began to scurry into action. I looked up into the dark sky as a large object came into view. I strained my eyes in the downpour trying to figure out what it was. Were we stopping at another island? Suddenly another bolt of lightning cracked the sky, lighting up the darkness all around us. I looked up at a dark mass hovering over the boat. The USS CHAFEE popped in big black letters on the metal side of the ship. I breathed a sigh of relief. They were Americans.

The sailors hoisted us on board and I was immediately in a hallway on the main deck. I gasped for air as the cloth was removed from my mouth and the cuffs from my legs, but the zip ties stayed. Someone slipped a navy sweatshirt over my head, then guided me out of the hallway and onto a covered deck where a few dozen sailors stood around. They stared wide eyed as we walked by and I looked shyly at the ground to avoid their glare.

A very decorated officer descended the stairs from the bridge of the ship. He looked me up and down straight faced, but somewhat amused.

"Haley, right?" He asked, but didn't wait for an answer. "Welcome aboard the USS Chafee." He then turned to his mate behind him. "Go ahead and take her to the room and then batten down the hatches. We need to get moving." He turned to me again. "You're lucky it was us," he snapped, nodding to the special forces unit that surrounded me. I said nothing, but returned his cool stare.

Gram pulled my arm and we followed his mate into the ship. Everything was metal including the floor and I almost tiptoed down the hall because my feet were freezing. The mate guy stopped in front of bunk room 207, clipped off my wrist ties and opened the door for me. We walked inside a tiny space with a flip down bed and porthole.

"There's clean PT clothes on the bed and a shower in there," he said pointing to a door. "It's almost 3 am, so I would shower quickly and get in bed. There's a category three hurricane that's passing to the north of us, so we won't get to Oahu until lunch time. Also the ship might get a little crazy tonight with the storm so if you need anything, someone will be stationed right outside your door."

"Thank you," I muttered as they both left, shutting the door behind them. I heard the key turn and a bolt click into place. Did they really just lock me in here?

I got the towel and the soap they provided and jumped in the shower quickly. By the time I was out, my eyes felt heavy. It had been almost a month since I had a hot shower and it felt amazing. I threw on the sweat shirt and socks they gave me and started looking for my phone, realizing quickly it had been left on the island with the rest of my stuff. Now I had no way to contact Johnny or my family to let them know I was ok.

I woke to the sound of someone banging on my door. The plastic mattress crumpled underneath the thin sheet I was laying on as I rolled over and rubbed my eyes. Rain pelted the little porthole window and the knock came again. I got up and slipped on the sweatpants they had provided and opened the door. A young dark sailor, with thick black rimmed glasses greeted me shyly.

"Hello Airman Haley," his eyes sparkled. "I've been asked to bring you this."

I looked down at the tray of food in his hands. It smelled amazing. "Thank you," I smiled.

He lowered his voice. "Also, can I get you to sign this? It's for my little sister. She's a huge fan."

I glanced at him bewildered as he handed me a sharpie, two 5x7 photos and a small clipboard to write on, all while balancing the food tray. I looked down at them. They were both the same photo of me as I was landing at Dillingham field with Kirsten. It was actually a really cool black and white photo and I wondered who took it.

"Where did you get these?" I whispered.

"A souvenir shop in Honolulu," he said, nonchalantly.

I nodded my head, completely in shock. "Oh," was all I could say. I opened the Sharpie, silently lecturing myself on how to sign it. Autographs were not my thing and I had no idea even where to begin. My hand shook slightly as I whipped up a little heart and then signed 'Airman Claire Haley' at the bottom of both. This was so surreal. I gave it back to him and he thanked me three times, while shaking my hand profusely.

"You're welcome...what's your name?" I asked.

"Adrian," he smiled.

I gently took back my hand. "Well, it's nice to meet you Adrian."

"It's so nice to meet you...and I'm...I'm sure we'll meet again in the future and don't forget to get your things."

I looked down to where he was pointing and noticed a white box beside my door. Inside I was thrilled to find a lot of things from the island including my phone and charger.

"Here, I'll carry the box if you want to grab the food," he said, handing me the tray.

Adrian took the box and placed it gently on my bed and then turned back to me. "I'm sorry, but I'll have to lock the door when I leave again. Orders from the top."

"It's ok," I assured him. "Can you at least tell me how far we are from Oahu?"

"About two and a half hours. The hurricane set us back." He walked towards the door. "Thanks again, Claire. It was nice to meet you and I'm glad you stayed safe on the island."

"That's really kind Adrian. Thank you," I smiled. "It was nice meeting you."

He gently closed the door and I heard the lock click again. I looked in my box and found my charger and phone and plugged it in. On the upside of all this, I could turn my phone on without fear of being found. I sat on my bed and pulled the rest of my belongings out. They had pretty much grabbed everything that was personal and left all the perishables. At least I had all my clothes and some of the things I purchased at the village.

The egg casserole creation and bagel they had brought was amazing and after I ate, I sat back on my bed and watched as the waves splashed against the side of the ship. My mind wondered and I began to guess how they had found me. Did I leave my cell phone on too long? Maybe it had something to do with the helicopter from the other night? Either way, I was on this ship headed straight for Oahu and would soon have to face the higher ups and Lt. General Gray, who I especially did not want to disappoint.

TWO

THE HORN FROM the USS Chafee blared across the gray clouds that covered Pearl Harbor. I looked out of the porthole window at the familiar scenery as we cruised into the main channel and docked, then gathered my things into my backpack and waited patiently for someone to come get me.

The ship shuddered and I picked up my phone, eager to see if I had a signal here. It sprang to life, but still no signal. I couldn't believe this. How could I have no signal at Pearl Harbor?

Seconds ticked into minutes and minutes to an hour and still no one came. By this time I had laid down on the bed and began to drift to sleep, when someone knocked lightly on my door.

"Come in."

The bolt clicked open and Gram walked in carrying a garment bag. "Hi Haley. Command Master Chief said to put this on and be on the deck in 20 minutes."

"Ok thanks." I said, trying to hide the dread in my face.

Gram winked at me, "It's all good, Claire."

I smiled at him as he walked out the door. Inside the bag, I found a new service uniform and boots. I threw it on quickly, pulling my hair in a tight regulation bun, then went through the white box and stuffed my backpack with only the items I wanted to keep. Luckily I didn't have a lot on the island and so I didn't have much to throw away. The special forces unit had left my blankets and a few clothes I had drying there, but that was it.

Exactly twenty minutes later another knock on the door came. I gave myself one more look in the mirror. I had gotten so dark over the last month, I almost looked like an islander, which is crazy considering I've always had pale skin. I didn't know I could tan like this. It really popped off my dress blues.

I scanned the room, checking around one last time for any personal items I might have left. I smoothed the couple of wrinkles that were still on the bed, even though I had made it back as perfectly as I could, then scooped up my backpack and headed to the door.

I turned the handle half expecting it to be locked, but it opened right up. My tummy dropped immediately and I jumped back in surprise as I looked into the smiling face of Mr. Lucas.

"Mr. Lucas!" I gasped.

"Claire," he smirked, chewing on his ever present toothpick. "You got me flying here in a hurricane?"

I shrugged sympathetically. "Sorry?"

He nodded for me to follow him, then turned and headed down the narrow hallway, back in the direction of the deck we were on the previous night. "You gonna run away and hide on an island, you may wanna check the weather beforehand, genius. That cave you were in is partially flooded now." I didn't say anything, but followed silently behind him. "I swear, you and Zhao make me crazy," he said, stopping at the end of the hall and straightening the tie on his ever present black suit.

I was just about to argue my case when the door popped open. Gram was there to usher us out to the deck.

"Stick close," Mr. Lucas instructed me and I skipped a couple of steps to catch up.

They opened the door to a bright and sunny deck and my heart dropped when I realized we were surrounded by a sea of white uniforms. Most of the sailors had a duffle beside them and were waiting impatiently to get off the ship. An eerie quietness fell across the deck as their attention shifted to us and I noticed some of them had their phones out trying to inconspicuously video.

"Come on Claire," Mr. Lucas instructed me under his breath.

"The Sky Walker," I heard one of the sailors whisper into her phone as she recorded us walk by.

"You guys, seriously, this is the Oahu Supergirl," I heard a deep voice narrate into his phone.

"I can't even believe this. She's on our ship, bro."

I dropped my head and held onto the bottom of Mr. Lucas' suit jacket as I followed him toward the gangway. This was one of those times that I didn't feel like a superhero, but instead a freak show. In that moment, a heavy wave of sadness washed over me and I caught my breath to push back the tears. I don't know if it was the dread of knowing what was coming my way from the top brass, the loss of my sweet friend Annessa or the sadness I felt having to leave my island, but it left me feeling lost and defeated.

We neared the gangway where a group of officers stood in line to separate us from the crowd. I faced forward, directly behind Mr. Lucas, not looking up.

Suddenly a popping sound started somewhere from the back of the deck. A slow clapping noise came like a wave and grew louder, echoing across the bay. What were they clapping for? I glanced up to hundreds of smiling faces eager to catch my eye. Then a chant began to trickle into the air. "Haley! Haley!" They began to yell as loud as possible. My face froze in shock and I did my best to not smile, because I knew the amount of trouble I had caused. I just couldn't help myself though. How did they even know my name? But I knew what they were doing and it was so sweet. They knew about the punishment I would soon be facing and they wanted me to know I had their support. I blinked back tears and smiled, giving an awkward wave in appreciation. Mr. Lucas turned around and looked down at me, smirking and playfully rolled his eyes. I shrugged my shoulders in disbelief. I was as shocked as he was.

The Captain approached Mr. Lucas and I, and attempted to talk above the chatter. "Look…the media is here," he yelled above the noise. "We don't know how they were tipped off, but they're waiting."

My heart dropped, while Mr. Lucas calmly nodded unfazed. Above us, two fighter jets streaked across the sky adding to the chaos of the moment.

"We'll get you off the ship as safely as we possibly can," he said, nodding toward the exit.

We followed him to the gangway. "Stay close," Mr. Lucas repeated himself as we got close enough to see below. I gasped as a sea of reporters swarming the end of the gangway came into view. Their cameras flashed and the noise level rose again, as I walked close to Mr. Lucas. This felt oddly deja vu. I stared at the ground the whole time watching the back of Mr. Lucas' shiny black shoes, wishing I had something to cover my face with as we slowly descended the ship.

The questions they asked came at once and fast as we reached the bottom.

"Airman Haley, how did you get your flying power?"

"Can you tell us more about your rescue of Kirsten Crew?"

"Does your flying power have anything to do with the UFO sightings off the California coast the last few years?" (That one made me give a side glance at the reporter and shake my head in disbelief.)

Mr. Lucas turned and wrapped an arm around me and pulled me in closer. "You guys need to move back," he instructed the crowd as he firmly nudged a few of them out of the way. He pushed us safely through with the help of a few MPs, to the familiar black SUV waiting not far from the gangway. The door opened and Mr. Lucas lifted me slightly off the ground, pushing me quickly into the back seat and slammed the door.

Once we were inside, I let out a huge sigh of relief and realized I had been holding my breath almost the whole walk off the ship. I looked out the window stunned at what I was witnessing. Where did they come from? How did they know I was on this ship?

I looked over at Mr. Lucas and stared at him for a moment, my eyes wide in shock as the reporters swarmed the SUV, pressing the camera against the tinted window in hopes of getting one last pic.

"How did they know Mr. Lucas? Did someone leak my name to the press?"

"Yep," he said coolly, looking straight ahead as we slowly pulled out of the crowd.

"Someone on the ship?" I pressed.

"Nope," he paused, then looked me in the eyes. "It was Gray."

I gasped. There was no way that could be true.

The SUV drove us straight over to Lt. General Gray's house.

I noticed two MP vehicles stationed at the beginning of the long driveway. They were definitely expecting me. I took a deep breath as Mr. Lucas walked me up to the familiar glass doors. I couldn't believe it had only been a few months since I left here. It felt like a year ago.

Corrin answered the door and her warm smile immediately put me at ease. She wrapped me up in her arms as soon as I got through the door.

"Are you ok?" She asked quietly in my ear. "I'm so sorry about your friend, Claire."

"Thanks Corrin," I said, my heart sinking at the thought of Annessa.

"Hi Lucas," she said, nodding to him. "You guys come on in the kitchen. I've got some food ready for you. You must be famished."

I let Lucas follow her in first. Somehow I was half expecting it to be full with Captain Crew, Major Wang, Lt. General Gray and maybe even Dr. Zhao, but we walked into a large and very empty kitchen.

"Lt. General is going to be here shortly, but in the meantime help yourself," she instructed us.

"Thanks Corrin. This looks amazing," Mr. Lucas said and immediately got a plate, helping himself to the lasagna and bread. I, on the other hand, had no appetite, dreading the meeting that was to come.

"Come on Claire, even just a little bread?" She urged me.

"No thanks Corrin," I smiled.

"Claire..eat," Lucas said firmly.

I looked at him for a moment, deciding whether I wanted to argue with him or not. I never had, so I didn't know what would happen if I did. In the end I didn't want to find out, so I reluctantly grabbed a plate.

"It might be a while before you get to eat again," he explained in a softer tone as I sat down beside him with a small portion.

The phone rang and Corrin excused herself to the living room, but I could still pick up small parts of her conversation.

"No, they're here now," she said. "She's eating....she looks fine."

"I'm not going back to the compound," I whispered to Mr. Lucas.

"What makes you think you're going there?" he asked, taking his last bite.

"Where else would they send me? Lt. General told the media I'm here."

Mr. Lucas turned and faced me. "Claire, you're in the United States Air Force. You don't have the privilege of telling them where you're going." I sighed in frustration because I knew he was right. "I'm just telling you because I live the same life you do."

"What do you mean?" I asked curiously.

"You know...the secrecy," he reminded me. "Going somewhere even though you don't feel like it. You think I wanted to fly here in a hurricane warning? I do what I'm told because I work for our country...just like you." He leaned back in his chair and popped a toothpick in his mouth. "You don't question it. You just go. You should know that by now girl."

I shrugged in agreement with him as the doorbell rang. "I guess," I said.

"Claire, you gotta stop running away from everything. You're bigger than that. There's a reason why all this happened to you and you've gotta find out what that reason is."

I let what he said sink in as I heard Corrin answer the door and let whoever it was in. I looked up and was relieved to see Zhao's sweet smile come around the corner.

"Claire!" he exclaimed. "Are you ok?"

I got up to greet him. "Yeah," I said as he squeezed me in a big bear hug.

"Oh hey Mr Lucas," he said, peeking over my shoulder.

"Hey Zhao," Mr. Lucas said dryly, standing up and adjusting the weapon on his belt and then began his normal routine of checking the windows and doors of the house.

Zhao raised his eyebrows at me as if to ask "*what's his problem?*"

"He's grumpy," I whispered.

"Maybe it's because he had to fly here in a hurricane, Claire," Zhao smirked.

"Touche'," I agreed. "Speaking of hurricanes, why didn't you tell me the other day it was coming?"

"Claire, I'm not a weatherman, nor do I know where your island is. Besides, I honestly knew nothing about it."

"Grab a plate Zhao," Corrin invited him and he did

so immediately.

Zhao had only sat down with me for a few minutes, when we heard the front door open. I recognized Lt. General Gray's voice talking to someone. He soon appeared in the kitchen door with Captain Crew behind him. Lt. General didn't look my way, but made a beeline for Corrin and wrapped her up in a bear hug. I smiled to myself, thinking how lucky they were to be here together and how much I missed my Johnny.

Both of the guys grabbed plates and sat down at the table across from Zhao and I. There was an awkward moment of silence as I could tell Lt. General was thoughtfully thinking over what he wanted to say. Captain Crew said nothing, but began eating in silence.

"Well, what I should do is punish you both," he said finally, as though he was finishing a thought out loud. "Haley, you know better than this and Zhao I trusted you to help her make good decisions. I even sent you all the way to Texas to keep an eye on her."

I stole a glance at Zhao. He never told me that.

"Lt. General," I interrupted, "Zhao had nothing to do with me leaving...in fact, in fact he even tried to talk me out of it."

He looked at me sternly. "That doesn't change anything, Airman Haley. You both went against orders and you will both suffer the consequences. I don't know what it's going to take for you to realize how much your life is in jeopardy. Apparently, the botched kidnapping last time didn't convince you."

I knew better than to open my big mouth again. I sat in silence with Zhao, feeling terrible that he was facing this with me. I still didn't regret my decision to leave, but I did regret dragging Zhao into it.

Lt. General took a deep breath. "You will both be stripped of rank and demoted one level down. Zhao, you will be given further detail duty with Mancuso here at Hickam." He tapped his pen on the table a few times, took a deep breath and then looked at me. I swallowed hard and stared down at the table, waiting for the dreaded punishment I knew was to come. "Haley," he sighed as I looked up for a moment, catching a trace of what I thought was a smile. "Major Silva has been instructed to do the same for you...at Campbell."

My mouth dropped open and I looked up at him in complete and total shock. Did he really just say Major Silva and Ft. Campbell? Tears filled my eyes and my voice shook as I repeated what I had just heard. "Lt. General, I'm going home?"

"Yes and you can thank Captain Crew and Major Silva for that one. The higher ups were all ready to send you to an even more remote location, but they both went to bat for you."

I looked over at Captain Crew. I had always felt his deep dislike for me, even after I saved his daughter Kirsten.

I listened closely as Captain Crew began to mumble his explanation. "I just feel it will be safer for you," he said, stealing a look my way. "Besides that, you saved my daughter's life... so I want to try in some way to save yours."

I stared in stunned silence again and tried to process what he was saying as a cold chill ran down my back. I was finally going home and the reason I was going home was because of Captain Crew.

"Captain Crew," I almost whispered. "Thank you...I don't feel like the words *thank you* are enough, but I thank you so much."

Captain Crew smiled slightly and shrugged it off. "Well, you know how Anna and I feel now," he mumbled.

I blushed and turned my attention to Lt. General who was looking up something on his phone. "Ok, it's about 4:30. Your flight leaves at ten tonight, Claire. You'll remain here until then and Mr. Lucas will escort you back to the airport. Zhao, Mancuso knows you're here so you can stay with her if you like."

"Thank you Lt. General," he answered.

I cleared my throat nervously. "Lt. General, can I ask you something?"

"Of course," he answered, not looking up from whoever he was texting.

"How did you guys know where I was? Where my island was?"

He slowly looked up, while Captain Crew smirked at my question. "Really Claire? That's almost insulting. We knew the whole time. We had eyes on you the whole time you were there."

"What do you mean by *had eyes on me*?" I asked, surprised. "Who had eyes on me and how?"

"Oh come on," Lt. General laughed. "We are the United

States Military. We knew where you were the day after you left. We have an Army Major who specializes in tracking down AWOL soldiers. You were no problem for him to find."

"Was he on the island with her?" Zhao asked.

My heart dropped at the thought of that. I had taken baths outside and certainly didn't do it with my bikini on.

Captain Crew looked at me. "No, he just found you. Major Reacher is very skilled at tracking down AWOL's. You will have to meet him someday."

"We also had three secret weapons-an underwater navy spy, a cruiser stationed about three miles to the south east of the island and our eye in the sky on you," Lt. General added.

I shook my head in disbelief. "Then why didn't you come get me and make me come back right away?"

Lt. General shrugged, "Well a couple of times we almost did, for example," he paused and then looked pointedly at me, "the almost shark attack." (I smiled bashfully at his sarcasm. *They really saw that?)* "But we thought after what happened at the compound you would be better off alone for a bit...then the hurricane warning came in and we had no choice but to get you out."

I sat back in my chair dumbfounded at how quickly my life had just changed. Twenty four hours ago I was swimming in the ocean on my island, with uncertainty swirling in my head as to what was to come. Now I sat in Lt. General's kitchen and just another short twenty four hours away from being with my family and my Johnny. Life was so utterly amazing that way.

THREE

I SPENT THE rest of the day watching 80's movies with Zhao that he had never seen before. How does any American kid make it through their childhood without seeing *E.T.* or *The Never Ending Story* at least once? Finally around 8, I grabbed a quick shower and threw on my PT sweats for the long flight home.

By 9 p.m. I was saying goodbye to Zhao, Lt. General and Corrin for what I knew would be a long time this go around. Zhao promised to come and visit me in Tennessee by the spring and Lt. General and Corrin made me swear to check in with them every couple of weeks.

At precisely 10:05 pm, the private jet lifted off the runway. I looked down as the island of Oahu grew smaller, its lights eventually fading away in the Pacific. My heart sank for a brief moment, because although

I had missed home tremendously, I had grown to love Hawaii and the people and culture it offered. I would miss my fellow Airmen, the command staff who had watched over me so diligently and most of all, my Zhao. Saying goodbye to him tonight was particularly hard since although we both knew we would be seeing each other again, we would never live close. Our hang out days and training time together were over.

"Claire, please be careful," he had said to me as we hugged under the roar of the jet engines. "I'm worried about you."

"I'll be careful," I promised. "I'll miss you Zhao."

I looked out of the jet window early the next morning as the hills of Tennessee rolled beneath us. It had only been 6 months since I left but it seemed like forever ago. What a crazy six months it had been.

"You ready to be back home, Claire?" Lucas asked.

"Oh Mr. Lucas, you have no idea," I smiled.

"I don't blame you at all on that. Tennessee is beautiful country."

I nodded in agreement with him. "True, but more so for my family and Johnny."

"You're a lucky girl Claire," Mr. Lucas gazed past me in thought as he spoke.

"Mr. Lucas," I paused, hesitant to get too nosey and in his business. "You have family, right?"

He chuckled, "You can't have family with this job, Claire. It's just not possible."

My heart sank at his words. How can someone find happiness with no family in life? My family, friends and Johnny were my everything. I looked at him sympathetically. "Well, you're a part of my family now and I expect you to be at every wedding, birthday party, Christmas and holiday celebration you can possibly make it to."

He smiled. "Thank you Claire. I appreciate that."

The captain's voice from the cockpit interrupted us. "Lucas, we'll be on the ground in 20 minutes."

Mr. Lucas got up to talk to the pilot, while I looked out the window again to catch a glimpse of the Tennessee patchwork fields below. Acres and acres of farmland very quickly gave way to city highways and finally the flight tower of Campbell Army Airfield. My mind began a flashback in vivid detail of some of the best and worst moments of my life there. It was in that hangar that now loomed into view, that I was cut and infected with the flying potion. I could still smell its metallic fumes and feel the burn that shot from my wrist up my arm. On the flipside, that was the first night Johnny had ever kissed me too. I closed my eyes to try and remember what his lips felt like on mine. I missed him so much. It had been six long months since I had seen him or felt his strong arms around me. He always made me feel so safe and I needed that so bad right now.

The tall trees that surrounded the airfield were bare in

the mid-winter wind. I looked at the forest below as we sailed downward on our approach and remembered my arrest there as I attempted to break into the hangar in search of more of the potion. Shawn, Alicia's fiance and Johnny's roommate, had tackled me in the woods in my escape and I'll never forget the look of horror in his eyes when he realized it was me he had chased down.

The wheels of the plane touched the tarmac softly and I breathed in deeply, my heart fluttering at the possibility of seeing Johnny. I had no idea if he even knew I was coming home. Everything in the past two days had happened so fast and with the hurricane hitting the outskirts of the island, my phone service was barely working.

Lucas came out of the cockpit and began his usual thorough check of himself, starting with his gun and belt which he casually adjusted. He then took the earpiece that dangled from a small spirally cord and popped it back in his left ear.

The ever present toothpick in his mouth was discarded in the garbage can and then he slid the shades that were resting on top of his head down over his eyes. He once explained that you never want anyone to see where you are looking and the dark shades prevented that. With this cloudy December sky, they certainly were not needed.

At last the seat belt lights shut off. I pounced from my seat eager to step onto the Ft. Campbell runway. I couldn't believe I was home and just in time for Christmas, now only four days away.

"Just a minute Claire," he instructed me as usual.

I paused, then grabbed my backpack and slung it over my shoulder.

Lucas spoke to someone in his earpiece and then very slowly opened the door to the jet, which doubled as a small stair step.

"Are you going with me?" I asked him, as I zipped up my jacket in anticipation of the cold December wind.

"Not this time sweetie," he said, nodding outside. "But I think he's got you covered."

I looked down the stairs and had to catch my breath. There stood Johnny, completely decked out in his dress blues and looking as incredibly handsome as ever. I stood there for a moment frozen in place. His bright smile brought me back to earth and I bounced down the small stairs and into his open arms.

Johnny hugged me tightly and I felt every muscle squeeze me in close. I smiled as his familiar scent filled my nose. I loved the way Johnny smelled and I'm not referring to any kind of cologne. He had this natural gingerbready smell to him that was one of the sweetest smells I had ever experienced and I missed it so much. When we first started dating, Johnny would lend me one of his shirts and I would sleep with it under my pillow, breathing it in during the long weeks we sometimes had to spend away from each other.

"Oh my goodness girl. I've missed you so much," he whispered in my ear and over the noise of the jet engines winding down.

I was so overcome with emotion, desperately trying to

swallow the lump in my throat, as if that would stop the tears from coming.

"You're never leaving me again, you got that?" he smiled.

"Yes Sir," I laughed, burying myself into his arms again.

"Well, it looks like you're good to go here," Mr. Lucas laughed from behind me. I turned to see him walking up to us. "Johnny," Mr. Lucas greeted him, giving him a high five.

"Thank you for taking good care of my girl Mr. Lucas," Johnny smiled.

"Not gonna lie, she certainly keeps me busy," Mr. Lucas smirked, looking down at me.

I blushed, cringing at his words. "I'm sorry, Mr. Lucas. I definitely know that's so true."

"Job security," he smiled. "Get over here and say bye to me."

I walked over to Mr. Lucas, pushing his hand that was up for a fist bump aside and hugging him instead. I felt him hesitate, not sure of what to do. I don't think he'd had too many hugs lately, but that was too bad. I was a hugger and I had a feeling this would be the last time I saw him for a while. I soon felt his arms squeeze around me, a little awkwardly, but it was a hug nonetheless.

"I feel like I'm not going to see you for awhile," I said, looking up at him as we let go.

"That's what you said last time," he laughed, then put his hand in mine. "As long as you need me, I'll be here. You have my card, so call me anytime, ok?"

"Ok," I smiled, sadly.

Mr. Lucas nodded farewell to Johnny, "Take care of her."

"Yes Sir," Johnny said, giving a little salute.

I joined Johnny and we watched as Mr. Lucas boarded the plane, the steps closing behind him.

Johnny slung my duffle over his shoulder. "What a life he must lead," he said, as he grabbed my hand and led me to the MP squad that awaited.

"Where are we going?" I asked, after we got in the back seat.

"The gatehouse please," Johnny instructed the driver, answering my question. "We're going to get you settled and then we have a meeting at 4."

I sat back in the seat and kept stealing glances at him. My heart raced with excitement, still in disbelief that I was here with him. The higher ups could have sent me anywhere. I could be on my way to some foreign base in the middle of nowhere again, but I was home. I felt so grateful and couldn't help but believe that God had somehow moved on my behalf. Why He cared enough to bail me out of my mischief was beyond me, but I couldn't thank Him enough. He was so good to me.

I wasn't surprised when we passed through the gates of the base jail and then to the guest house that sat behind it, deep in the woods. I had stayed here just six months ago for a few nights before they sent me to Hawaii. It's crazy all I had done and been through in that short period of time. I had changed so much and had grown into a totally different person. In June I left shy, timid and unsure of myself, but with the help of Professor Corral and all my hard work training with my company, I was not only physically stronger, but very capable of defending myself if necessary.

We pulled through the gate and around the circle driveway to the beautiful brick stairs that led up to the fancy French doors. Major Silva had told me in June, this was the most secure home on the whole base and had even housed a couple of Presidents during their visit here at Campbell. I knew I had no business staying here and it was strictly for my protection, so I didn't let it go to my head.

"I'll return around three Sir," the driver called after us.

"Great! Thanks!" Johnny replied, then looked at his watch. "It's already 9:30. At least we have a little break."

Our footsteps echoed on the marble floored foyer that greeted us. I noticed a large American flag that stood prestigious beside the cherry wood staircase. I followed Johnny up the white carpet that lined the middle of each step and to the room I stayed in last time.

Johnny plopped my duffle on the bed and immediately turned and wrapped me in his arms. I had to catch my breath from the mixture of excitement and butterflies I was feeling just being around him. Plus he was just so strong and I don't think he realized how tight his grip was.

I snuggled in close to him, burying my face into his

neck and kissing it over and over. Soon his lips found mine and I pulled him in, balancing on my tiptoes to get as close as I could. Johnny is the best kisser ever. I can't help but believe he took kissing lessons or something (even though he swears he's only kissed one other girl before me and that was on a dare at a friend's house in 6th grade.) When he finally set me on the ground, I felt dizzy and out of breath and had to sit on the bed.

"Are you ok?" he asked softly, sitting beside me and removing a curl that had fallen out of place.

"Yes," I said, breathing deeply. "I just got a little dizzy."

"Me too," he smiled with his beautiful emerald eyes, tracing my cheek with his fingers to my chin, then lifting my lips to his again. My hands found his and then moved over his arms and up the back of his neck, running my fingers across his freshly shaven head and into his thick dark hair on top.

I always lose track of time when I'm with this guy and kissing him. I could kiss him all day and not ever need a break. Occasionally I would open my eyes, just to make sure this was real. As much as I loved my island, I did not want to wake up there and all this be just a dream. On a stormy night a couple of weeks before, I had dreamed I was lying beside Johnny and was sorely disappointed to wake up and find myself alone in my cave.

Johnny and I finally laid back on the bed. He wrapped me up in his arms and before I knew it we fell fast asleep. I slept so hard, mainly because I knew I was safe and I felt happy. It was the best sleep I had in a long time.

FOUR

I WOKE UP to Johnny's sweet smile, leaning over me and kissing my cheek.

"Claire Bear, we've got to get moving. It's already one and you said you want to hop in the shower before we leave."

I rubbed my eyes, feeling so rested and warm. I remembered how Johnny was like a personal furnace, his body always radiating so much heat.

"I do need a shower," I yawned and stretched.

He leaned down and softly kissed my nose. "I'll tell you what. You get ready and I'll go downstairs and see what I can pull together for lunch."

"Really?" I asked, surprised. "You can cook?"

"I think they have PB & J down there," he laughed, then hopped off the bed. "Just joking. I can cook."

I slowly sat up and stretched again watching him head

towards the door. He turned and smiled at me. "Be down in an hour, ok?"

"Yes Sir," I smiled.

He disappeared down the hall and I breathed a deep sigh. I couldn't believe he was mine.

Exactly an hour later I pounced down the stairs, my damp curls bouncing and half dressed in my dress blues with my shirt untucked. I had barely put on any make up, because my skin was still glowing from the Hawaiian sun and I wanted to keep it moisturized. I did however add a little eyeshadow, mascara and pink lip gloss, because I wanted to look my best for Johnny. I couldn't wait to be with him again and I was more than eager to see what he was cooking.

He greeted me with a big smile as I slid into the spotless white kitchen in my fuzzy socks. Bob Marley's "*Could You Be Loved*" played on the bluetooth and spread across the counter in various tupperware bowls was a variety of chopped veggies and grilled chicken. It smelled incredible and I built the most amazing Caesar salad.

"So what do you think?" He asked as we sat at the kitchen bar.

"Mmmmm…" I replied, unable to talk with the huge bite I had in my mouth. "I'm sorry," I said, when I finally swallowed. "This is the best salad I've ever had, Johnny. Where did you learn to cook chicken like that?"

Johnny wiped his mouth. "At home on the island. I worked at this little cafe on the beach and Caesar salad was their specialty."

My mind went back to last spring and my little vacation I had with Johnny and his family in his hometown of Anna Maria Island. This beautiful island was tucked in the gulf coast just to the south of Tampa. I had the best time sailing and vacationing with him there and sneaking in secret night flights over the Gulf.

"You never told me that," I smiled. "So let me get this straight…you're incredibly hot *and* you can make a mean Caesar salad?"

"Whatever…" Johnny smiled, shrugging me off bashfully.

"No really," I interrupted him. "Can you get any more perfect?"

He smiled at me again, then slid his seat close to mine, making my heart pound hard in my chest. "You know what makes my life perfect? You. My life is perfect because of you."

Johnny had a way of catching me off guard with the incredibly sweet things he said. I always tried to equally return the compliments, but sometimes felt nothing I could say was good enough. I was better with actions. I wrapped my arms around his neck and squeezed him tightly.

"I love you Johnny," I whispered.

"I love you too, Claire," he whispered back, kissing my forehead. "I'm never letting you go again."

"Good, because I'm not going anywhere," I smiled.

He held out his hand. "Deal," he said. We shook on it, then he lifted my hand and kissed it princess style. "Well, except now. You have to go to that meeting."

I rolled my eyes. "Oh yeah. Another meeting. Do you know what it's about?"

"No idea. I literally just found out you were coming home last night."

"I don't care," I shrugged. "They can hide me in some hole in the middle of the woods as long as I'm home and I get to see you and my family and my friends."

He winked at me. "Oh Claire. Always my little drama queen."

"Whatever," I laughed, then looked at him skeptically. "Johnny, isn't it weird how they just suddenly decided to send me home? The same place they rushed me out of just six months ago to keep me safe?"

Johnny shrugged. "Not really. I mean, Major Silva and I have been very vocal about getting you back here, especially after the Texas catastrophe. But I didn't think we had that much pull. Major Silva is the one who really went to bat for you on this side of things and made sure the base stepped up its security."

"He did?" I asked, surprised.

"Oh yeah. Well think about it Claire. He had your mom in his ear and she was so worried when you took off…besides," he looked at me slyly, " you might be more than just one of his Airmen in the future."

I squinted at him, amused because I knew where this was going, but I just wanted to hear him say it. "What are you talking about?"

"Seriously? Come on Claire. He's got the hots for your mom."

"Johnny!" I exclaimed, punching his arm lightly.

"*Johnny*!" He mocked in a girly voice, then grabbed and tickled me. "Like you don't know it's true!"

"Ok…yeah," I giggled, trying to free myself from his strong hands. "Well, don't just blurt it out like that! You're talking about my mom! Show some respect!"

"Ok Claire Silva," he teased, tickling me harder.

"Shut it, Johnny!" I choked out, trying to catch my breath between laughs. "You're such a brat!" I pushed back on him, making the bottom of the chair slide out from underneath. We tumbled to the floor and luckily he broke our fall.

"Are you ok?" I gasped, as we laid on the shiny tile, laughing again.

"I'm fine," he said sitting up, "but seriously girl, what have you been doing with yourself?"

I sat up beside him. "What do you mean?"

Johnny grabbed my arm and put it into a muscle flex. "Let's see it," he commanded.

I proudly flexed my muscle, as Spandau Ballet's "*True*" flowed through the kitchen.

"Claire," Johnny gasped. I could tell he was genuinely impressed. "You've got some muscle action going on."

"There wasn't much to do at the compound except the gym," I explained, then grabbed his arm. "Your turn."

"Maybe later," he laughed, jumping up and then lifting

me effortlessly off the floor. "We gotta get out of here soon. Go finish getting ready and I'll get this cleaned up."

I gave him one final kiss and then did as he instructed. Upstairs I pulled my hair in a tight bun topping it off with my blue flight cap. I slipped on my dress blues jacket over my crisp uniform shirt and blue pants then checked myself out in the full length mirror. Not to brag, but I looked pretty sharp. The navy blue popped off my dark island skin and my new uniform fit just right. I smiled at myself in the mirror, so proud to be wearing this uniform and serving my country.

Downstairs Johnny stood in the foyer talking to the driver who had returned at exactly three to pick us up.

"Oh wow, they moved you into that position quickly," I heard Johnny say as I quietly gasped at him standing so tall and handsome in his dress blues. He towered over the driver who hung on to Johnny's every word.

They turned their attention to me and I smiled as Johnny's eyes grew wide with approval.

"Claire, this is Justin. He just transferred here from Ft. Hood."

"Nice to meet you," Justin said wide-eyed, reaching out to shake my hand.

"Nice to meet you also Justin." I noticed his hand quiver in mine as we shook. That was weird. Did they tell him about me? He continued to shake my hand and as I gently pulled my hand away I noticed his last name, Newman.

"Well, let's get this party started," Johnny said, grabbing

my hand and leading me out.

Johnny and Justin talked about Campbell as we drove the short five miles to headquarters. Justin was an MP and had only been at Campbell a couple of weeks. He had plenty of questions about my neighboring hometown of Clarksville and all it had to offer and I did my best to give him the hot spots to visit and hang out while he was here.

Soon we pulled in front of the large building that housed headquarters and my heart leapt in excitement as we walked up the sidewalk and to the round front entrance. The screaming eagle with the word *Airborne* etched in stone welcomed us. I was officially home.

FIVE

"AIRMAN HALEY!" I heard Major Silva's voice boom through the busy foyer. I turned to see him walk quickly toward us dodging soldiers who entered and exited the main door. Many were just mingling, drinking coffee and chatting, but all eyes were on us.

"Major Silva!" I smiled, excited to see him.

He stopped short as he reached us and we both paused for a moment, unsure of how to greet each other. He finally wrapped his arm around my shoulder and squeezed slightly in an awkward side hug, while Johnny smiled inconspicuously. Oh well. At least he tried.

"Where's mom?" I asked, as we headed toward the elevator and up to General Collin's office.

"We're processing soldiers in from Korea today so she had to be there. I'll bring her and Kass to the house

4□

tonight for dinner though."

"I'm not going home?" I asked, as the elevator door slid open on the second floor. Major Silva ignored my question at the sight of General Collins walking out of his office.

"Well, hello there gang," General Collins smiled at the three of us. One of the many things I admired about him was his laid back attitude. We always saluted and paid him the respect he deserved, but he seemed uninterested in all the formality and more interested in getting to know you personally. We stopped in unison to salute him, but he waved us off with a half salute.

"Come on in and shut the door," he said, smiling at me in particular.

I immediately noticed two unfamiliar faces standing in front of the General's desk. They both looked at me the same way everyone had been lately. That familiar glazed-over stare of curiosity before snapping to their senses, followed by an attempt to treat me as normal as possible.

"Airman Haley, Warrant Officer Angel," General Collins nodded in their direction. "I would like to introduce you to Major Simmons, operations manager of safety here at Campbell."

Major Simmons, a tall and stocky, bald headed man greeted me with a kind smile. He reminded me so much of my cousins on my dad's side of the family. I could imagine he had a Harley sitting in his garage at home.

"Major Simmons," Johnny said, saluting and then shaking his hand. "Major Simmons," I echoed, doing the same.

"Pleasure," he smiled.

General Collins continued. "This is Captain Lewis. He handles our media across the board and that includes everything from social media to any national press and beyond."

Johnny and I greeted him as well. His attendance here totally piqued my curiosity. Maybe it was because of the media blow up since my beach landing with Kirsten.

We all found our seats at the small conference table and I smiled to myself when I saw Johnny go out of his way to get the seat right beside me. I sat between him and General Collins, who sat at the head of the table and directly across from Major Silva. I felt Johnny's hand grab mine under the table in reassurance. I was so thankful he was here with me.

The door to the office opened and the General's secretary entered. She pushed a button on the wall and a screen slid down in front of us. She then flipped the lights off and quickly left the room.

I turned my attention to the large screen where the beaches at Dillingham came into view. I knew what was coming, though most videos I had seen of it were grainy and jumpy. Whoever took this one stood directly in front of the firetruck and had a clear image of the sky. I squeezed Johnny's hand tighter as if to warn him of what was to come. I was sure he had already seen it, but for some reason I felt protective of him, like it would hurt him to see it. I glanced at him and then all of the men whose eyes were glued to the screen.

"*I think we got a plane in distress coming in,*" I heard what I assumed to be a fireman say. "*Keanu, make sure that second rig is on standby.*"

I took a deep breath and twisted the bottom of my jacket with my spare hand. Johnny smiled slightly recognizing my nervous habit, then gently took both of my hands reassuringly in his.

"Don't wrinkle your jacket," he whispered in my ear.

"*What is that Chief?*" A different voice on the video asked, snapping our attention to the screen.

"*What is what?*"

"*There!*" An arm extended toward the sky and the camera panned from the beach to the cloud line. Voices began to rise and a commotion with the camera occurred, temporarily losing sight of us. Suddenly we came into focus and boy did we come into focus good. Johnny sat up straighter in his seat watching intently as I descended from the sky. Kirsten's bright red hair popped against the clouds and every line on my face creased with worry. I landed on the beach exhausted and Zhao ran up and took her from my arms, followed by my desperate attempt to run and Mr. Lucas scooping me off the runway in the SUV.

"Lucas?" Johnny whispered. I nodded yes.

The beach scene cut off, then immediately rolled internet shorts from around the world. I gasped when the footage stated my video with Kirsten had been shared over 300 million times. Next came interviews with people speaking all different kinds of languages. My picture was on their tee shirts, tumblers, bumper stickers, and even fan clubs had been formed. It was so overwhelming, I had to look down and catch my breath.

Johnny squeezed my hands again. "It's ok," he mouthed to me.

I did my best to smile back. The screen turned to black for a moment, then a face from the past slowly faded into view.

"Yeah, I know her." Tracy said smugly. "We went to high school together. Her name is Claire Haley and I believe she's in the Air Force now." She cocked her head sideways and gave the camera a snide smile and sarcastic wink.

"*Why that little…,*" I thought to myself.

Another face popped up. "Oh yes. We know Claire," Lillian's sweet wrinkled face smiled. "She used to stop by and visit me and my late husband all the time."

"Were you aware of her flying super power?" The interviewer asked.

She looked at the camera shoved in her face, stunned and gulped hard. "Excuse me?" she asked.

My heart sank as the interviewer said nothing. Lillian seemed so confused as she stared blankly into the camera. She was my elderly neighbor down the road. I felt terrible for her. How did she even get involved in this? What did they do, canvas the whole neighborhood? And what's even worse, I hadn't seen her in almost a year and had no idea her husband had died. "*Claire, you're a bad friend,*" I scolded myself lightly.

Suddenly another thought entered my mind that shook me to the core. If they knew of Lillian, then they knew where I lived. My body trembled at the thought of that.

The video then began popping images of me, one after another over the last two years, as suspenseful music played quietly in the background. Whoever put this together, was definitely trying to prove a point. Everything from my first "official" sighting at the Aerosmith concert, to the accident at the bridge, the blurry image of me flying above the buildings in Clarksville when I beat up the creepy guys, and finally a couple of pics I didn't even know existed.

The video ended abruptly and everyone sat in silence for a moment, soaking it all in. I felt a twinge of guilt over my lack of discretion, even though I felt like I was on ground 90% of the time.

The General got up quietly and turned the lights on, while the screen slid back up. I looked down at the table, almost ashamed of the past two years. Clearly I hadn't gone out of my way to stay out of the spotlight, although I could say I handled everything the best way I knew how.

General Collins cleared his throat, the way he did every time he spoke to us. "So this is obviously why I invited Captain Lewis and Major Simmons here. Simmons is overseeing your security now Claire. Major Simmons?" He nodded at him, giving him the floor.

"Airman Haley, I've been put in charge of your security from now on. Some of the responsibilities I have had include overseeing the protection of some of our nation's most notable dignitaries, including two of our own Presidents, plus leaders from around the world during their stay here. I just want you to know that I take my job seriously with you under my care. I will keep you safe," he said firmly.

"My family too?" I asked, thinking back to Lillian's interview and how close she lived to my mom.

"Of course," he answered.

"Claire," Major Silva interrupted. "We're moving your mom and sister onto Campbell. Major Simmons feels it's what's best for now."

"At least until the hype about you subsides," General Collins added. "And believe me, it will subside."

I was not expecting that one. We were moving? "How does my mom feel about this?" I asked. "What...what about our house?"

"We'll talk it out tonight," Major Silva assured me.

My heart sank. I didn't want to lose our house. It wasn't much, but it had become our home since my dad died. I knew mom and Kass would be devastated and I felt terrible. We were losing our home and it was all my fault.

The room was quiet again as I took it all in. General Collins opened a brown leather notebook, then looked at Captain Lewis. I watched them both intently, scared of what they were going to throw at me next, but nothing could have prepared me for what was to come.

"Second thing we need to discuss is the media," General Collins said.

Captain Lewis took that as his cue. "Airman Hailey, just a little background on me; I graduated from USC. My resume includes being the spokesman for three Governors and two Senators and also many other politicians and celebrities that have found themselves in…well, in a bad place. I'm basically going to be a buffer between you and the public. I'm now in my seventh year here at Campbell and I'll be handling your press conference."

I did a double take. Did he just say a press conference?

"Press conference?" I heard Johnny ask in disbelief. "Claire's having a press conference?"

I looked wide eyed at General Collins and softly shook my head no.

"Hear us out Claire," he said, leaning in closer to me. "We, all of us here, including the top brass from Hickam and Austin, think it would be in your best interest to introduce you to the world. It is now obvious who you are, as was clearly seen in that video. We feel that hiding you would put you further in danger." He then addressed Johnny. "We're just going to try and make Claire and her flying power a norm in this world. Look at it like this. A hundred years ago, the thought of someone flying across the world in a jet would have been unheard of. Now it's just as normal as driving a car. We want to try and do the same for her. The human race has an incredible way of adjusting to the abnormal."

"With all due respect Sir, I don't understand how that

would keep her any safer," Johnny said, squeezing my hand a little tighter. "Claire's a living being, not an object."

"It's the timeless safety in numbers kind of thing," Major Simmons explained and then looked at me. "At this point we can either put you under government watch and hide you away for the rest of your life *or* we can throw you in the ocean with all the rest of the fish and hope you adapt while we do our best to keep you safe."

"And from what we know about you Haley," Major Silva said in his thick, Hispanic accent, "you are not one to be tied down. Even if we tried to keep you hidden, it wouldn't be fair and you would find a way to break free."

I nodded my head in agreement with him. They were so right. There was no way I could ever be tied down again. The thought of being able to fly on a whim and openly use this gift I had been given to do good for people, sounded very inviting .

"So the best we can come up with is to get you and your family moved to base," Major Simmons concluded. "We have housing arranged in a home that's close to the MP station and will have your family under constant watch at least until we can find some sort of new normalcy for you. I'll also be giving you a strict list of rules you must follow," he looked at me sternly, "and I mean follow Airman Haley. There will be no bending of the rules or we will have to look for an alternative for you and I'm afraid it won't be anything you like."

I nodded in agreement with him and mumbled a quick, "Yes Sir."

General Collins stood, signaling the end of our meeting. "Just know Haley, you're our responsibility and we take that very seriously."

Johnny stood up face to face with him. "So basically, it's the press conference or she's sent off somewhere to hide out the rest of her life?"

"Pretty much," Major Simmons answered.

I watched as Johnny's jaw line tightened, a clear sign he did not like that answer. Major Silva stood up and joined them, placing his hand on Johnny's shoulder.

"Johnny, I know you're worried, but you're going to have to trust us on this one."

After an awkward moment of silence, I walked over to them and slipped my hand into Johnny's. "It's ok. I'll do the press conference and everything will be ok. I just don't want to leave again."

Johnny sighed in disapproval, but I think he realized it was a no win on either side of it all. He didn't want me leaving again and if it took a press conference to make sure that didn't happen, so be it. At this point I was just happy to be home and with Johnny. I would do whatever they asked of me and try my hardest to be on my best behavior.

SIX

"IT LOOKS LIKE you're my little shooting star now," Johnny whispered to me as we sat in the back seat of Justin's squad.

"What do you mean?" I laughed.

"Everyone is really going to know who you are now."

"Oh," I rolled my eyes. "I wouldn't go that far, Johnny."

"Well, after that press conference, it's on," he said. "Everyone's gonna know your name."

"I can't believe they're even...even doing a press conference," I stammered, still in disbelief.

Johnny nodded in agreement. "I get what they're trying to do, but I'm not sure about that whole safety in numbers thing."

I put my head on his shoulder. "I kind of get it. I mean, the more eyes the better and the alternative road of seclusion would be devastating."

"Well, at least they're waiting until after Christmas, so you can have one last weekend of normalcy before the storm."

I sighed, wrapping both my arms around his one arm and pulling him closer.

"Where are we going?" I asked, noticing the car turn in the opposite direction of the house.

"To get my truck. I'm tired of being driven around like a schmuck. No offense, Justin," Johnny laughed.

"None taken," Justin smiled.

A couple of minutes later we pulled up in front of Johnny's barracks. I looked around at the familiar building, again so thankful to be home.

"I'll just wait here then," Justin said, as we climbed out.

Johnny took my hand and led me to the steps. "I just need to grab something first."

"Is he going to be with us all the time?" I asked, looking slightly back over my shoulder at Justin, who was now casually leaning back on his squad and scanning the parking lot. "I'm with you, so I find it a bit unnecessary."

"Not all the time," Johnny said, holding the door open for me.

"Oh good," I breathed a sigh of relief.

He winked at me. "I'm sure they'll have to change shifts at some point."

I punched him lightly in his arm as we went inside. We walked down the hall and past a rec room that was full of soldiers hanging out, watching tv and shooting pool.

"Johnny!" One of the soldiers yelled as we walked by.

Johnny paused in the door. "Hey guys. What's up?"

I stood behind Johnny, trying to be as invisible as possible, but that didn't last long.

"Is that Claire?" I heard a familiar voice ask.

Johnny moved to the side to reveal a very red-faced me.

"What in the world?" Tater said in his thick southern drawl as he made a bee line across the room. The next thing I knew he was picking me up and spinning me around.

"Hi Tater," I smiled. Tater was one of Johnny's closest friends and had dated one of my close friends Lexi for a while.

"Careful with her man," Johnny laughed. "She's still nursing some bruised ribs."

Tater put me down and looked at me mischievously. "So I guess we finally figured out who the mysterious ghost girl is."

"Yeah," I cringed.

"What a trip, huh Claire?" he asked. "Don't worry girl. We all talked about this. We got you."

I looked around at the room full of smiling faces, nodding in agreement with Tater. Maybe General Collins had something with that whole fish, safety in numbers thing. I felt untouchable in this moment.

One of them, a short, dark haired freckled face kid, approached me slowly and held out a notepad. "May I have an autograph please, Airman Haley? My little brother is a huge fan."

I smiled awkwardly at his request. "Of course."

I signed the best I could and before I knew it, I was signing tee shirts, hats, and even a ping pong paddle.

Johnny waited patiently by the door as I signed for all 22 of them. The guys were so kind and thanked me profusely.

At last Johnny grabbed my hand. "We gotta go Claire."

I said bye to all of them, then Tater joined us on the walk upstairs.

"This is a trip, Claire," Tater said again as we reached the second floor.

"You're telling me," I laughed, as we entered the hallway.

"Does Lexi know?" He asked as we waited for Johnny to unlock his door. I smiled back at him. I knew somehow he'd bring her up.

"Ummm, I'm guessing by now she does, but I never got a chance to tell her to be honest. They made me promise not to, otherwise I would have."

"Oh no, I get it," he said.

We walked into the room Johnny and Shawn shared. I was so excited to see Shawn standing by the sink in their kitchenette.

"Shawn!" I exclaimed.

"Hey Claire," he winked at me.

"Hey Claire," I heard a sweet familiar voice echo. My mouth dropped open as Alicia popped out from behind him and in a split second had her arms around me.

"Mony!" I tried to squeak out, in my excitement. "Oh my goodness!"

"Clairey!" she squealed. "I've missed you so much!"

We jumped up and down in our excitement and I felt the tears immediately begin to fall as I squeezed her tight. In fact we both started sobbing while Johnny, Tater and Shawn watched us in amusement.

"I missed you so much too!" I cried into her shoulder.

Alicia put my face in her hands. "These past 7 months were *so* lame Claire. You are never leaving here again!"

"I'm not!" I agreed as we wiped our tears. I heard a snicker behind me and turned to see the guys covering their mouths and turning away quickly in an attempt to hide their laughter.

"What?" Alicia asked, blowing her nose into a napkin and looking at Shawn.

"Nothing sweetie pea," he said, trying to keep a straight face.

Johnny cleared his throat and covered his mouth, but I could still see his smile in his eyes.

"Johnny," I sniffed, trying to be serious, but his face was making me laugh. "It's not funny," I said, muffling a giggle.

Johnny walked over and wrapped me in his arms. "I know, I'm sorry." He kissed me on my forehead. "You guys are just so cute and dramatic."

I looked over at Alicia and we both smiled knowingly. She had been calling me dramatic since middle school. It was nice to hear her put in the same category for once.

Alicia grabbed my hand. "Let's sit for a minute," she said, leading me to the frumpy 1980's couch the boys had in their living space. "Are you ok?" she asked as she pulled a curl that had fallen out of my tight bun behind my ear. "I'm so sorry to hear about Annessa, Claire. She seemed like such a sweet person."

The guys followed quickly and pulled chairs up to join us.

"Oh Mony, she definitely was." I looked over at the boys. "I promise you guys, I had absolutely nothing to do with her death. I didn't want any part of her flying… but it was forced on me."

"Oh Claire we know," Shawn reassured me. "Silva told us everything."

"Hey," Johnny said softly, as he came over and knelt in front of me. "You had no choice. You were following orders and that's all you could do. Annessa was a grown woman. That was her choice and she could have declined."

My mind flashed back and in an instant I was in the sky over the desert again. Johnny's face disappeared and all I could see was myself shooting through the clouds, desperately looking for Annessa. I saw the earth approaching quickly. I saw her final moments in the air as I plunged head first in an attempt to save her. I remembered turning my head to avoid her final moments before she hit the water. I screamed her name and knew in an instant she was gone. The agony of my cries that flowed from the deepest despair of my soul were so horrifying, ringing through the crisp air and into my headphone mic. I hung in the air, as the radio buzzed an eerie quiet distraction.

"Claire," Alicia said quietly, grabbing my hand and bringing me back to the present.

"I'm so sorry," I whispered, feeling an overwhelming heaviness in my heart. I had been so busy running since Annessa died, I didn't have the chance to dwell on the pain of it all. And I was very good at running from hurt. I had been doing it since I lost my dad, when I realized I could physically run the hurt away. Maybe it was the wrong way to handle tragedy in life, but in this case it had saved me for a while. Mr. Lucas had warned me that I couldn't keep running away from everything and I was learning he was right. It eventually catches up to you and you will eventually have to face it. At least now I was at home with the people who loved me most and I wouldn't have to face it alone.

Johnny sat beside me and wrapped me in his arms while I cried quietly. Four weeks of built up hurt and guilt escaped me as I allowed myself to mourn the loss of my sweet friend.

"Claire," Alicia said, at last. "It's ok to feel hurt and regret, but please don't allow the guilt to take over. You don't deserve that. You did all you could."

I nodded in agreement with her. "I honestly did, Mony."

"You did," Johnny agreed, kissing my cheek. "And you know what? I'm going to insist on canceling that press conference Claire. I just don't think you're ready for all that."

"What press conference?" Alicia asked.

Johnny and I looked at each other. He raised his eyebrows at me as if to ask permission to tell Alicia. I shrugged my ok with him.

"Well, General Collins and whoever else, thinks it might be a good idea for Claire's identity to be revealed to the world."

We heard a silent gasp from Alicia and Shawn, as Tater's eyes grew wide.

"That makes absolutely no sense," Alicia snapped.

"It's a safety in numbers thing," I tried to explain. "They think it would be safer for everyone to know who I am instead of hiding me away."

"Doesn't everyone already know?" Tater asked, confused.

"No…I get it," Shawn said. "Back home, we always rolled in a group. There's definitely safety in numbers."

"How do you feel about that Claire?" she asked.

I paused thoughtfully for a moment, my face wrinkled deep in thought. "I don't feel like I have a choice," I sighed at last. "The alternative is to be hidden away, stuck in some out of the way government compound thing again."

"Everyone knows who you are anyway Claire," Tater said.

I nodded my head in agreement with Tater, but Alicia and Johnny didn't seem convinced.

"How about if we all get together for dinner tonight," Shawn suggested, breaking the tension. "I'll grab some food and we can just all be together. Would you like that?"

"That sounds amazing Shawn," I smiled, gratefully. For

the first time in weeks I felt lighter, like I could breathe again. Whatever guilt that had been weighing me down was mostly gone. I knew deep inside I was not at fault, but for some reason I just needed to hear it and from the people who mattered the most. I was so glad to be home and I'd do whatever it took to stay here.

SEVEN

THAT EVENING I sat in the spacious living room of the Presidential house on top of the world, having been reunited with my family. Kass and mom sat on either side of me on the couch, Kass holding my hand and not letting go, while mom wrapped one arm around my waist, squeezing occasionally. Alicia sat close by, while the guys, Johnny, Major Silva, and Kyle (Kass' boyfriend) gathered outside, bundled up on the patio watching Shawn grill chicken.

We talked quietly about the past six months and everything I had been through, from my first few months at Hickam to the past month on the island and finally Annessa. I did my best not to be too depressing, especially since we had just been reunited, but talking it all out was definitely helpful.

My mom, always the encourager with all the right words, reminded me that I couldn't control everything and I had no choice but to do what I was commanded. I loved having my mom here with me and even though I was an adult, I still needed her guidance. She made me feel loved and protected.

"I can't believe Christmas is only three days away," Kass said, trying to change the subject and cheer me up. "And Danielle and Tessa will be here tomorrow night!"

I was so excited to see my older sisters, but in the craziness of everything going on, I hadn't even thought about Christmas. I was not even close to ready. There were a few gifts I had bought while visiting Zhao during my stay on the island, but not much as I had to fly with them all the way back to the island. I needed to do some shopping.

"We're going shopping tomorrow," Alicia said, reading my mind as usual. "Your mom already cleared it with Major Silva."

"Oh good," I sighed in relief.

"Dinner's ready!" Shawn called as he entered the patio doors.

We all gathered around the kitchen island and to my surprise Major Silva led in grace.

"Father in heaven, we are truly grateful for all your blessings on our family," he began. (That definitely got my attention as I snuck one eye open and gave Kass a questionable look. Did he just say *our* family? Kass smiled slyly at me, muffling a giggle.) "We pray that you will bless this food and the hands that prepared it.

We thank you for bringing Claire home and we ask for guidance and protection over her as she and all of us in leadership, navigate the next chapter of her life. We ask in your Holy name. Amen."

"Amen," we all repeated. I smiled at Major Silva in appreciation. That prayer opened my eyes to a whole new view of Major Silva, a side I didn't know existed and made me ok with putting total control of my life in his hands. I knew he wanted nothing but the best for me and apparently mom felt that way too, as I saw her grab his arm and squeeze it in approval.

Dinner was amazing and afterward we all sat in the family room discussing the next week and what it would bring.

"So when is this press conference supposed to happen?" Mom asked Major Silva.

"Well, we thought we would wait until the New Year," he answered. "That way we can at least ensure a somewhat normal Christmas for Claire and the family."

"Do I have to say anything?" I asked.

"No…well, not unless you want to and even then it will have to be cleared with the General."

I nodded my head like I agreed, but there was so much to this I still didn't understand.

"I'm not trying to disrespect your leadership Sir, but I just don't see the point of it," Johnny interrupted. "I worry for Claire's safety. I can take care of her, but I can't always be around."

"That's exactly why more people need to be aware she

exists, Johnny. If she lives here and our soldiers know about her, you better believe they will be watching out for her. People will be more apt to pay attention to her and report anything suspicious." Then he peeked at mom. "I'm not trying to frighten anyone, but I'm just going to be honest. If someone wants to find Claire, they will do everything they can to get to her no matter where she is. We don't want a repeat of Hawaii."

My mind flashed back to that day a few months back. Images of my near abduction from the shack were still very raw in my thoughts. I could still see the landscaping guys, feel their arms around me and the pounding of my heart watching Zhao and Prof. Corral take them both down. Major Silva was right. If it could happen on Oahu at a secret training area, it could happen anywhere.

The room grew quiet as he turned his attention back to Johnny. "You just have to trust us on this one, Angel. She's going to have all the security she needs and you will be a very big part of that."

Johnny nodded his head in agreement, though I knew he totally didn't agree. I had never seen him so defiant. "Yes Sir," he mumbled. I remembered the conversation we had earlier today in the car. "*I swear Claire, if I didn't have to abide by their rules, this press conference wouldn't be happening,*" he had said.

By the end of the evening I pretty much knew how the next week would unfold. January 4th was the day set for the press conference. It would be held at headquarters and only 2 major news outlets, plus our own local Nashville station would be allowed in. Mom would join me, as well as Johnny. In the meantime, we would all go to mom's house the day after Christmas and move her. Our goal was to have her and Kass completely moved out and onto their base house before the 4th. With all the help we would have, I knew that would be no problem.

"Mom and Kass, I'm so sorry you have to move out of our house because of me," I had told them earlier.

"Oh honey, please don't worry about that," Mom reassured me. "We're going to be just fine."

"It's just a new adventure," Kass smiled. I couldn't believe how much older she looked. Her face had thinned out and the baby cheeks she had kept through her highschool years were almost gone. She was simply beautiful with her long golden blonde hair and perfect tan. Seriously, a tan in December. Who could possibly have such beautiful skin tones in the winter without some kind of a tanning bed, which I knew she would never use.

Around midnight, we said our goodnights.

"Ok, I'll be here tomorrow morning at 9 sharp to get you and then we'll stop and scoop up Kass, ok?" Alicia said.

"No girls," Major Silva interrupted. "Kass first, then Claire." He looked at me sympathetically. "Too many eyes on your house," he explained. "One more thing, shopping at the Exchange only. We don't want Claire off base."

"But we're going to the mall," Kass sighed.

"I'm sorry," he said. "Base only."

Mom lightly took his arm. "Sebastian, do you think if someone went with them, they could go to the mall? There's not many shopping places at the Exchange and who knows when Claire will get to go again," she countered.

Major Silva looked at all three of our pleading eyes. "Well…I guess it'll be ok," he said at last. "I'll explain it to the General and I'll tag along…far behind." he added quickly.

"Thanks Sebastian," Kass said, hugging him in appreciation. She certainly seemed to have changed her tune about Major Silva. I was eagerly anticipating my talk with mom about them two and what exactly the 411 was on that situation. Oh well. Maybe after Christmas.

Johnny and I stood at the door watching them all leave. Major Silva turned and pointed out the two military squads that sat on duty for the night. "If you need anything, call," he said to Johnny.

"Thank you Sir," Johnny said, then softly closed the big wooden door, securing the three bolts.

"Two guards?" I asked, looking up at him.

"Of course," he smiled. "Claire, you're more important than the President of the United States at this point. You better get at least two guards."

That night Johnny slept on the sofa downstairs. "Extra security," he argued with me when I told him how dumb I thought it was. I didn't care how many guards were outside, all I needed to feel safe was Johnny. I slept so peacefully that night, at one point even waking up just to peek down at him sleeping.

SN

Eight short hours later, I was up and in the shower, excited to spend the day with my girls. At exactly 9:01 am, the chiming doorbell rang through the house and shortly after I heard Alicia call up to me.

"Claire, let's go!"

I bounced down the stairs to Kass and Alicia waiting below. They both wore matching Santa hats and Kass plopped one on my head as soon as I hit the bottom step.

"Seriously?" I laughed. "Do I have to?"

"Yes you do," a tiny voice said from behind me. I turned around to see Lexi, our sweet friend, pop out from behind a pillar in the same Santa hat we were wearing.

"Lexi!" I gasped. "Omg!" I grabbed her and pulled her close. It had been almost a year since we had seen each other.

"I missed you so much, Miss Supergirl!" she giggled, her eyes full of wonder. "How did…I just can't even believe this," she stammered. "I saw the video online and I knew it was you, but it just didn't seem real."

"Lexi, I'm so sorry you had to find out like that," I apologized, taking her hands in mine. "Kass found out on accident and then when I told Alicia you weren't in town. I never meant to exclude you."

Lexi squeezed my hands. "It's ok Claire, really. Alicia explained everything to me. I would have done the same thing."

"That was an interesting conversation," Alicia laughed

as we headed outside to the waiting SUV. "*Mony*," she said, mocking Lexi's tiny voice in monotone and replaying the conversation. "*I think I just saw Claire on Tiktok flying.*" We laughed so hard as we settled into the SUV with Major Silva at the wheel. "It was just so emotionless. Just so matter of fact," Alicia laughed.

"I was in shock!" Lexi giggled.

"Alright girls," Major Silva called from the front seat. "I'm not gonna put you on a time schedule, but you need to get done as fast as possible. Claire, we have four undercovers there so just be mindful that they are following you. Again, I'll be three steps behind."

"Ok, thank you Sir," I said, rolling my eyes at the girls. Four undercovers? Really?

Twenty minutes later, Major Silva pulled to a stop in front of Governor's Square, our local shopping mall.

"Do you girls have a list?" Kass asked, as we jumped out.

"I do," I said, pulling out a long one.

As soon as we walked through the back entrance of the mall, I immediately saw the first "undercover" Officer. He stood against the wall just inside the door with his arms folded, one leg tucked under and propped up on the wall and his shades on. Yep, his shades on inside. He had that familiar swept up hairdo and stared straight ahead, not even acknowledging our entry, except for a little inconspicuous nod he and Major Silva exchanged.

"Well he's not obvious at all," I whispered to Major Silva, who in return smirked at me.

The girls and I immediately got busy, deciding to

start at the south end and make our way north. I hadn't laughed that much or been that relaxed in public in a long time. In fact, I hadn't been in public in a long time, at least not in such a busy setting. The mall sparkled in glowing Christmas lights and glittery red and green ribbons and bows. The Santa hats turned out to be a great idea, as they seemed to blend us together with each other and the hundreds of other people who were wearing the same thing, but still I kept my head down.

By noon, we had pretty much marked everyone off our lists and headed to a couple of more stores to buy some clothes, because unfortunately I didn't have many. I had bought a few summer clothes in Hawaii, but at the compound I mostly stayed in my uniform or PT clothes. I had a few sweatshirts, but nothing nice for Christmas dinner with my family.

"Claire, look at that," Alicia almost whispered as we walked by a novelty shop. My eyes followed her stare to a tall window display that was dedicated entirely to me. I gasped, wide-eyed and walked slowly to the window. There were two large banners, one of them showing a cartoon character of me, long brown curly hair and all, while the second also showed another picture of me mid-descent at the beach, but somehow they had managed to edit Kirsten out. I stood in front of it wide-eyed while Lexi snapped pics of me from behind with the window display in front.

"This is crazy Claire," she smiled. "Stand in front and smile. I want to get your pic."

I turned and glanced at her, while several people walked by casting long glances my way, then looking up at the window.

"Girls, let's move on," Silva said, looking around clearly worried about someone making a connection.

We obeyed him, but not before I stole one last long glance at the window display. That was me. I couldn't wrap my mind around it. Maybe the press conference would be a good thing. Everyone seemed to already be accepting the idea of a flying girl.

Our next stop was American Eagle, one of my favorites in high school and after finding a bunch of clothes, we headed to the dressing rooms to try them on.

"Ok you guys, just remember Silva is waiting so we don't want to take too long," I reminded them.

"Oh he's totally fine Claire," Kass smiled. "He's got a jumbo pretzel, a coffee and a bench just outside. He's a happy guy."

We each tried on ten different outfits as quickly as possible, modeling for each other and after much deliberation, I decided on a few pairs of jeans, sweats, tee shirts and sweaters (plus an adorable black beret I thought would never be my style.) For Christmas I found a black and white skort with a black sweater and matching tights. I couldn't remember the last time I wore a dress of any type and I had this overwhelming desire to dress up.

We checked out and grabbed a very patient Major Silva, who by this time had struck up a conversation with one of the soldiers who was supposed to be there undercover.

"What do you think girls, are you hungry?" he asked as we climbed in the SUV.

"I'm starving," said Lexi. "Can we hit a buffet?"

"Lexi!" Kass laughed. "I see you still haven't lost your appetite."

We all agreed what a crazy amount of food Lexi could consume for her size. She was this petite little blond from California, who stood just over 5 feet and weighed no more than 110 pounds, but boy could she eat.

We finally agreed on our favorite burger joint *Johnny's*, then crammed into a booth in the back. I admired all the adorable Christmas decorations and the walls that were painted red and white in honor of our hometown university, Austin Peay.

After ordering, we talked about our adventures over the last two years. It was nice for once to hear what the other girls had been up to and not all about me and my flying power. It had only come up once and Major Silva shut it down fast. (He also crammed me on the inside of the booth in the corner, facing away from the door and any curious eyes.)

Major Silva had gone to pay the bill and we had pretty much finished up, when Kass looked at me, her eyes wide. "Don't look," she said through clenched teeth, "but Tracy is standing by the counter and she's looking this way."

"Tracy?" Lexi asked a little too loud. "Tracy from high

school?"

"That's the one," Alicia whispered, a little irritated. "She also blabbed it to the whole world that Claire is the Supergirl."

"And…here she comes," Kass smirked.

Tracy approached our table cautiously, another girl tagging along behind. "Hey Kass, I thought that was you," she said, then looked around the table. "And Alicia, Lexi…" then her eyes stopped on me, "and Claire."

We all sat in silence for an awkward moment, before Kass finally spoke up.

"Hi Tracy," she smiled, sweetly. "Wow it's been forever. I haven't seen you since..well, since I saw you blowing Claire's cover on national TV."

I looked at my baby sister, in shock at her forwardness. Kass was never a confrontational person, so hearing her take on Tracy like this was surprising to say the least.

"How…how was I supposed to know it was some big secret?" Tracy snapped, obviously thrown off by Kass' forwardness. I could tell her attitude hadn't matured much since high school.

"We don't know…maybe common sense?" Lexi added.

Alicia nodded her head in agreement. "You could have put Claire's life in danger, Tracy," she reasoned.

Tracy stared at us for a moment, finally shrugging her shoulders and rolling her eyes. "Whatever," she said, turning to leave. "I don't have time for this drama. Good luck with your alien…" she muttered as she walked away, so I didn't catch the end.

I waited until she was out of earshot. "Kass!" I tried not to laugh, while I lightly scolded her. "You know better than that."

"*Whatever*," Lexi said, mocking Tracy. "I'm sorry Claire, but sometimes people need to be called out."

"Kass was only doing her duty as your sibling," Alicia added.

Kass smiled at me, completely pleased with herself.

"Alright girls, let's roll," Silva said, approaching the table and throwing down a twenty dollar tip.

"Ok," I laughed as we all slid out of the booth. "And girls, thank you, but don't let it happen again. I have a superhero reputation to live up to."

"Anyways...," Alicia smiled at my cockiness, as the rest of the girls groaned, keeping my ego in check.

EIGHT

THAT AFTERNOON WE were thrilled to find Shawn and Johnny putting up our family Christmas tree back at the President's house. I hugged Johnny completely floored at his thoughtfulness.

"That way you can have a bit of home since we have to celebrate here," he said, kissing me on the forehead.

I looked up at our eight foot tree, that suddenly seemed so small in this massive great room. At our house it went all the way to the ceiling. "Thank you so much Johnny," I gasped, squeezing him tighter.

"Claire," Shawn called from the kitchen as he, Alicia, Lexi, Kass and Kyle came in from the garage. "Do you know where a ladder is around here?" He held up our family angel. "I can't get Gabriel up top without it. I tried a chair, but that was a no go."

I rolled my eyes, looking at them all. It was so obvious what they were up to. "You want me to fly it up there, right?"

"You did it last year," Kass reminded me.

I looked at Johnny who was smiling down at the ground, avoiding eye contact.

"Fine," I smirked, snatching the angel from Shawn. "But this is it. I'm not hanging lights."

"Mom, come here!" Kass yelled. "Claire's gonna fly the angel up!"

That didn't sound weird at all.

Very quickly, my mom, Silva and my two Aunts and Uncle joined us in the living room.

"Oh wow Claire, be careful," Lexi warned, though I knew she was excited to watch.

"I think I got this Lex," I laughed, then lifted softly off the ground and just to the top of the tree. I heard everyone gasp as I leaned in to securely fasten our angel. It was so nice to be in the air again, even at only 8 feet. I straightened up a few ornaments and a strand of lights while I was at it, then did my favorite backflip out of the sky, landing safely on the floor.

"Wow," Lexi gasped. "Unbelievable Claire."

That evening all my family began arriving. My sister Danielle first, then Tessa and her husband Ryan. I loved watching their expressions as they walked in this massive house, but still felt bad that we weren't able to have Christmas at home.

"This house is a trip Claire," Ryan said, looking around. He was a Master Sergeant now and stationed in North Carolina. "We don't have anything like this at Bragg. How long are they keeping you here?"

"I think just until after the press conference and they can figure out what to do with me," I shrugged.

"Whatever they decide, I'm sure it's in your best interest," Ryan said, putting one arm around me. "Everything's going to be ok." I loved Ryan. He was like the big brother Kass and I never had.

Tessa slid up beside Ryan, stealing his other arm. "Claire," she whispered and looked into the kitchen, "what's with mom and Major Silva?"

I turned and looked behind us at mom and Silva who were busily preparing dinner together, along with my two aunts. I looked back at Tessa and smirked, "What's it look like?"

"Seriously?" Tessa gasped.

"I mean...I think so. Mom hasn't said anything yet, but it's obvious he really cares about her." I glanced at both of them who were talking and smiling. My aunts seemed to like him a lot too. Major Silva was definitely at ease with my family and it was fun to watch him blend in so well. I knew being around a family wasn't the norm for him, but my mom could make anyone feel at home. In fact, home was wherever she was and that's why celebrating Christmas here was just fine for all of us.

"As long as he's a good guy." Ryan flexed his triceps and stood a little taller, while giving Silva a stare down.

"He is Ryan," I laughed. "From what I know about him, he's never had much family or been married for that matter. I think even talking to mom is a pretty big deal for him."

"Well, I'm sure mom will let us know whatever it is, in her own time…which I hope is this weekend," Tessa winked at me.

S
N

Christmas eve and Christmas Day was the best holiday I had in a long time. My whole family was there, plus Christmas night Shawn and Alicia were able to join us for dessert. Everyone had dressed up, which was not the norm for my family on Christmas. We usually settled for Christmas PJs or an ugly Christmas sweater and jeans, but somehow being in this house made us all want to look our best. I was so glad I picked up a dressy outfit and best of all, Johnny seemed to like it because he kept telling me over and over again how nice I looked.

That night after the celebration was over, we sat around the fire and I let my family ask me as many questions as they wanted. I felt bad that so many of the people closest to me didn't know of my flying power, but they also knew I had no choice in the matter. In fact mom and Major Silva once again reminded them of that.

It was amusing to sit back and listen to Kass and

Alicia, Johnny and Shawn tell everyone their stories of how they first found out I could fly. Kass and Alicia had us laughing hard as they retold the craziness of those two days, Kass finding out by accident and then us purposely driving Alicia out to my grandma's farm to tell her. Then everyone sat on the edge of their seats as Shawn gave a play by play of the night I broke into the hanger.

"We knew a ghost girl was hanging around the hanger, but we had no idea it was Claire," Shawn explained. "And then when I tackled her in the woods and flipped her over I just…," he looked over at me. "I just lost it."

Shawn's eyes met mine and immediately I was on my back in the woods, his heavy body on top of me with his gun belt pinning me to the ground. "*Claire!*" he had yelled at me. "*What are you doing?!*"

I looked around the room at 14 pairs of eyeballs staring intently at him hanging on to his every word. Shawn should definitely have been a story teller. Some parts of his story had them gasping, while other parts made everyone laugh. He remembered every detail of that night, even some things I had purposefully pushed out of my mind.

"So Claire," Danielle asked, when Shawn was done and everyone was quiet. "The rocks? The flying rocks from another planet?"

I nodded, cleared my voice and was ready to answer, when Major Silva interrupted. "Zeta Reticuli," he answered. My eyebrows raised in curiosity at him. What the heck was that? "Zeta Reticuli, that's a star system

39 light years away from earth and where we think the floating rocks came from."

"*Interesting,*" I thought. No one had ever mentioned that to me.

Major Silva continued, "My partner, Major Bryan Kearney, his father and his grandfather, all biochemists and scientists with NASA, worked together to make the flying potion both he and Claire were infected with. Unfortunately it didn't work on him, nor does it appear to have any success with anyone other than Claire."

"You mean Claire is infected with alien matter?" Kyle asked, astonished. I saw Kass lightly nudge him then look in mom's direction. I knew she was thinking what I was thinking and that was to not worry mom anymore than need be.

"Well…yes," Major Silva answered, "but alien meaning 'not of this world' and she is still completely normal and healthy. Her body has adjusted to it well."

"True," I agreed, to reassure my mom. "Plus I get the added bonus of flying." I looked around at my family who didn't seem too convinced. "Seriously you guys. I'm totally fine."

"She's absolutely fine," Major Silva reiterated. "And we're doing everything in our power to make sure Claire is healthy and safe."

"Well, Ryan and I are staying here until the press conference, Claire," Tessa said. "We want to support you in any way we can."

"That goes for me too," said Dani. "Plus we can help

mom move."

"Are you sure?" I asked, not wanting to put anyone out, but excited to have them around longer for whatever reason.

"Of course!" They said in unison.

The press conference. The thought of it sent shivers down my spine and I noticed Johnny shift uncomfortably in his seat and squeeze me closer.

"You're all welcome to come," Major Silva said. "But we have to keep it on the down low until then, ok?"

Everyone nodded in agreement.

"What happens after that?" Dani asked. "What are you guys doing with Claire then?"

"She's under our watch now," Major Silva smiled at me. "We'll take care of her, one hundred percent."

That answer seemed enough for my family, as everyone relaxed a bit. Soon we were able to move on to other subjects, which I was thankful for. All my family seemed to be adjusting to this craziness, so if they could find normalcy in who I was now, maybe the rest of the world could. I guess I would be finding that out in just eight short days.

NINE

THE NEXT FEW days were extremely busy for us. I spent the whole week meeting with the General, getting checkups with Dr. Enroe at Blanchfield hospital and weirdest of all, media classes with Captain Lewis. In those sessions, we did mock press conferences and interviews and I was drilled over and over again on what I could say and what was strictly forbidden.

"Never, under any circumstance are you to bring up the rocks and who and what led to the pink potion or that the potion even exists for that matter," Captain Lewis emphasized. "You have no idea why you are the way you are. You woke up with this power and that is the end of it."

If for any reason I went off script or gave too much away, I would be exiled from Ft. Campbell and forced

79

to live protected in a place of the government's choosing. My heart sank at the thought of that, but that didn't seem so hard for me. My worry was someone else messing it up. I had to give General Collins a list of everyone who knew about the potion and everything I had shared about my super power. Thankfully I had only shared it with those I truly trusted, which was only a handful, but even that seemed pointless since so many people knew now anyway.

My family spent the week at our house packing and then getting mom and Kass moved to the south side of Campbell. I was not able to go to our old house off base, but was allowed to help move into the new one because it was on base. I watched mom closely as she unpacked, just to make sure she was taking this all ok and thankfully she seemed to be fine.

Johnny and I unpacked my room that next cold and rainy Saturday afternoon, while my family was busy scattered about the new house helping out. It was New Year's Day. Just three days away from my press conference.

"I don't know why mom insists on me having a room here," I laughed. "I have a feeling, I won't be living in it."

"I guess she wants it ready, just in case," Johnny said, then winked at me, "but who knows…maybe you won't need it after all."

I looked at him inquisitively, unsure of where he was going with that. Did he mean me living on base somewhere or at another base entirely or maybe…maybe with him? I tried not to let my mind wander too much toward the latter, because although I wouldn't want to be with anyone else ever, I got the impression the few times it had come up, that he was focused on his career right now and marriage was far down the line for us. Besides, I wouldn't wish the responsibility of me right now on anybody. At least with us living separately, Johnny was not responsible for my safety. I decided to just smile and act like I knew what he was talking about.

"So what do you guys think of the new house?" Major Silva asked, as he walked in my room.

"It's beautiful Sir," I said, looking around my room. This house was a little bigger than our last house. The ceilings were higher and it had more of an open concept than our little white cottage in Clarksville.

"You know, this is the first time they have ever allowed a civilian family to move here, especially in this neck of the woods," he smiled.

That made me giggle, hearing him use redneck slang in his thick hispanic accent. "Neck of the woods?" I asked. "You've been hanging around us way too long Sebastian."

"Is that what I said?" he chuckled.

"Don't worry Major Silva, I caught myself saying fixin' last week and I had to check myself," Johnny said, putting one hand on his shoulder. "Hey, by the way, thanks for helping get this house for Claire and her family. I know you had a huge part in it."

"Yes, thank you Sir," I echoed him. "It's such a relief to know my family will be safe here. I'll definitely sleep better at night."

"My pleasure," he simply said, but I could see appreciation in his eyes. The wall he built was quickly crumbling and it made me so happy. Everyone needs somebody and it made me sad to know how long he had been alone. "So are you ready for Tuesday?" he asked, quickly changing the subject.

"I guess as ready as I'll ever be," I gulped.

"You're gonna be fine Claire," Major Silva reassured me.

Johnny kissed my forehead. "Of course, you'll be fine."

I smiled at them both as Johnny wrapped an arm around me and pulled me close. He had certainly changed his attitude about the press conference since Christmas and I had a feeling the higher ups had a lot to do with that.

Monday night I laid in my bed in the President's house wide awake. The wind blew lightly, scraping a tree branch up against the shutters outside of my room. It was unseasonably warm for a January night, only dipping into the 50's. Tomorrow the high would be close to 65 for the press conference. I looked at the clock. It was already 12:30 and I had been laying here for two and half hours imagining every possible thing that could go wrong tomorrow. I threw my blankets off, as the thought of that made my body temperature climb drastically. Maybe if I got something to drink that would slow my brain down. I slipped out of bed and walked to the top of the stairs overlooking the great room. Johnny lay on the couch fast asleep. Poor guy. Between his job and dealing with me, I could tell he was exhausted. "*Good thing I'm so in love with you,*" he had teased me earlier in the day, when I had brought it up. "*Otherwise, I would have quit a long time ago.*"

A flash of light in the distance caught my eye in the tall glass window. I could see a storm moving in from the west. What I wouldn't give to be up in the clouds watching it roll in. I walked quickly back to my room to check the radar on my phone. It was still about 20 minutes out. Maybe, just maybe I could pop up in the sky for a moment to catch a glimpse.

"*It'll be ok Claire,*" I told myself. "*Ten minutes. Just ten minutes and then right back to bed.*"

It didn't take much to convince myself and five minutes later I was bundled up and standing on the sill of my bedroom window. Outside the wind was picking up and I assumed anyone on guard outside would be sitting out the storm in their car.

I gently slid the window shut leaving just a crack to get it back open, then flew up and around the gutters. Once I was on top of the house I peeked over the side. To the left of the circle driveway, an MP's car sat inconspicuously, under a large oak tree. Inside I could see the light of a phone, so I knew it was safe to go. I walked the point of the rooftop to the back of the house and then shot off into the crisp air. In the distance I could see the rotating light of the airfield tower, as I soared quickly to 250 feet, high enough to not be seen and low enough to get a good view of the storm.

I popped in my earbuds then sat back watching the beautiful light show, smelling the fresh ocean air it was bringing in from the gulf. Phil Collin's *"In The Air Tonight"* filled my ears and I breathed out a deep sigh of happiness and contentment. As much as I dreaded the press conference and all the publicity it would bring, if it meant giving me more freedom to fly I would be all for it. I dreamed of a life where I will be able to pop in the air at anytime and anywhere.

As my song came to an end, the storm quickly moved in closer. A bolt of lightning flashed from the cloud striking something on the ground, while lighting up the sky as if it were daylight. I took that as my cue to head back down. I allowed gravity to leave my body and began free falling toward the earth on my back, letting the wind take control for a moment, occasionally flipping me around and then lifting me up and down. At fifty feet I paused to get my eyes on the MP and once I knew it was clear, slipped silently into the bedroom window. It closed with a snap, locking shut. I then slid off my shoes and sweatshirt and made my way to bed. Suddenly, lightning flashed, sending a bright light streaking through the darkness. It lit up my bed where a male figure sat waiting, stopping me in my tracks. My body froze in terror, sucking the breath out of my lungs. I backed quickly toward the door fumbling for the light, before finally noticing it was Johnny.

"Have a nice flight, Claire?" he asked dryly.

"Johnny!" I scolded him. "You scared me to death!"

"Good." He was obviously mad at me. "What are you doing?"

"I couldn't sleep," I shrugged, as I turned on a lamp.

"So you thought getting struck by lightning might help?"

I sighed loudly and sat by him on my bed exhausted, all that fresh air getting to me. It was after one now and the day was finally catching up, plus flying made me even more tired.

"I'm sorry," I muttered. Johnny had been on edge a lot lately and definitely not his normal, relaxed self.

He slowly got up from the bed. "Claire, you are too much."

"Johnny?" I said, grabbing his hand. "Will you… please stay with me tonight? Please? I can't sleep."

Johnny ran his hands through his hair, the way he did when he had to think something over. I knew he wanted to stay with me, but so much responsibility came with that. I knew he wanted to keep me safe, but we had never made it a habit to sleep in the same bed together. With my body being compromised like it was, he worried about doing any harm to me physically and emotionally, so he clearly set the boundaries a long time ago.

He walked back over and sat on the bed again. I moved closer to him and slid my arm through his. Johnny's arms were waves of muscle and I loved feeling ever crease of them. He leaned over and kissed my forehead as I put my head on his shoulder.

"Please?" I whispered again.

Johnny's other arm wrapped around me. "Ok," he finally agreed.

I melted into the bed as he wrapped me up in his arms. I felt very lucky laying beside him. Somehow I knew that no matter how difficult tomorrow's press conference or the days to come would be, I was going to be ok. I had Johnny.

TEN

I WOKE EARLY the next morning without my alarm. Johnny was already up and gone, having to report to his unit before we met for the press conference at 10. I sat in the silence of the big house all alone, except for the security team outside that had grown to five MPs overnight.

The bagel I had toasted for breakfast sat cold on my plate at the kitchen bar. I stared down at it, unable to even take one bite. The clock on the wall said 7:30 and loudly ticked the seconds away. I knew in just two and half short hours, my life was going to change forever and I gulped at the thought of it. I had always been a blender and had no idea how to live my life so openly.

My phone rang and my heart jumped when I saw Zhao's number pop up.

"Zhao?" I squeaked, before he had a chance to say anything. "Oh my goodness! How are you?"

"Hey Claire!" he exclaimed. "I'm good. I just wanted to call and check on you."

"Just calling to check on me? Isn't it like 2:30 in the morning in Hawaii?" I smiled.

Zhao laughed. "Well…that, plus I heard you're *only* telling the whole world you can fly today."

"Yeah," I sighed. "I'm so nervous Zhao."

"I know you are Claire, but it's going to be ok."

We were both quiet for a minute. I appreciated Zhao's encouraging words, but at the end of the day, no one could guarantee that I would be ok and he knew that as well as I did.

"Claire, you know Major Silva would never do anything to put your life in danger…I mean, of course with the power you have, there's going to always be some danger, but I know that guy would walk on water for you."

"I know, Zhao."

"And look at all the positives that come with it. No seclusion, no more flying in the middle of the night and hiding from everyone…plus you're going to be famous, girl!"

"Oh gosh Zhao," my voice cracked. "That's the worst part."

"Why? Everyone in your life loves you Claire." His voice grew softer. "I know I do. The world will fall in love with you too."

I paused for a moment at his sweet words. Zhoa had

told me he loved me many times, but not like *that.* Something in his voice had changed. This time it felt different. I shook it off though, not wanting to pause too long and make the conversation uncomfortable.

"I love you too, Zhao. You're one of the bestest friends I've ever had. I don't know what I'd do without you in my life."

I heard Zhao sigh quietly into the phone with almost a soft flare of agitation. "Well you know I'll always be here for you Claire. If you ever need to get away, you can come find me."

"I know I can and…and I'm sure with my crazy life, that is always a possibility."

I hoped I hadn't hurt him and was so glad he called. By the time we hung up my nerves had calmed. He had a way of bringing calm into my stormy life. He was so right about the best part of this, the no seclusion side. I loved being in seclusion on my island and am one of those people who loves spending time by myself, but living a reclusive lifestyle was a whole different story and one I feared more than any spy or foreign enemy.

The black SUV began the ten minute trip to Headquarters as I sat in the back seat all alone. I didn't mind it so much though, as it gave me a chance to clear my head. General Collins made sure I wore my dress blues and Johnny told me he thought that was so everyone would know I was in the military and under the protection of the US government.

The SUV pulled into the main entrance of Headquarters. I looked in the front of the building where several news vans were parked and their crews waited patiently outside the building to enter. It was only 9 and a full hour before it was to start. We drove around the back where another MP was waiting to escort me inside the building and up to the General's office. Headquarters was unusually empty for a Tuesday morning. Usually the main lobby was bustling with soldiers coming and going and secretary's answering phones that seemed to ring constantly. Today I noticed only one main receptionist and a lone podium standing in the middle of the circle lobby.

We took the lobby elevator to the 3rd floor where General Collins, Major Simmons, and Captain Lewis greeted me in the hallway. The MP who escorted me saluted, then left quickly. Captain Lewis gave me a quick review of what I could and couldn't say. I remembered them all, but especially the part where I had to pretty much lie and say I had no clue where my flying power came from. Captain Lewis would open up with a short speech and explain who I am and how I came to fly, as vaguely as he could, then open up the floor to questions. If he felt the vibe was right, he would allow me to answer a few.

After a while, all three of them left the office to finish the final preparations for the press conference. It was now 9:45 and I stared out of the General's tall window that stretched from ceiling to floor. I was scared. I was so scared my throat went dry and I felt nauseous as heat rose in my body, breaking me out in my red blotches. Just perfect. I was going to greet the world looking like I had the measles.

As I stared outside, a red cardinal suddenly flew in front of me. It hovered and we stood eye to eye, eventually perching on the window sill. I moved closer to get a better look at him and in return he cocked his head sideways, the crest of his head popping straight up. He stared back at me, almost cross-eyed making me giggle. I know this sounds weird, but I could have sworn he smiled at me laughing. He gave me one more long glance and shot into the air. I pressed my nose against the window and watched him as long as I could, jealous of his freedom to fly whenever he wanted. That's what I wanted. A new determination filled my soul and all the jitters began to calm down as I looked up into the clear blue sky. I would give the best and most professional press conference I could give.

Johnny and Major Silva joined me and General Collins in the elevator for the short trip down to the lobby where Captain Lewis and Major Simmons waited. My family was gathered at my mom's new home, tuned into the local station where the press conference would air nationally. General Collins had thought it would be best to keep them away from headquarters to avoid the media from possibly following them home.

Johnny squeezed my hand that was holding tightly to his. "You're going to do great Claire Bear," he whispered down to me. "And you look beautiful. I love your hair like that. You look like you just stepped out of a 1940's ad."

"Thank you," I whispered as I glanced at myself in the elevator mirror. I had my hair pulled back into a sleek bun, while what little bangs I had peeked out from under my flat cap in a little wave curl. My red lips did tie it all together for a 1940's vibe.

Major Silva gave me a reassuring wink, as the elevator door chimed and slid open. I took a deep breath and paused, then everything seemed to move in slow motion as I eventually followed the guys out of the elevator. One step at a time my heels echoed on the empty foyer floor, as cameras began to snap and pop catching our every move. Finally at the podium, at least a dozen reporters waited in silence, their curious glares staring right through me. I smiled slightly to make them feel a little more comfortable. General Collins had not told them what the press conference was about, but the rumor had spread and it was pretty much known it had something to do with the flying girl. Since I was the only girl present, that was obviously me.

I stood in formation where I had been instructed, just to the left of General Collins at the podium and squeezed in between Major Silva and Captain Lewis. Johnny stood just off camera to the side, with the thought that maybe I'd be more recognizable if we were seen together.

I definitely agreed with that. Johnny was an eye catcher and a guy whose face you couldn't forget. When we were out together, he was always a standout in the crowd, especially with the girls. I could just see it now; someone would record him off TV and he would become a Tiktok with every girl asking who he was.

Crazy side note; little did I know (and had I known I would have died) the President of the United States and his staff sat in a room at that very moment tuned in at the White House!

Then the moment was here. General Collins was given his cue and so he began.

"Good Morning. My name is General Collins and on behalf of our command staff here at Ft. Campbell, I want to thank you for allowing us this time to connect with the American public and answer some questions… maybe put some rumors to rest. I would like to first introduce my fellow Command staff here," he said turning to his right, "this is Major Simmons, head of security of the 101st, Captain Lewis, who is in charge of public relations, Airman Claire Haley (I glanced up and smiled then my eyes fell immediately back to the floor), and Major Silva."

I stole a peek at Johnny who returned my look, his face in a slight worried scowl. He didn't like this at all, but he smiled reassuringly at me to ease my jitters.

General Collins continued. "Over the past two years, we have been asked to address rumors and comment on sightings of an unknown object or person in the skies above Clarksville and the Ft. Campbell area. We have not been in a position until recently to share any information with you, mainly because at the time, we were not even completely sure of what was happening ourselves and we had little information to give you. Well as of today that has all changed. At this time, I'd like to have Captain Lewis come and speak to you."

"Thank you General," Captain Lewis said as he reached the podium. "Two years ago, we received our first notification of an unknown UFO sighting over the downtown area of Clarksville. Some were reporting a large bird, others a witch-like image and we even had reports of a supergirl, after several unexplained, but helpful interventions with the Clarksville Police Department. After months of investigating we have cleared up the mystery, so to speak."

The lobby grew deathly silent, as everyone awaited his announcement. I took a deep breath, knowing this was my last moment of living a life of anonymity. I could see Captain Lewis take one as well.

"Ladies and gentlemen, I would like to introduce you to Airman Claire Haley." I lifted my chin up and stood up as straight as I could. "Let me first say that Airman Haley above all is a top notch asset to the United States Air Force. She is extremely intelligent and serves her country well and we consider ourselves very lucky to have her aboard. Airman Haley came to us a couple of years ago, when she was just a high school senior, after realizing that she possessed what we've considered an impossible human ability, until now, and that is…at various times to defy gravity."

A large gasp echoed through the air and every eye in the building rested on me. The enormity of the moment was so heavy and I bit my bottom lip under the pressure of it. "*Keep it together, Claire,*" I reminded myself.

Captain Lewis cleared his throat. "We have very little information on how this is even possible, but we are working with the best research team available to figure things out. She is being monitored at all times and is seeing the best medical doctors to make sure she stays healthy and well, because above all that is our number one priority." Then his tone changed and his voice grew stern. "On behalf of the United States military I want to make it absolutely known that Airman Haley is under our care. Again she is being monitored and protected at all times and anyone who crosses our restrictions or puts her life in danger will be punished to the utmost degree." The room was quiet, as Captain Lewis paused to let his words sink in. "Now, I'll take a few questions."

They all started asking at once and Captain Lewis gave the go ahead to a familiar blonde lady I had seen reporting on me in the past, from a local Nashville station.

"Captain Lewis, can we just verify when you say 'defy gravity' are you saying that Airman Haley…can fly?"

Captain Lewis nodded his head yes. "That's what I'm saying."

"Excuse me Sir," she tried again. "You mean fly as in her having, sort of a Superhero flying power?"

"Airman Haley's exceptional human ability is unlike any fantasy movie. We are dealing with an unknown reality and we are working hard to figure it out."

I noticed Captain Lewis refused to use the words "superhero" or even "flying." He kept avoiding them through each question. Major Silva told me later, it was to keep everyone grounded and I guess that meant calm.

Another male reporter spoke up. "Can you confirm that the video that came out of Hawaii a couple of months ago, was in fact Airman Haley and also explain a little about what was happening in that video?"

"I think we are all aware that it is her," Captain Lewis answered, somewhat annoyed. "But that's all the information I can share on that, to protect other parties involved."

"Will Airman Haley be stationed at Campbell from now on or will she be transferred out?"

"We prefer to keep her permanent whereabouts unknown," came Captain Lewis' quick reply.

The questions kept rolling in one after the other.

"*Can you tell us where her flying ability originated from?*"

"We're still figuring that out."

"*Do you believe Airman Haley will possess this ability forever?*"

"We have no idea."

"*How has it affected her health?*"

"Airman Haley just passed a physical with flying colors. She's very healthy."

And then the question we all knew was coming.

"*May we direct some questions to Airman Haley?*"

Captain Lewis turned to me. "Claire?" He quietly asked for my approval. I looked up at Major Silva, who gave me a quick nod of approval.

I walked to the podium, as Captain Lewis slid over. He was going to stay beside me the whole time in case I got backed in a corner.

"Good Morning," I said, as confidently as I could. I saw the blonde lady's eyes soften, almost as if she felt sorry for me.

"Good Morning Airman Haley," she smiled. "First of all may I ask how old you are."

"Yes Ma'am, I'm 19. I'll be 20 this spring."

"And you're from Clarksville?" She asked.

"Yes Ma'am."

Another man jumped in, with a mischievous grin on his face. "So it's safe to say you are the mysterious flying girl that's been seen in the area over the past two years."

"Perhaps some of them," I answered vaguely.

"Have you been in touch with the Clarksville Police Department yet?" Another woman with a stern face asked.

"No, I have not."

"No? I'm sure they would be interested in talking with you about your many assists to them over the past two years," she pressed further.

"I have not heard from them," I repeated, "but of course I'm open to that conversation."

Another question came from the back. I looked to find

a face, but the glare from the camera lights were starting to blind me a bit. "Airman Haley, can you explain how you fly, the process of it and how you got this flying power?"

"It's pretty basic," I shrugged. "It's like walking. If I want to fly, my body just does it and I'm not exactly sure where my power comes from. They're working to figure it out." I hoped that was gray enough.

"Airman Haley, how long have you been like...like this?" a man in the front asked, looking me up and down, almost disgusted. "And how do you expect to just fit back into society?"

I slowly looked down at myself following his gaze, the tiny smile I was wearing quickly faded. I did not know what to say and felt very insulted, almost bad about myself. At first I wanted to snap back at him, but what good would that do? America would forget his snarkiness and instead focus on mine. I had to be better than that.

"It's been almost three years," I said, smiling coolly at him. "Three of the best years of my life and I'm proud of who I am. I think...I think Americans are some of the most accepting kind of people in the world and I'll find my place just fine."

I glanced over at Captain Lewis who nodded his approval at me. Several reporters shouted more questions, but General Collins approached the podium, dismissing me much to my relief. I stood beside Major Silva, exhaling the breath I felt like I had been holding the whole time.

General Collins thanked the press and before he could

finish, Major Silva took my arm and we were surrounded immediately by MPs who escorted us to a car in the back. Behind me I heard cameras begin to click and glanced quickly over my shoulder to get one more peek at the reporters. I don't know why, but for some reason that snapshot is the one that caught on and by 7 o'clock that night, was spreading around the world.

ELEVEN

I JOINED MY family that night in my mom's cozy living room. We had just watched the press conference together and they were reassuring me what a great job I had done. I appreciated the encouragement, but I could tell that despite my efforts to be brave, I was terrified. Luckily, I was mostly hidden behind the podium and my nervous habit of twisting the bottom of my shirt was concealed.

"Shhh!" Kass hissed at everyone.

We turned our attention back to the news station we had tuned into all day. Except for a few stories sliced in between, they had been running everything about "the supergirl" all day including clips of me flying in Clarksville over the downtown area, the notorious bridge car accident I had rescued a teenage girl from, Nashville at the Aerosmith concert, and all the Hawaii footage with new angles I had never seen before. They had interviewed anyone that was willing to come forward and all the people involved with anything my flying power had ever touched. The Chief of Police in Clarksville was especially kind and had nothing but nice things to say and I was so excited to see the girl I saved from the bridge doing well.

Major Silva gave me special permission to stay at mom's house that night since my two older sisters would be flying out the next morning. Both Danielle and Tessa had begun making plans to move back home to be with our family and that made me so happy.

I was just about to get up and walk Johnny out when Major Silva stood up and cleared his throat. "Excuse me everyone," he said, drawing every eyeball in the room in his direction. "Can I speak with you for a moment?"

I glanced quickly at mom, who seemed oblivious to what was happening.

"Oh this should be good," Johnny whispered in my ear, squeezing my leg, while I jabbed him in the side.

I had never seen Major Silva so uneasy. He was usually so in control and laid back and cool, kind of the leader of the pack.

"So I just wanted you all to know that I am going to do everything I can to keep your family safe and I appreciate your flexibility as we adjust to this new norm. I know it's been a little difficult for you all and especially your mom..." he paused and looked over at my mom. "And I...I want you to know that I care very much for her and I'm going to always be here for her. For all of you."

My mom smiled and got up to hug him. He wrapped her in a big bear hug and kissed her forehead softly. Major Silva didn't have a way of expressing himself with words, but we all knew exactly what he was saying. This was his way of telling us they were together. It was official now.

"Ok, now!" my brother in law Ryan said, laughing and clapping. We all laughed with him and stood up to gather around them.

"I knew it," Kass smiled, obviously proud of herself. "I knew it from the very beginning, didn't I Claire?"

"Oh yes Kass," I smiled, wrapping her in my arms. "You definitely did."

That week I started in my new duty station and in a new company that was known for its elite members, much like the company I was stationed with in Oahu. Major Silva had given me the 411 on them and had assigned me to this unit for number one, my protection and number two, to train me to be as strong and resilient. Between training with them and continuing Jiu Jitsu with Professor Corral every two weeks, I would stay very busy. I was thrilled when I found out Professor Corral would be coming down from Indiana every other week for two full days of training. I had learned so much from him and the skills he had taught me had been essential in saving my life the night I stole back Kirsten from the drug lords.

Winter quickly melted into Spring and between work, family, Kass' graduation and helping Alicia plan for her June wedding, I was extremely busy. Extremely busy and extremely happy. I was so thankful she had decided to wait for me to come home, because I wouldn't have missed it for the world.

On a bright Saturday morning in May, Kass, Lexi and I were escorted to a bridal shop to meet Alicia for a final fitting of her wedding dress and to pick up the bridal dresses. I pulled my hair in a high bun and donned my dark aviator shades to attempt to blend, but that was nearly impossible with the two armed MPs at the door.

Alicia had chosen a beautiful periwinkle blue for dress colors and let us choose our own style. Mine was a long strapless gown that gathered at the side, with a slit just high enough to give me some breathing room. Alicia looked stunning in her Italian lace gown and all of us girls were immediately crying as soon as she stepped out of the dressing room.

"Two weeks Mony," I reminded her as I helped straighten the sash around the middle of her dress. "Are you nervous at all?"

"Oh no way Claire," she smiled. "It can't get here fast enough. I can't wait to marry Shawn."

I winked at her, almost envious. I knew it would be a long time before Johnny and I could even broach the subject.

"You know, you're next," she reassured me.

"I don't think so," I said, bending down and smoothing

out a wrinkle. "That will be a long time from now, if ever."

"Oh…my…God," she almost whispered.

I stood up beside her. "No seriously. Not until we can figure out…" I tried to finish my thought, but saw her staring wide-eyed at the front of the store. I turned to see the two MPs closing and bolting the front door. Outside a large group of people had their noses and phones pressed up against the glass window recording us.

"Back up!" One of the MPs yelled at the crowd as they pushed into the glass doors making them bow slightly.

Our sales associate walked over to Alicia and I, her eyes wide. "You're the flying girl, right?" she asked in awe.

"Yes," I said, then looked toward the glass door. "I'm so very sorry."

"No, it's fine!" she said in awe. "You saved my baby sister from the bridge accident. My family has been dying to meet you. I'm Celeste. Her name is…"

"Maci," I finished for her. "Oh my goodness, I have thought about her so much and wondered where she was and what happened to her."

"She's just fine," Celeste laughed.

"Claire, we gotta go!" Justin the MP yelled from the front.

I frowned at Alicia who was stepping down from the little stage she was standing on.

"It's ok, Claire," she smiled. "Go. I'll meet up with you later."

I sighed in disappointment and hugged my sweet

friend. "I'm so sorry. Today was supposed to be your day."

"It's our day," she reassured me. "Now go. Be safe."

I looked over at Celeste. "I'll be getting in touch with you and Maci soon."

"Thanks," she smiled. "I'll let her know."

"Claire!" Justin yelled again.

I grabbed Kass and headed to the front of the store. Outside the Clarksville Police had arrived to help us push through the crowd of people to the SUV. I put my head down and held tight to Kass as hands grabbed me and we were pushed back and forth.

"Claire!" they yelled. "Can you sign this please?" others asked, pushing paper and pens in my face. Suddenly, I felt an arm go around my neck. My mind went back to Oahu, to the day I was almost kidnapped and being put into a choke hold.

My body took over and immediately went into defense mode. I tucked my chin so I couldn't be choked and lowered my base. I dropped to my left knee and using his arm as a fulcrum, hip tossed him high over my shoulder hard onto the ground. The crowd gasped and moved back, forming a circle around us. I looked down to see a very buff police officer on the ground.

"Oh my God," I exclaimed, reaching down to help him up. "Are you ok?"

"I slipped," he smiled, bashfully. "I was just trying to get you in the car safely, but I shouldn't have grabbed you like that!"

"Sorry Sir, just reflexes I guess," I said, trying to make

him feel better, as all around us muffled snickering could be heard.

Once we were safe inside the SUV I leaned back in my seat. Kass sat in silence beside me catching her breath.

I looked over at her. "Kass, you ok?"

"Yeah," she said, her eyes in shock. "Are you?"

"Sure," I shrugged.

"What was that?!"

"Jiu Jitsu," I said calmly.

"Claire, are you going to have to deal with that the rest of your life? That was insane."

I lowered my voice. "Better than being stuck in a compound out in the middle of Texas alone. Kass, please don't make a big deal out of it. The minute I act afraid they'll take it as their cue to send me away. Be brave with me ok?"

Kass stared at me for a moment, realizing what I was saying was true. "Ok Claire," she agreed. "Consider it dropped."

The day of Alicia and Sean's wedding arrived. We gathered at a whimsical garden spot along with Alicia and Shawn's family and three hundred guests. It looked almost fairy like with the white lights and white strands of flowers hanging from the ceiling . Alicia, Lexi, Kass and I had spent the last month, late nights at my mom's house helping her make the homemade decorations, since I couldn't get clearance to go to Alicia's house. She was on a tight budget, but you wouldn't have known it with the way her wedding turned out. It was very classy and looked very expensive. Alicia had great style.

Inside the bride's dressing room, we were busy getting ready and helping Alicia with the finishing touches on her dress. I stood back and admired her. She was stunning. I couldn't believe my best friend was getting married.

"Claire," she said, turning around and peeking at me from the side of her veil. "Do you ever wonder where we would be and what we would be doing now, if we hadn't driven into the fairgrounds that night? I mean…I wouldn't have met Shawn and you wouldn't have met Johnny and you would have never been able to…to…"

"Fly," we said together.

I had to catch my breath with that one. Not so much because of the flying part, but because of Johnny. I had never thought of that. One little thing could have kept us away that night and our paths would have never crossed and the reality of that terrified me.

"Wow Mony, I never thought of it that way."

She grabbed both of my hands in hers and we stood face to face. "Thank you Clairey. Thank you for always being here for me. I can't imagine my life without you, most of all."

"Same for me Mony," I said, blinking back a tear. " I don't know how I would have made it through all this craziness without you. I'm so happy for you and Shawn.

I know he's going to take care of you and you deserve nothing but the best."

"Now I get to live by you on base!" she smiled.

"I know! I can't wait!"

Alicia's mom opened the door. "Alicia, it's time."

"I'll see you out there," I said, kissing her cheek.

She took a deep breath and smiled. "See you soon."

I don't think Alicia's wedding could have been any more perfect. Her family and Shawn's family, the Jackson's, blended so wonderfully, despite their differences, his being from New York and her family from Tennessee. Johnny was Shawn's best man and Tater one of his groomsmen. I wasn't surprised to see Tater and Lexi reconnecting after he walked with her down the aisle. Weddings have a way of bringing people together.

Later that night Johnny took my hand and led me to a corner of the crowded dance floor. Elvis' "I Can't Help Falling In Love With You" played softly from the tall speakers. He looked so incredibly handsome in his classic black tux and his matching periwinkle tie.

"How do I have the most beautiful girl in the universe in my arms tonight?" he asked.

"Oh no, I'm the lucky one," I smiled up at him.

"Oh no," he repeated. "Every single guy in this place is staring a hole through you. They know what's up."

"That couldn't possibly have anything to do with

seeing me flying on the news last week, right?" I laughed.

He looked thoughtfully at me for a moment. "Yeah, you're probably right," he teased, pulling me in closer. I rested my head on his shoulder while he leaned down to kiss the top of my head. "Seriously though Claire, you know I plan on this being us one day, right? Just because we're not talking marriage right now, does not mean I'm not thinking about it."

I looked up into his kind eyes. "I understand," I said, though deep inside I wish this could have been us tonight. I would marry Johnny tomorrow if I had the chance, but I knew he was waiting because he thought it was what's best for me. "We have time," I reassured him.

Johnny pulled me in close again and I thought about what Alicia had said earlier. I was so thankful he decided to step in front of our car that night, almost three years ago and do his goofy little dance for me. I trembled at the thought of ever losing him.

TWELVE

OVER THE NEXT few weeks, I slowly adjusted to my new life at Campbell and to my new life being back home. Kass joined Kyle and Lexi at the University of Tennessee where she decided to major in Elementary Education. Getting used to not having her home was a huge adjustment for me and I couldn't even imagine how it was for mom now that she was an empty nester.

I grew even more comfortable with everyone knowing about my flying power, at least at Ft. Campbell. I rarely ventured off the base and since it was a closed base, not many civilians were around. My company treated me like any other Airman and I was able to go to the Exchange with my mom and Alicia without too many people approaching and even still, they were mostly friendly. General Collin's prediction seemed to be right in that people were getting used to my superpower.

One Saturday at the end of August, Alicia picked me up from the President's house to go grocery shopping with her. Shawn and Johnny were returning that afternoon from three days of field training, so we decided to fix dinner for them at Alicia and Shawn's new apartment, knowing they would be starving after four days of eating MREs.

"They're still following you?" Alicia asked as the Military Police's SUV followed us out of the driveway.

"Yeah," I sighed, snapping my seat belt closed. "I asked General Collins how much longer and he said, '*As long as necessary.*' Whatever that means."

"Oh wow, that's lame," she said, looking in her rear view mirror.

At the grocery store we began our quest for the ingredients for chicken enchiladas.

"Do you need enchilada sauce?" I asked, picking up a can.

Alicia rolled her eyes at me, grabbing the can and putting it back on the shelf. "Si, but not from a can. We're making our own sauce, carina."

"Claire?" I heard a familiar voice from behind.

I turned around and to my complete surprise saw Jason from the compound, smiling broadly at me.

"Jason! Oh…oh my goodness!" I stammered, reaching up to give him a big hug. "What are you doing here?!"

"I'm…umm…here for training believe it or not."

"Training?" I asked, surprised. "What kind of training could have possibly brought you to Campbell?"

"Some kind of copter training...I don't know," he shrugged off. "Look at you though! You look great Claire," he smiled. "I've been pretty worried about you."

I saw Alicia turn and pretend to look at the shelf beside her out of the corner of my eye. "Thanks, I'm ok though. Are you ok? I know you and Annessa..."

"Yeah, I'm good," he said, cutting me off.

There was an awkward pause and then I turned to Alicia. "Jason, this is Alicia. Alicia, this is Jason. We were in Texas together."

"Ahh...the famous Alicia," he smiled, shaking her outstretched hand. "Claire spoke of you often."

"It's nice to meet you Jason," Alicia said, as gracious as always.

"How long are you here for?" I asked, still completely in shock to see him. "Maybe we can get coffee or something."

"Yeah definitely. That would be great," he smiled, then lowered his voice. "Are you sure it's ok? I mean, I'm surprised they're letting you out like this."

"I'll clear it with my Major, but they have me under such strict surveillance, as long as I stay on base it should be ok."

"Well, you still got my digits right? Give me a call and we'll make it happen."

"Ok," I smiled. "It's so good to see you Jay."

"You too," he said, turning to leave. "Nice to meet you Alicia."

"Nice to meet you too," Alicia said loudly, as he was already half way down the aisle. Then she turned and looked at me skeptically. "There's obviously a story here I need to hear all about."

But I just stood there stunned, watching him leave the store. I couldn't believe he was here. "I'll tell you while we're cooking." I grabbed her hand. "I'm out of time, so let's go."

S
N

The enchilada sauce bubbled on the stove inside of Alicia's small kitchen, while Michael Buble played on the blue tooth speaker I had sent for her birthday last year. The kitchen and living room combined was the size of her old bedroom, but it was her home with Shawn and I'd never seen Alicia so happy. I was so envious of her too. I'd live in a VW van as long as I got to be with Johnny.

"So Jason had a thing with Annessa?" she asked.

"I think so," I said, stirring the yummy sauce. I took a sniff and the spices and tomato sauce scent made my mouth water. "I think he was more into her than she was him though."

Alicia took the tortillas out of the warmer. "You think Johnny's going to be ok with you meeting up with him? I mean, especially after the way he came onto you that time?"

"Well…" I hesitated, "he doesn't exactly know about that. There was no reason to tell him since I wasn't around Jason that much anyway, plus I don't see why Johnny would want to know about me meeting up with him just for coffee."

Alicia turned and faced me putting her hand on her hip, a sure sign she was going into mom mode. "Claire, you're going to meet up with this guy and not tell Johnny? Think about it, would you be ok with him meeting up with a girl who was interested in him in the past?"

I stared down at the sauce while I stirred, taking in what she said. I had never thought about it that way. Johnny had been my whole world for the last three years and I had never even looked twice at another guy since I met him. I was sure Johnny was aware of that so he never worried. "Honestly Mony, I wasn't thinking about it that way. I was more so, just trying to not make Johnny worry."

"I'm sure you were," she said, wrapping an arm around my shoulder. "I just know what Shawn would be thinking and they are two peas in a pod."

I was about to agree with her when my phone rang. "Hello? Kass? Kass, calm down...he what? Where are you guys? Ok, I'll be right there!" I hung up quickly and grabbed my purse and flung it over my shoulder. "I gotta go Mony."

"Claire, what's wrong?"

"It's Major Silva," I said, catching my breath. "They think he had a heart attack."

"Oh no," she gasped, as she began to turn off the stove top. "I'll take you."

I walked quickly to the door. "Thanks, but I'm flying. I know the guys will be here soon so you should wait for them. Can you let Johnny know we're at Blanchfield?"

She followed me onto the small porch as I stepped off and into the fresh air. "Of course."

"Thanks," I said, spinning around and waving, then shot into the dark summer sky.

"Claire!" I heard Justin's voice yell from below as he jumped out of the SUV he had been sitting in keeping watch. I soared higher. "Where is she going?" He asked Alicia.

I almost felt sorry for him as his frantic voice faded below. Justin had been guarding me a lot lately and I didn't want him to get in trouble, but there was no way I would drive the twenty minutes it would take to get to the hospital, when I could be there in three minutes flat.

My heart raced as I glided over the base. Below me the military houses, barracks, and the bright lights of the shopping district sparkled and while I was beyond thrilled to be in the air, I couldn't get to the hospital fast enough.

At last the tall building split the horizon. I descended to the main entrance, where a couple of dozen people stood outside lingering and then slowed down on approach not wanting to scare people too much. To the left I noticed a security guard and a nurse deep in conversation, while on the other side a family sat on the brick ledge eating a snack and enjoying the warm evening. Everyone else was on their phones or walking in and out of the automatic doors that kept opening and closing with the flow of traffic. Once I got close enough, I softly touched down on the sidewalk, coming in just like a plane would land.

Around me I heard gasps, followed by excited chatter.

"Mom, it's the super girl!" a young teenager exclaimed.

I didn't say a word and as soon as my feet hit the pavement, I ran straight into the hospital and up to the fifth floor just as Kass had instructed me to.

Upstairs, I jumped off the elevator and followed the signs to the waiting room where Kass sat with Kyle waiting for mom to come out.

"Claire!" she said, jumping up and wrapping me in a hug. "That was so fast. How did you get here so quick? We literally just got off the phone."

"I flew," I explained, catching my breath. "Where's mom?"

"She's with Sebastian and the doctor."

"Is he ok? What happened?"

"We don't know. He just showed up at our door, pale as a ghost and having breathing difficulties. Luckily Kyle was there to get him inside, because he almost passed out on the porch."

"He was out of it," Kyle said, in his deep, gruff voice. "He was clammy and sweating. I'm pretty sure he was having a heart attack."

"Oh my gosh," I said, catching my breath. "I'm so glad you guys were in for the weekend."

"Claire!" I heard mom's sweet voice behind me. My heart melted when I saw her face. Very few times had I seen her this hurt and worried. The last time was when my dad died and then again when we had to move out of our home after his death. It brought back horrible memories and a very familiar pain.

"It's going to be ok Mom," I said, wrapping her in my arms. "How is he?"

"Well, he's resting. The doctor said he doesn't think he had a heart attack, but they do think whatever it is that made him sick, put a strain on his heart."

We all sat close together on the waiting room couches.

"What could have made him that sick?" I asked, confused.

Mom shook her head, clearly worried. "They're not sure, sweetie. They're going to run some more tests until they can figure it out. They want to keep him overnight, so I think I'm going to stay with him, ok?"

"Ok, that's fine mom," I reassured her.

Then she looked at Kass. "Kass, I want you to stay with Claire overnight. Everything is still pretty new here to us and at least I'll know you're safe. That will be one less thing to worry about."

"Yes Ma'am," Kass agreed.

"I got her mom," I reassured her.

Suddenly a voice boomed from behind me. "Claire!" We turned to see an irritated and out of breath Justin standing in the doorway.

"Hey Justin," I said meekly.

"What are you doing? Why did you leave like that? Do you know how much trouble you could get me in?"

I walked over to him. "Justin, I'm so sorry."

His eyes bulged in anger, ignoring my apology. "Seriously Claire! This is not some game. If something happens to you I'm…I'm dead."

That was dramatic, I thought to myself. "Justin, I really

don't want to get you in trouble, but just so you know, I'm not going to check in with you every time I want to go somewhere."

That really irritated him. His face turned into a deep scowl. "Well you need to figure things out with the higher ups then." He moved closer to me. "It's hard enough babysitting you all the time."

I stared up at him, my own irritation creeping in and I was just fixing to tell him how insulting he was when Kyle's 6 foot 5 inch frame stepped in between us. He looked down at Justin.

"That's a little too close my friend," he warned.

"Kyle, it's fine," I whispered.

"No it's not," Kyle said stiffly, not taking his eyes off Justin. "Rank or no rank he better never approach you like that again."

Justin backed off, slowly walking backwards towards the door, keeping his eyes on Kyle the whole time. "I'll be waiting downstairs," he said bitterly, before disappearing behind the wall.

"What happened Claire?" Mom asked, coming over to me and Kyle.

I shrugged my shoulders. "I guess it's because I flew here instead of riding with him."

"Is that what you're supposed to do?" she asked.

I squeezed her in close. "Mom, I didn't go on national TV and tell everyone my secret, just to be ducking down in the back of someone's MP squad. This is who I am and people are just going to have to get used to it."

THIRTEEN

THAT NIGHT KASS and I sat alone in the President's house eating popcorn and watching our favorite 80's movie, *Can't Buy Me Love*. Mom had called and let us know Major Silva was doing better and that made us relax a little, though she reiterated he was not out of the woods yet.

"Oh Patrick Dempsey," Kass sighed, watching him on the screen. "Isn't he so perfect Claire?"

"Yeah, he's ok," I agreed, "But nothing compared to Johnny."

Kass rolled her eyes and threw a piece of popcorn at me. "Whatever," she laughed. "You can shop without buying, Claire."

"Really Kass?" I laughed.

"Hey, did you ask General Collins if you can go to

119

Kyle's game this weekend?"

"Not yet," I sighed. "I thought I should leave that up to Johnny. He has more pull with the General than I do."

Kass whipped her legs off the side of the recliner and sat up straight. "But Claire, you have to go! This is a big deal! I mean…Kyle is the starting quarterback for the University of Tennessee! You guys being there means the world to him."

"I know Kass. I know," I reassured her. "Trust me. Johnny and I will do everything we can to go, especially since mom and Sebastian can't come now."

A soft knock at the door interrupted our conversation. Kass and I looked at each other skeptically, as we were not expecting anyone tonight.

"Stay here," I instructed her.

I tiptoed to the door and peeked through the peephole cautiously, despite Ft. Campbell's secret service being just outside. I was almost expecting Johnny, but was surprised to see Justin there. He wasn't on duty now and he almost looked like a different guy in his civilian clothes. I opened the door slowly.

"Hi Claire. Can I come in?"

"Of course," I said, closing the door behind him. We stood in awkward silence for a moment, after what had happened earlier at the hospital. "Would you like to sit down?" I asked, finally.

"No thanks. I don't have much time. I just came by to…just because I wanted to say that I'm sorry about today. I'm under a lot of pressure and I feel terrible for the way I treated you."

I smiled. "It's ok Justin. I can relate. Really. I know I should have told you and I promise to do better in the future."

"Thank you," Justin said, grabbing my hand. "Claire, I promise you I'm a good person. No matter what, just know that. I do what I do and what I will do because I have no choice. I have to obey orders."

Hmmm…ok. I really didn't know how to respond to that. "No really Justin, it's fine. Everything's fine. I know we're all just doing the best we can with all of this."

Justin squeezed my hand and stared hard at me for a moment as if he were trying to tell me more. "I've gotta go," he said, at last. "I'm not supposed to be here, but please just remember that."

I looked at him curiously. He had a unique way of apologizing, but I appreciated him clearing the air. We would be seeing a lot of each other and I didn't want anything to be weird between us.

Monday morning I woke bright and early to get to jiu-jitsu. Professor Corral was in for his one week a month training and I didn't want to miss a moment of it. I had come so far with him this past year and out of everything I had learned, knowing the art of Jiu Jitsu made me feel safest.

The gym we were training at was still empty and the sky a twilight blue as I entered the doors at exactly 5:30

am.

"Super Claire!" Professor Corral greeted me with a bear hug. "How are you?"

"Hey Professor Corral," I smiled.

"You're looking great! You been practicing that throw we went over last month?"

"Yes Sir. I tried it on Johnny," I laughed.

"And?"

"And he said he liked it, but for all the wrong reasons."

"Of course he did," he laughed. "And how are you doing with everything else? Is the public starting to accept you more?"

"I guess," I shrugged. "I mean, at least on Campbell they do. I don't go off base too often, because the last time I went, it was a madhouse."

Professor Corral nodded. "I know. I saw that awesome hip toss you did on that Officer on Youtube," he laughed. "But still, I bet that's frustrating."

"Yeah, but at the same time, if I knew I'd be safe, I wouldn't mind the crowds. I like to meet new people and make new friends. I've even heard some of the local schools have requested me to come and do a meet and greet with the students."

"I can help you do that," he said nonchalantly.

"Seriously?" My eyes popped wide.

"Of course. I'm sure I can talk General Collins into it as long as I'm with you. I can take a few guys from class with me too. No one would ever get past us to you, Claire."

I smiled big in appreciation. All I've ever wanted through this whole flying fiasco is to be able to use my gift to help other people, especially kids. A lot of them faced big problems and if I could help them through a tough spot that is exactly what I would love to do.

"Speaking of protecting you Claire, I'm going to put you on the mat with Taylor today."

"Taylor?" I gulped, sitting on the bench to take off my shoes. Taylor was a big guy. Probably the most built guy in the special forces. And he was good at everything. From shooting practice to survival training and now jiu-jitsu. Taylor would put me to shame.

"Yes Taylor," he said firmly. "Claire, we've been back at jiu-jitsu for 6 months now. You're a year into your training and with your unique circumstances, you need to be able to defend yourself against guys like Taylor. You think some enemy of the U.S. is going to send some wimp to kidnap you? Not happening. It's going to be the best of the best like Taylor and you need to be prepared. Plus if you want to do stuff like school visits you have to prove to the General you can protect yourself if need be."

I was quiet while the reality of his words sank in. Of course everything he was saying was true, but I was a little nervous to roll with Taylor.

Professor Corral sat down beside me. "I don't mean to be harsh Claire, but I feel like I need to help you stay vigilant. What happened to you in Hawaii could very well happen again and I would never forgive myself if it did."

"You really think I can take Taylor?" I asked.

"I know you can."

"Ok, Professor Corral. I trust you."

An hour later we were stretched out and ready to hit the mats. I looked over at Taylor sizing him up. He wasn't much bigger than the guy I had tangled with on the yacht when I rescued Kirsten. That guy ended up with a broken arm, so maybe I had a fighting chance against Taylor.

I watched a few duos grapple, going over each move in my mind, taking notes on everything they were doing right and each mistake being made. Four matches in, I heard him call my name.

"Haley…Taylor!" Professor Corral demanded.

I snapped to my feet, as Taylor remained in his knelt position on the mat. He raised his eyes at Professor Corral questioning if he had heard him correctly or not.

"Problem Taylor?" he asked.

"No Sir."

"Well then get into position."

"Yes Sir," Taylor said, jumping to his feet. He stood across from me on the mat and for a moment we locked eyes. I could tell this poor guy was even more nervous than I was.

Professor Corral walked over and stood face to face with him. "Don't go easy on her. This class is a matter of life and death for Airman Haley. You understand?"

"Yes Sir," Taylor almost whispered.

"I'll start the clock," Professor Corral told us as he backed quickly out of the way.

I immediately went on the defensive, because I would most likely be the one being attacked. Taylor began, shooting in for a double leg take down. Before he could get my legs, I "air sprawled", a move Professor Corral taught me after he found out I could fly. An air sprawl is like a regular sprawl, when you kick your legs back to avoid a take down, except I just float my legs back and fly around my opponent's head into a better position. I easily took Taylor's back and worked on choking him out. He defended the choke for a bit, trying to better his position, but no matter how hard he tried to escape, I was able to control him and keep the dominant position. The rest of the round I used what I had learned, along with my super power.

"Good job Haley," Corral nodded at me in satisfaction, as we rolled up on our knees trying to catch a breath. "Just remember, you start out on the defense, but you need to flip that switch to the offense as soon as possible. You did that nicely and maintained control."

"Yes Sir," I said, still surprised I had managed to hold my own with Taylor. This gave me so much hope that I could lead a somewhat normal life knowing I could take care of myself.

Professor Corral dismissed everyone for the day and while I packed up my belongings, Taylor walked over to me.

"Hey Taylor," I said, unsure of how he was feeling about everything.

He held out his hand to fist bump mine. "I'm not going to lie, it's not easy getting manhandled by a girl, but on the flip side of that I'm glad you can hold your own."

"Thanks," I blushed. "You are some tough competition though. I don't think without my flying moves, I would have stood a chance against you."

"Don't be so sure about that," Taylor laughed, in his deep baritone voice. "You did just fine."

"Well Claire," Professor Corral said as we began to walk towards the door with Taylor. "Tomorrow I'll hit the General up about the school thing and maybe Taylor could tag along as a bodyguard."

"I'm so down!" Taylor agreed.

"Awesome!" I smiled.

Friday night Johnny waited patiently for me while I packed my overnight bag for Knoxville.

"What are you wearing to the game tomorrow?" he asked, watching as I stuffed as much clothes as I possibly could into the small suitcase.

"I'm not sure yet. Probably just some shorts and my UT tee. You know, the one Kass gave us all for Christmas with Kyle's number on it?"

"What shorts?" Johnny asked.

"Probably my white ones."

"Oh good, I like those. They really pop off your tan."

"Ok Marc Jacobs," I laughed at his new interest in my choice of fashion.

Johnny's phone rang and he answered quickly. "What's up Shawn? No, we're almost ready. No…I know Justin's going, but I'm not sure who else they're sending down." His voice dropped and he walked away from me toward the bathroom, making me listen even harder. "No, I'm all good," I overheard him say. "Yep, I've got everything. Cool, we'll be there to pick you guys up in twenty. Bye."

I looked at him curiously while attempting to zip my overstuffed suitcase, wondering why he was being so weird.

"Did you let Justin know we're leaving?" he asked, flattening the zipper down with one hand and zipping it in one quick tug. "I promised Major Silva there would be no more surprises this weekend."

"Yeah, he knows," I replied, sliding on my Vans he had given me for my 19th birthday. "Did you get to see him yesterday?"

"Yep and he looks so much better Claire. They're sending him home Monday. He's really worried about you though."

"I know. I told my mom not to worry, I'm fine. I think General Collins is sending the whole 101st with us and plus…" I moved in closer to him, wrapping my arms around his neck, "plus I'll be with you."

Johnny leaned down and kissed me softly. "And I would breathe my last breath to protect you, Claire."

FOURTEEN

THE NEXT MORNING Kass knocked on our hotel suite door, bright and early. She was in her Freshman year at the University of Tennessee and at long last able to be with Kyle more.

"Rise and shine!" Kass exclaimed, jumping into my arms as I yawned and hugged her tight.

"Oh my goodness Kass! I miss you so much!"

"Me too, Clairey. I'm so excited you guys came!"

My baby sister's eyes were sparkling and it made me so happy to see her flourishing here.

"Where's Lexi?" Alicia asked, giving Kass a big hug.

"She's going to meet us at breakfast. Is Tater still coming?"

"Yep," called Shawn from the other room. "He's going to meet us at the game. He's just coming off guard at the hangar."

Johnny came out of the bathroom, toweling off his face from a fresh shave. "Good, cause I'm starving," he said, giving Kass a squeeze and a wink. "Let's see if Mr. Kyle is as good as everyone's making him out to be."

The vibe in Neyland stadium was electric. The stadium was packed, with orange and white as far as the eye could see and the smells of grilled food and sweet bread baking filled the air. Alicia and I stood in awe as we watched all the pregame pomp and pageantry on the field. These people were so dedicated to their school and team and it was fun to watch it all high above the crowd. General Collins had arranged to have us seated in a secure section for safety that included plush chairs and standing tables. This section was normally reserved for special guests and celebrities, but the fact that we were there at the request of the starting quarterback helped General Collins get us in here.

Lexi said that word of our arrival had spread throughout the school and friends of friends were asking if they could do a meet and greet with me. I know it sounds like I'm bragging and I don't mean for it to, but it was very sweet and very flattering. My goal was to meet and befriend people and not come across as some snooty, recluse. Again, that was the whole purpose of the press conference.

On the flip side of that, I reiterated to Kass and Johnny that this day was about Kyle and I didn't want to do anything to take away from it. Unfortunately, that didn't happen. A few minutes before the Vols took the field, a wave of cheers began to spread through the crowd. Alicia and I strained our necks to see what we were missing.

"Oh my goodness Claire!" Lexi yelled above the roar and pointed to the jumbo tron at the end of the field. Alicia and I followed her direction to the very large screen. The camera man had zoomed in on me, my face in shock as I realized it was now covering the whole screen. People began to yell my name, some of them chanting it, while turning around and looking up into our section.

"Oh wow," I whispered, looking like a deer in headlights.

"Don't just stand there looking goofy Claire!" Kass laughed. "Wave to them!"

I looked at my group of friends who were all smiling and encouraging me with Kass, then turned back to thousands of people below who were waving, their cell phone cameras pointing our direction. I smiled in appreciation and waved back and in return they yelled even louder.

"See? They all love you!" Lexi smiled.

Much to my relief, the camera only stayed on me for another few seconds, then at last it was over and everyone focused back on the field again.

"What just happened?" I asked, catching my breath.

"Get used to it," Alicia laughed, wrapping her arm around me and squeezing me in close. "They're getting used to you, just like you wanted."

At kickoff time Kass joined Alicia, Lexi and I in our seats looking over the balcony, while Johnny, Tater and Shawn grouped over with some other young men standing at a table to watch and discuss the game.

"What number is he?" Alicia yelled to us above the roar of the stadium.

"Seven!" Kass smiled, then pointed down to number 7 who was sprinting across the field, ready for the first play. She grabbed my hand and squeezed it, not letting go until Kyle threw his first pass of the game. I could tell she was so nervous for him, but Kyle was in total control as usual.

By half time, the Vols were leading 21 to 7 and a big part of that was thanks to Kyle's ability to deliver under pressure. We sat back in our seats at halftime breathing a sigh of relief and bragging to Kass about how well Kyle was playing. She seemed much more relaxed now. I looked over at Shawn and Tater who were grinning from ear to ear, talking over each other, discussing play by play the first half of the game. Then I turned around looking for an absent Johnny. He must have stepped out to get a drink or something.

"Lexi, go with me to the bathroom," Kass said, standing up and grabbing Lexi's hand.

"Ok," Lexi agreed, while Alicia and I kicked our feet up on the rail and leaned back in our seats. The autumn Tennessee sky was a bright blue today and at that moment I would have given anything to be able to jump off that balcony and fly over the Smokeys.

"Are you hungry?" I asked her. "Wanna go get some food?"

"Yeah, but let's wait a minute…to avoid the crowd."

"Ok," I agreed. "Alicia, do you think it will be ok for me to do a meet and greet with Lexi's friends? Do you think it will be safe?"

Alicia looked at me and lifted her shades. "I think so. How many guards came with Justin?"

"Seven, including Justin."

"Oh yeah, Claire. Plus you have Johnny, Tater and Shawn. Why? Are you feeling weird about it?"

"No," I shrugged. "This will just be my first time meeting the public up close."

She squeezed my hand. "It'll be fine Claire. There's no way Johnny would ever let anyone hurt you." A familiar tune filled the stadium, catching Alicia's attention. "Oh my goodness! I love this song!"

I placed my hand over my heart as Elvis' "*I Can't Help Falling In Love With You*" echoed through the loudspeakers. "Oh Mony, his voice melts me."

"Claire," Alicia whispered, nodding up the stairs behind us.

I turned around to see Johnny walking down the stairs with a dozen long stemmed roses in his arms. Standing across the top of the room were all of my sweet friends. Shawn, Tater, Kyle (still in his uniform), Lexi, Kass and

Alicia joined them. My mind was spinning, trying to take it all in and figure out what was going on.

Johnny stopped half way down the short staircase and smiled nervously at me. "Come here, Claire Bear."

I slowly got up and walked towards him. What was going on? It wasn't our anniversary. My birthday was six months ago. Did this have anything to do with the meet and greet later? Maybe the flowers were from the school. Then another thought crossed my mind. Wait a minute…was he? There's no way. We had talked about the "M" word (as we jokingly called it) and he had made it clear, now was not the time.

I joined him on the stairs and took the beautiful roses he placed in my arms. He looked down into my eyes and suddenly the whole stadium disappeared. Everyone. It was just Johnny and me.

"Claire, I knew from the very first day I met you, that I was going to marry you. I remember telling Shawn that night after you left, you were the one. The perfect girl for me. I don't know how I knew it, but I did. I know these past few years have been crazy for you, but you handle yourself with so much maturity and grace and I admire that so much. I want you to know I'm so proud of you. I want to cover you and protect you and love you for the rest of my life." Johnny pulled out a box from his pocket and I caught my breath. This was it. He opened it for me and inside was the most beautiful ring I had ever seen. A perfect round diamond sparkled brightly, surrounded by tiny emerald stones. I couldn't have picked a more perfect ring. Johnny then went down on his knee. "Airman Haley, I love you so very much and you make me so happy. More than anything in the world, I want you to be my wife. Will you marry me?"

I paused for a moment, still unsure if this was really happening. "Yes!" I said quickly. "Yes Johnny! A million yeses, over and over again."

To my delight, Johnny let out a big sigh of relief, almost as if he thought I would say no. He slid the ring down my finger, a perfect fit and stood up. Then he wrapped me in his arms and sealed it with the most perfect kiss.

"Thank you Claire," he whispered. "Thank you for saying yes."

A loud round of applause began to rumble through the stadium, snapping us back into the reality of over ninety thousand faces peeking into our world. We looked out to see Vols fans clapping and cheering us on. I waved and then buried my head in Johnny's chest as he laughed. The next thing I knew our friends were surrounding us offering their congratulations. Kyle bent down and hugged me.

"I'm sorry Kyle," I whispered in his ear. "This day was supposed to be all about you."

"Oh no," he laughed. "Johnny and I planned this one ourselves. This day was all about you Claire and you deserve it." Kyle then high fived Johnny and scurried back to the game.

I was thrilled to see Kass had mom and Major Silva on Facetime, while Shawn held up his phone so the Angel family could watch the proposal. Johnny and I both took time to talk to them as we beamed with excitement. I noticed Johnny kept using the words *my fiancé*, as many times as he could and I loved hearing it. I couldn't have been any happier. I was officially his.

SN

Kyle led the Vols to an easy 35-17 victory. The whole rest of the game, I kept holding my ring up and staring at it.

"Did you help him pick this out, Mony?" I asked.

"Oh no. That was all Johnny," she reassured me.

"Hey Claire!" I heard Johnny yell.

I turned around to see Johnny and Justin and a younger male student standing at the top of the box.

"I'll be right back," I told the girls.

"Claire, this is Austin. He is the President of student body life here at UT," Johnny said as I reached the top of the stairs. Austin and I shook hands and he smiled brightly.

"Nice to meet you and congratulations," he croaked out. I watched in amusement as his face turned bright red and his skin blotchy. This guy was just like me!

"Are you up to doing a small meet and greet with some of the students after the game?" Johnny asked.

"Well…" I said unsure. "What do you mean by meet and greet? What is that?" I asked.

"Just a few students and our media department," Austin assured me. "Just some publicity for our school and a huge thrill for some of our students. It will only be about twenty minutes."

"Ok…" I agreed and looked at Justin. "But did you guys check with…"

"Silva cleared it," Justin reassured me, then looked at Austin. "But we'll need to secure the area prior and no more than 20 minutes."

"Sure! We can go do that right now," Austin smiled. "Thank you guys so much!"

Johnny put his arm around me and pulled me in close as we watched Justin follow Austin out of the box to go inspect the press room.

"You sure you're ok with this?" he asked.

"It's fine," I assured him. "Besides, some of the students are friends with Kyle, Kass and Lexi and I don't want to let them down."

After the game, we were led down the long tunnel hallway by our security team to a conference room, where the press and about 200 prescreened students were waiting at the meet and greet. Everyone seemed genuinely happy for me and Johnny, and I took time to meet each of them, sign autographs (something I don't think I'll ever get used to) and answer their questions. I had the best time and was invited back for another meet and greet as soon as my schedule permitted.

Justin and the security team did a great job of balancing my safety, yet giving me space to be personable and that meant the world to me. I knew if General Collins and the higher ups in Washington could see there was a way to balance my safety with my public life, they would be much more likely to give me more opportunities like this one.

FIFTEEN

THAT EVENING WE gathered at a small pub just off campus for dinner. The guys were shooting pool while we waited for our order and the girls sat at the table discussing the crazy day we just had. The sun was just beginning to set, casting a warm glowing light through the window and on to our table. I put my hand in one of the sunbeams and watched as my new ring made rainbow prisms of light on the wall and ceiling. Lexi, Kass and Alicia laughed and teased me about it, but I didn't mind at all. This was one of the most incredible days of my life.

The heavy wood door chimed behind us and I heard Kass whisper, "What the heck?" not taking her eyes off the entrance. I turned around to see what looked like a park ranger and a couple of Officers from the Knoxville Police Department. They made a beeline for our table, but we're quickly intercepted by Justin and two of his guard friends.

"Can we help you?" Justin asked.

"Yes, we need to speak with Miss Haley," the Sergeant said, looking over at me.

"She's not.."

"I'm Claire Haley," I said, walking over to meet them, with Johnny, Shawn and Tater right behind me.

"Miss Haley, I'm Sergeant Chandler with the Knoxville Police Department. We are assisting the park authorities and the county sheriff in the search and rescue of a four year old little boy who went missing about two hours ago from the Caney Creek Campsite about 10 miles from here. We've pulled together all our resources to find him, but now with just about an hour of sunlight left, we are feeling desperate. We fear he won't make it through the night in the mountains."

"We need your help," the park ranger added. "We've been using drones, but as you know, they can't see down into the trees. We saw you on the news this afternoon and hope that you can join our effort."

I looked back at Johnny who nodded his approval. "Of course," I said.

"Shawn," Johnny said. "I'm going with Claire. We'll meet you guys back at the hotel later."

"No, Tater and I will go with you to help search. We'll send the girls back." Shawn said, handing Alicia the car keys.

I turned my attention back to the Sergeant. "I'm going

to go now. The car ride will cost me at least twenty minutes of search time and I can fly there in five. What's the little boy's name?"

"It's Cody. Here's a picture of him taken just this morning. He's still in those clothes."

I looked at the brown haired, blue eyed little boy, smiling so big, holding up a fish he had just caught. "Ok, feed me information over my phone. My boyfri… ummm finance, Johnny has my number." Then I quickly headed to the door.

"Claire!" Johnny called after me. "How are you going to know how to get there?"

I held up my phone. "GPS of course!"

I ran out into the parking lot and jetted into the sky. People in the shopping district stopped and gasped and I heard several yell my name. I had never flown in the mountains, so this was going to be quite an experience.

I followed my GPS instructions along the highway, green mountains towering on either side, while a deep woodsy earth smell enveloped me. Five minutes later I was flying over the Caney Creek camp sign entrance where more than a dozen police, fire and EMS vehicles were parked. A crowd of people were gathered in front of a firetruck and I was careful to land a little distance away, so as not to startle anyone. I found the guy who seemed to be in charge and asked in which area Cody had last been seen.

"Over there by the brook," the guy replied in a thick southern accent. "But this area around here has been searched several times. We're going to go out further now."

"Ok Sir. Thank you." I walked quickly toward the brook, trying to put myself in a four-year olds place. If I were him, where would I go exploring? I decided to fly along the small stream to make sure he wasn't stuck somewhere close to the water. I pulled my long curls into a tight bun and stepped off the small embankment and into the crisp air. Although it was still early fall, a cool breeze was blowing out of the thick woods and across the water, blowing droplets into the air, making me shiver. I was still in my white denim shorts and Vols tee, so I had nothing to protect my arms and legs. The brook bubbled quietly as I slowly flew north toward the big mountain it flowed from. My eyes scanned the banks from side to side of the stream that was only about 15 feet wide. At some points I could see to the bottom of the brook through the crystal clear water and at other points the creek was too deep. I shivered even more when I thought about Cody possibly falling in, but stopped myself. Panicking was not going to help any.

"*He's alive Claire and you're going to find him. God help me find him,*" I kept repeating to myself.

I had reached the bottom of the mountain and was on my way back to check the south side of the creek when Johnny called me.

"Claire, where are you?"

"I'm checking the brook first. I just wanted to make sure he's not near the water."

"Smart girl," Johnny encouraged me. "Listen, you don't have to worry about the area down here. We're covering the base, if you can stick to the bottom of the mountain. He's been gone for a couple of hours so I don't think he could get that far."

"Who's we?" I asked.

"All of us guys, the girls too, and a bunch of kids from UT are on their way over."

"Oh wow," I whispered. I should have known my friends would show up.

"Be careful Claire Bear. We only have about 40 minutes of sunlight left."

"Yes Sir," I said. "But Johnny, I'm not leaving here until I find him. I'll check in soon."

I hung up the phone somewhat discouraged. Forty minutes was nothing I thought as I floated in the air, just above the trees looking over the vast forest. A humming noise caught my attention and I looked above to see a drone scanning the area. It seemed to catch me in the camera, because it moved softly down just above my head and we stared at each other for a moment before it quietly zoomed away.

I dropped just below the tall tree line. No wonder why they couldn't get the drones in here. I had barely got in zigzagging my way through the trees, dodging limbs and sticky pine cones. Then I got busy flying back and forth at the base of the mountain, careful to dodge the trees, while trying to cover as much ground as I could. At one point my heart skipped a beat as I looked through a clearing. The biggest black bear I had ever seen trudged along the forest floor, occasionally looking over his shoulder like he knew someone was watching him. I flew down a little closer to follow him, because as morbid as this sounds I had to at least check and make sure he had not come across Cody. I startled him as much as he did me and at one point he stopped to face off with me. I gasped as he stood on his hind legs. He was a big guy standing at least 7 feet tall. He snarled up at me and gave me the death stare before finally taking off into the thick brush.

The forty minutes passed quickly and darkness settled onto the forest floor, as frogs croaked loudly and katydids began to sing. In the distance I could hear many voices calling out to Cody. I continued to search desperately until finally I couldn't see anymore and had to get a flashlight.

I found a clearing in the trees and flew straight up, pausing to take in the view once I was in the open. A black sky stretched above and the bright stars twinkled. There were so many thousands of them and no lights around so you could see them everywhere. The moon was bright and cast a beam down that sparkled on the stream trickling down the mountain. I pulled my phone out of my back pocket and took a short video to show the girls later, because no matter how hard I tried, I could never explain in words the incredible views I was privileged to see from above.

I quickly flew back to the parking lot where a few people lingered at the campgrounds office, then landed in the back behind the firetruck. I ran up and found the same firefighter I had spoken with before.

"Excuse me Sir, can I borrow a flashlight? A powerful one that can shine down from above?"

"From above?" He asked curiously, then his eyes lit up. "Oh, you're the flying girl."

"Yes Sir."

"Of course," he said, then went to the back of the truck and opened a large bin.

As I stood quietly waiting, the sound of a female sobbing caught my ear. A few parking spaces away a young woman leaned against one of the patrol cars talking to an officer. I couldn't make out what they were saying, but at one point I heard her say, "*this is all my fault,*" through her sobs. I assumed she was Cody's mom and my heart just broke for her.

"Is this too heavy?" The firefighter asked, holding up what looked like a small theater spotlight right in front of my face.

I carefully took it from him. The weight wasn't so bad. Nothing I couldn't handle after having carried Kirsten all that time.

"I think I can handle it," I smiled.

"Thank you for your help, Ma'am," he smiled back. "At this point, I don't know what we would do without you."

"My pleasure," I said, then lifted off the ground. I just

had to find this little guy, I thought to myself as I flew over the treetops. "God please help me," I prayed over and over again.

I searched and searched for the next hour. By 9:30 I had covered about a half mile up the mountain and was exhausted. I stopped to rest on a rock at the base of the mountain and set the spotlight down, feeling so discouraged. Doubt began to fill my mind. How was I ever going to find him and how could I ever face his parents if I didn't? Everyone's hopes laid at my feet. My cell phone ringing from my back shorts pocket, (that was now a dingy white) interrupted my thoughts.

"Claire Bear," Johnny said. "Where are you?"

"I'm about a quarter mile up from the bottom, by the brook."

"We're back at the truck. This whole area has been searched. The only place he could be now is up."

"Seriously? You think he could climb the mountain? It's so steep after the first turn."

"Well, he's used to the mountains, even though he's only four. Claire, maybe you should come down and take a break."

"No Johnny," I said, firmly. "I'm not leaving until I find him."

"Claire, you need to rest."

"I'm fine. I promise you I'll rest if I need to and check

in with you every hour."

Johnny sighed at my stubbornness. He had learned long ago to let me be in situations like this and did so respectfully. "Ok," he agreed. "I want to hear from you in an hour though."

"Yes sir," I smiled.

I hung up the phone and zipped up my sweatshirt Alicia had given me earlier. I grabbed the spotlight and flew up to just 10 feet above the ground. This would help me to not only see him, but hear him as well.

"Cody!" My now hoarse voice echoed through the darkness. "Cooodyyy!"

Back and forth I went, careful to cover every area and making sure I didn't look in the same place twice. By midnight, I had made it back to the brook, higher up the mountain and had to rest again. I sat down on a rock and pulled out my phone to call Johnny, but surprisingly he didn't answer and it just rang. I rested my head in my hands, carefully listening for any sort of footsteps around me. After that run in with the bear earlier, I didn't need that surprise again.

My phone echoed loudly through the small canyon I was sitting in.

"Johnny?"

"Claire, I'm so sorry. Somehow the sound on my phone got turned off."

"It's ok," I yawned.

"Are you ok?"

"Yes, but I want to keep looking," I said, before he

could even tell me to come in.

"I know you do," he laughed. "My first night engaged and I can't even be with you."

"I know and I'm so sorry," I sighed. "I just want a little more time. You guys should go back to the hotel and wait for me."

"Yeah right," he smirked. "Claire, I'm not leaving here without you."

I smiled because I already knew that was the response he would give me. We hung up the phone and I stood up to stretch, then bent down to get my spotlight. Just perfect, my shoe was untied. I was so tired, I dreaded even having to bend over to tie it. I sat back on the rock again and tied it, making sure to double knot so I wouldn't have to do it again. That's when I heard it. So slightly, but definitely not a sound common to the forest. Above me a small whimper echoed on the light breeze . I looked up in the tall buckeye tree that towered over, unsure of what I heard. I froze and listened, but there was just silence.

"Cody!" I yelled, then listened.

"Maaaa," came the sound again.

I grabbed the spotlight and jumped into the sky, then hovered over the brook. "Cody, where are you!?"

"Mommy!" came the voice from just up the hill.

"Oh my God," I gasped and then flew toward it as fast as I could, shining my spotlight back and forth on the rocks. At last I saw him. His little arm stretched up in the sky toward me. I flew down to the rock wall he was laying by, sat my spotlight on the ground and ran toward him. He reached out his arms and I knelt down to lift him up, but he screamed out in pain. His foot was wedged in between a rock from the ankle down. I tried to wiggle it loose, but it was really stuck.

"Hi Cody, I'm Claire. Your mommy and daddy sent me here to help you, so don't be scared ok?"

"Ok," he shivered. "I want my mommy."

"I know buddy," I said, taking off my sweatshirt and sliding it over him. "I'm going to call your mommy and some people to help get you out of here, but I'm not going to leave you, ok?"

I pulled out my phone and sat down beside Cody wrapping my arm around him while the phone rang in my ear. At last he picked up.

"Johnny?" I said, almost in tears. "I have him. I found Cody."

Johnny breathed a deep sigh of relief. "Oh baby, that's awesome. I knew you would find him."

I spent the next few minutes explaining to Johnny and the head medic why I couldn't move Cody and where we were approximately.

"Just follow the stream up." I instructed them. "I'll meet you when you get close. I don't want to leave him alone."

An hour later the rescue team completed the two mile trek from the parking lot up the mountain, having to walk the whole way because of the lack of road access.

"I can't believe he made it this far," the fire chief said

in disbelief.

When Cody was finally free and his ankle wrapped and stable, it was decided that I should fly him back down the mountain to his parents and the ambulance waiting below. I called Johnny to let him know the plan and that we would be down soon.

"Ready to fly like Superman?" I asked Cody, as he wrapped his arms around me and the firefighter strapped him to my waist for extra safety.

"Yes!" Cody yelled in excitement.

"Claire," the firefighter stopped me before lift off. "I just want to thank you. That could have gone the wrong way if it hadn't been for you." He patted my shoulder and I smiled in appreciation.

"My pleasure Sir. I'm just so glad he's ok."

"Well, be careful up there," he smiled.

"Oh I will," I said, my heart pounding inside my chest, so excited to have found him. "Ok, Cody. Let's gooo!" I said, launching us into the air. Cody gasped as we lifted off the ground to the sound of the medics cheering below. Now my heart fluttered in happiness as I watched his excited little face. Maybe this would be the part he remembered the most of this horrible night.

What would have been an hour walk, took me just five minutes. When at last I appeared over the trees carrying Cody in my arms, a loud applause rose up from the parking lot, as cameras began to flash and people began to surround Johnny.

As soon as my feet touched the ground, a young

woman came and snatched him out my arms. "Cody!" she cried.

"Careful!" I instructed her. "He may have a broken ankle."

The woman then grabbed me and hugged me tight. "How can I ever thank you?" she cried. "I was so worried about my baby."

"You're so welcome," I smiled at her.

I felt Johnny's strong arm wrap around my waist and pull me in close, as she let go and the crowd began to swarm around. Suddenly Justin and a few of his soldiers were at my side as well.

"Claire, can we just ask a few questions," a guy with a small mike and a bright camera light asked, shoving it in my face.

"Back up!" Justin said firmly.

"It's fine," Johnny agreed. "But just a few."

I stuck around for a few minutes and answered the reporter's question as best as I could, while Cody's mom stood beside me. I answered as many as possible and as quickly as possible, remembering everything I could and couldn't say.

At last Johnny took my arm. "We need to go, Claire."

I said goodbye to Cody and joined my friends who were waiting by the cars. We were all cold and exhausted, but talked excitedly in the car as we headed back to the lodge.

"Well Claire," Shawn said, as he drove us through the winding Smokey mountain roads. "I understand now why Johnny always says life with you is never boring."

I laughed as I rested my head on Johnny's shoulder and looked down at my ring again. "I know," I agreed. "He doesn't know what he's getting himself into."

SIXTEEN

MONDAY MORNING AT 9 am, I was back in a review meeting with General Collins and Dr. Enroe, that had been sandwiched in between my weekly physical and a field training exercise with my company.

"So you had an exciting weekend, huh Claire?" General Collins asked, leaning back in his chair.

"Yes Sir," I said, taking a deep breath and looking down at my engagement ring. I still couldn't believe I was engaged.

General Collins followed my gaze. "Well," he chuckled, "we knew it was coming. Angel couldn't stop talking about it. Congratulations Haley."

"Thank you General Collins. I was *so* surprised."

"You know a lot of work went into making that happen. Keeping it a surprise and safe was not easy…but you both deserve it. Angel is one of our best pilots and you, well you've been through so much, we felt you deserved whatever kind of proposal he wanted to give you."

I smiled in gratitude. "I'm so grateful for you allowing us to go and letting me keep some normalcy in my life." General Collins was good to me and I was so glad to be back under this leadership.

He then turned his attention to Dr. Enroe. "So, how was her health check up today?"

"Everything is still looking normal. I'm not seeing any changes on her blood tests and her vitals all came back fine. She did show some signs of fatigue, but I think that's just from all the flying she did Saturday night."

"Ahhh yes. The infamous mountain rescue." General Collins squinted at me, while I bit my lip nervously. I had not heard one way or the other his opinion on my involvement. "I guess under the circumstances you had no choice but to help, but Claire you do understand you can't be everyone's hero, right? I mean, if you say yes to everything you'll spend the rest of your life flying from here to there trying to keep up with everyone."

"I know…it's just when I heard it was a little kid…"

"I get it," he interrupted me, "but you need to let us help you make those decisions. Next time you need approval. At least while you're under our watch. Understand?"

"Yes Sir."

"Ok, so you're going to be in field training this week, but tomorrow morning you'll be meeting with Captain

Lewis beforehand to discuss a few media projects. Justin will be picking you up and dropping you off everyday. We still don't think it's safe enough for you to be out there overnight yet, so you'll be staying at the President's house."

"Yes Sir."

"Also, no check-ins with Dr. Enroe, until next week."

"Yes Sir."

"Alright Haley, you're dismissed. I'll see you next Monday morning."

I stood and saluted them both, then headed down stairs and out the main doors where Justin and another MP waited patiently.

"Claire!" I heard a familiar voice call. I turned around to see a surprised Jason walking up behind me.

"Jason!" I smiled, equally surprised to see him. "You never called me."

"Yeah, I know. These people here got me so busy. I can't wait to get back to the compound in Texas where things are much slower."

"Oh really?" I laughed. "When are you going back?"

"Wednesday. I have to wrap everything up tomorrow."

"Did you still want to try and get coffee later? I have field training until 5, but I can meet you after that."

"Sure," Jason said, looking over my shoulder at Justin waiting outside the SUV. "If it's ok with your entourage. Those guys are your only security Claire?"

I turned around and looked at Justin who was leaning up against the car, laughing at something on his phone. "Well…yeah," I said, turning back to Jason. "But that's just on Campbell. If I go off base, I'm surrounded."

"Not good Claire," he shook his head. "Not good. But yeah, I can meet for coffee tomorrow if that's ok."

Jason and I set a meeting place and time for the next day, then he hugged me and walked away abruptly. Things between us had been weird since I rejected his feelings towards me and I hated it. We had gotten along so well until then and now I guess this would be the new norm for us.

"Did you get in trouble?" Justin asked as I climbed into the back seat.

"No, not exactly," I sighed, buckling in. "I was just kindly, but sternly told to get permission before any more rescues."

"Ahhh," Justin said, driving out of headquarters. "I had a feeling that would happen. Not having eyes on you at all times is nerve wrecking."

"Justin," I said matter of factly and leaning slightly forward to make sure he heard me, "I don't know who told you that, but that's not ever going to be the plan. I'm not living my life under someone's eye all the time."

"Ok," Justin said clearly, then mumbled, "that's not what I heard," under his breath.

I just ignored him and popped my headphones on, then sat back in my seat to rest for the 30 minute drive out to the training field. Michael Buble's "Fly Me To The Moon," filled my ears, drowning out their chatter in the front seat. I looked down at my Saturn tatt that glowed brightly, reminding me I needed some more flying time stat. Maybe I could make that happen tonight.

Field training was draining, but I didn't care. I definitely needed it. As soon as I got back to the President's house that night I showered and grabbed a quick dinner, then threw on a light sweatshirt with my shorts and sneakers. I quickly pulled my hair into a tight ballet bun high on top, so I could catch the brilliant Tennessee sunset that was beginning to glow through the windows. In the past I would always wait until dusk, but I no longer felt the need to. Everyone knew about me now and I had no reason to hide anymore.

I grabbed my selfie stick to get some good shots for Kass and Alicia, my biggest flight fans. Outside on the back patio, I waited until the coast was clear, then flew into the dense woods for about a mile and up through the trees above several large farms that surrounded the base. Three hundred feet seemed pretty perfect tonight so I stopped and perched in the air to pop my phone on the selfie stick. Peter Cetera's "*Glory of Love*" played through my headphones and I was immediately taken back to my ballet dance recital in sixth grade. I had danced up until my dad's death and for that reason, lost my passion for it and pretty much everything else I was into.

Before I knew it and as corny as it may sound, I was dancing in the air. It was so much easier without the resistance of gravity and I moved much more fluidly.

I turned on my camera and recorded, sometimes with the sky above and some with the earth underneath as I twirled and flipped through the air. My split jump was phenomenal at this height and I was able to snap the most amazing pics with the fiery sunset behind me.

I finally settled in and watched the sun as it set over rows of Tennessee hills. I loved my home so much and hadn't been this content since I was on my island.

An hour later, I laid in bed gasping at the images and video I had been able to capture. Not to toot my own horn, but they were more than just good or beautiful. They were majestic and thrilling and I felt the need to share my world outside of crime fighting and alien theories.

I opened the TikTok app on my phone and went to my page. I hadn't really used it for anything besides watching my friends' and family's videos. In fact, I had all of seven followers and that included Kass, Lexi, Alicia, Danielle and Tessa.

First things first, I had to give my page a name. I kept Airman Claire Haley the same, but added the nickname the Clarksville Police Department had given me underneath, *The Sky Walker.*

I spent the next hour learning how to make videos and when it was all said and done, I was pretty proud of the video I put together. I added one of my favorite songs *Rocketeer* by Ryan Tedder to the background, then sat back to watch it play. I smiled to myself and as I came alive on camera, the joy on my face was undeniable. I was the happiest when flying. The fiery colors in the sky above contrasted so drastically with the cool colors of the earth below and I put on quite the show in between. I hash tagged a few things and then plugged my phone in. I had to get some sleep. It was already ten and Justin would be here at seven sharp to take me to field training.

I melted into my pillow as exhaustion flowed over me and I drifted off into a content sleep.

SEVENTEEN

THE SUN PEEKED through the lace curtain early the next morning. I rolled over in bed to the sound of my phone pinging an unfamiliar tone. I pushed the button on the side to shut it off, then felt my eyes droop closed and instantly drifted off to sleep again.

"Ping…ping, ping, ping." My eyes shot open again. "What is that?" I mumbled, slightly irritated, sitting up in bed. I opened my phone in search of the culprit. The TikTok app button lit up again and again, dinging at an even higher speed. Suddenly my flight from last night flashed into my foggy morning memory as I opened it to my page.

My face totally froze. *Did I just read what I thought I read?*

I blinked twice and rubbed my eyes, unsure of what

I was seeing, but yeah, it was still there. 2.2 million followers? How did I…was this even possible?! Where did they all come from? I looked down at my only posted video. Seven and half million views in just eight hours? I scrolled down. Comment after comment rolled by, each one more positive than the last.

"*Claire, this is unbelievable! Thank you for sharing your flying world with us!*"

"*Air ballet is my new favorite! This is unreal.*"

"*We are officially in another world, people. Who would have ever thought this was possible?*"

"*This girl is a supersonic half alien. Is there any way we can get your super power too? I'll pay whatever!*"

I read that one again. *Supersonic half alien.* If they only knew the half of it. I still couldn't believe myself. I had alien matter floating through my veins. The thought of that sent a shiver down my body and I pushed it out of my mind again for the thousandth time. It was just too overwhelming to think about and Zhao had wisely instructed me to let it go.

"*You have to let that go Claire.*" He had told me the day I found out my superpower had come from an alien asteroid that crashed to earth over 70 years ago. "*There's nothing you can do about it now. You're healthy and that's what matters most.*"

I missed my buddy Zhao.

An hour later, I stood in front of the bathroom mirror applying a light layer of mascara on my lashes. I usually didn't wear much makeup, but this morning I would be meeting with my publicity rep so I wanted to look somewhat presentable. I tied my sneakers and zipped up my PT jacket, then bounced downstairs as the doorbell rang. Justin was here and right on time.

"Ready to go?" he asked, poking his head in and looking around, as I grabbed my small backpack.

"Yep," I replied, joining him outside and bolt locking the door. "Where's your wing man?"

"Uhhh…they just have me today. I guess they couldn't get anyone else."

"Oh," I shrugged, jumping in the back seat. Maybe they were getting a little more lenient now. I had never been allowed to travel without more than two armed guards around, even on base.

My mind wandered to the day and what it would bring. I wondered first about what Captain Lewis would think of my TikTok video from last night. He had encouraged me to stay active on social media, to help the public connect with me more, but I wasn't sure what he'd think of me videoing an actual flight. So far that had been reserved for my family's eyes only.

My phone dinged and my heart skipped a beat to see a text from Johnny. Him and Shawn were returning this afternoon from a two day flight down to Fort Benning. I couldn't wait until this day was over. We made simple plans to make dinner and watch a movie tonight.

Johnny: Good Morning Beautiful

Claire: Good Morning Mr. Perfect

Johnny: So I'm back a little early from Georgia. We decided to fly out at three this morning instead of noon, because they're getting some bad storms over there.

Claire: Omgoodness, are you home now?!

Johnny: Yeah. Shawn and I are going to stop in and see Silva though. Are you on your way to meet with Lewis?

Claire: Yes. Justin's taking me.

An unfamiliar change of direction caught my attention and I glanced up as Justin turned the car west, instead of east towards headquarters.

"I hope it's ok if I stop at the airfield real quick," he said before I had the chance to ask. "General Collins needs me to grab something and I figured since we're a little early, I would get it now."

I sunk deeper in my seat, my intuition radar starting to go on high alert for some reason while my Saturn tatt turned a bright pink. "No, that's fine," I said as casually as possible and resumed my text with Johnny.

Claire: Change of plans-I guess he has to pick up something from the airfield real fast. Maybe I'll see you.

Johnny: Probably not sweetness. Shawn and I just cleared the Black Hawk and we're leaving the field. I'll see you tonight though, ok?

I sent a thumbs up emoji, then turned my attention to Justin who was approaching the guard's gate to the airfield.

"What's up man?" The guard asked Justin, then glanced

in the backseat at me. The two seemed like they knew each other and that put my mind a little more at ease from the weird creepiness I was feeling.

"Nothing. Just picking up something for the Sergeant."

That got my attention again. "You mean the General, right?" I corrected him.

Justin laughed, looking at me in the rear view mirror. "General, Sergeant…all the same."

I smiled back at him as best as I could and glanced at the guard who was giving him the same half smile I was.

"Is this our Supergirl?" he asked, squinting back at me.

"Yep. Donovan, this is Claire," Justin said.

I smiled again and nodded in his direction. "Nice to meet you," I said.

"You too, Ma'am. I know Johnny. We served together last year in Afghanistan, so it's nice to finally meet the famous Claire he always talked about. He's a great guy."

"Yes he is and thank you," I smiled.

"You're welcome," he smiled back, tipping his hat in my direction. "You guys be careful," he added, pushing a button as the gate lifted.

Shawn turned the key and the Humvee roared to life. Johnny sat back in his seat, exhausted from the overnight flight as they exited the airfield just before my arrival.

"Dude, I'm going to sleep for hours," Johnny yawned. "Are you going home after we meet with Silva?"

"Yeah, but I'm not going home to sleep," Shawn smiled mischievously, while Johnny rolled his eyes. "You know what's up," Shawn laughed. "I haven't seen Alicia in three days."

"Two," Johnny corrected him.

"Whatever. Same difference. Are you seeing Claire tonight?"

"Oh definitely. Hopefully she gets back from field training by 6. They try to squeeze so much into her days. I feel terrible for her."

Johnny's phone ringing interrupted their conversation.

"Good Morning Major Silva. Yes Sir, we're on our way. Yeah, we had a good flight, missed those storms so we were happy about that… Yep, I just talked to her. She's on her way to the airfield and then to meet with the General. The airfield…with Justin." Shawn watched as Johnny's eyes grew wide and his brow slowly creased with worry. "Well, she's with a guard so I didn't think… Yes Sir." Johnny looked at Shawn. "Turn around!"

Shawn whipped the Hummer around as best as he could. "Where to?" he whispered.

"The airfield. Step on it," Johnny said urgently, pointing ahead. "We're on our way back sir. Hold on…I'm getting a text from Claire."

Johnny's face froze. "It says HELP." The car went deathly silent for a moment while they caught their breath. "Let's go Shawn. I know Major," Johnny almost yelled into the phone. "We're five minutes away…Yes Sir!"

Johnny hung up the phone. "Major is putting the

airfield on alert and calling the MPs." He dialed my number, but no answer. He dialed again frustrated, but I still was unable to answer.

Shawn tried his best to weave in and out of morning traffic, but the wide Humvee didn't give much room. Across the base the eerie sound of an alarm began to echo, sending chills down their spine.

"That alarm…it's the tornado alarm right?" Shawn asked, bewildered.

Johnny shook his head no. "That alarm is for Claire."

I already had a bad feeling and knew I was in deep trouble. I noticed Justin grip the steering wheel as he passed the office hangar and drove out towards the furthest runway. It was an old one and seldom used, except to park the occasional out of service aircraft waiting to be moved to the junkyard.

"Where are you taking me Justin?" I asked, sternly, more anger than fear taking over at this point.

Justin said nothing, but stared straight ahead. I slid my phone out and quickly texted the word HELP to Johnny. Immediately it rang back.

"Don't answer it Claire. It's too late," Justin said, nodding ahead.

I looked down the runway at a large black helicopter with red blades sitting half way behind an old cargo plane. Outside the copter stood three men all in black uniforms, two of them armed with large guns strapped across their chests. I grabbed the door handle to try and escape but realized it was locked and Justin had control.

"Claire, I had no choice," Justin said, almost whispering. "Do you understand what I'm saying? It was either you or my mom and she's all I have. She's my only family."

I shook my head in disbelief at him as we got closer, then turned and looked out of the back window. No one was behind us or even seemed to notice us back here.

Justin quickly drove up to the copter, almost slamming on the brakes. Two of the guards came to my side and attempted to open the door.

"Unlock it!" one of them yelled at Justin.

The locks popped open and he reached inside for me. I swung my legs out and began kicking with all my might, hitting one of them where it hurts the most. He doubled over in pain as the second guard grabbed my arm.

"No!" I screamed and began fighting him with everything I had as he pulled me out and onto the ground. In the distance the flight tower stood tall above the treeline. If I could just break free from this guy, I could fly up to the tower for help. My Jiu Jitsu training kicked in and I easily flipped the guy on his side. I was just about to shoot into the air when a shadow loomed over us and knocked me on my back again.

"I told you to be prepared, that she would put up a fight," I heard a familiar voice say, as the guy jumped on me again. I looked up past the guy who was now sitting on top of me, pinning my arms to the ground.

The sun burned bright behind his body making it hard to see features, but I had no doubt about who it was. I gasped as I looked into his cold face.

EIGHTEEN

"JASON!" I SAID in shock.

"Hey Claire," he smirked and knelt down beside me.

"What are you doing!" I gasped under the weight of the man. "I trusted you."

"Sorry I can't make our coffee date today," he said, shrugging away my question. "I have a little package I need to deliver." He reached inside a small black bag he held in his hand. "And that package is you. Here, this will make your trip a little more enjoyable."

My eyes grew wide in horror as he pulled a syringe needle from the bag. I squirmed as he knelt down close to my face.

"So I made the ultimate mistake as a spy," he whispered close to my ear, his eyes dark in frustration. "Falling for the girl who's supposed to be my enemy."

My eyes squinted in confusion. "Annessa?.."

"Oh no…well she would have been a nice second choice if she could have at least gotten off the ground for more than a minute. But no, it's always been you Claire."

My lip quivered in anger. "You sick…"

"Dude, we gotta go!" A voice yelled from the helicopter as the blades popped louder and faster.

He slowly slid the needle into my arm. "But you've made it easy to refocus Claire. I don't handle rejection very well."

I felt the guy get off me, then Jason's arms come under and scoop me off the ground. My arms and legs began to tingle intensely and quickly turn numb. Above me the rotors of the helicopter began to disappear and then came Annessa's voice from the past. I remembered her warning to me about Jason. *"There's just something not right about him, Claire."* Then that was it. Everything went black.

"Open the gate Dononvan!" Johnny demanded, as Donovan started to salute.

"The gate! Now!" Shawn yelled, waving off his salute. Donovan quickly pressed the button and the hummer roared through.

"Where do we go Johnny?" Shawn asked.

Johnny looked around for a moment, gathering his thoughts then pulled out his phone. "Connect me to the air tower please...Good Morning this Warrant Officer Angel again, do you have any flights leaving..." Johnny stopped mid sentence as a loud engine roared in the distance. He and Shawn watched as an unfamiliar copter rose above the treeline at the furthest runway.

"What kind of copter is that?" Shawn asked. "Because it sure isn't one of ours."

"Sir," Johnny asked, his voice a little shaky, "where is that copter from and where is it heading? ...Texas? Where in Texas? ...Ok, I need it tracked on radar and for you to notify all airports in the vicinity to track it as long as possible. Also, I need a copter that is fueled and ready to go."

Shawn drove quickly to the hangars, keeping the copter in sight as it slowly began disappearing into the horizon. "Which hangar?" he asked, impatiently. Johnny held up his index finger, asking for a moment.

"Ok...go to 3. They're almost done with a Pave Hawk."

"A Hawk?" Shawn looked at him skeptically. "It's been a minute for us with that copter."

"I remember," Johnny assured him. "I'll do the flying."

The hangar door for 3 began to pull back as the Pave Hawk was slowly wheeled out. Johnny and Shawn jumped from the hummer and greeted the airman in charge.

"Ok gentlemen," the airman said. "She's all yours, but just a heads up. She hasn't been up since Afghanistan so you're flying at your own risk. I mean everything looks good, but don't fly her hot. Give her a minute."

"You got it," Johnny agreed, looking at Shawn for his

approval.

"Let's do it," Shawn said, thanking the guy and heading to the copter.

Ten minutes later the copter lifted safely off the ground with Johnny at the controls.

"I hope we can keep up in this guy," Shawn said through the headset.

"It's one of the fastest we have," Johnny reassured him. "If I know my Claire she'll find a way to bail out of there and when she does I want to be close by."

"Hawk 770 from tower control," a voice cracked over the airway. Johnny and Shawn looked at each other, neither surprised that it was Silva, who had made his way to the air tower.

"Major Silva, good to hear your voice Sir," Shawn replied.

"Yours too. Be advised, I'll be here in tower control if you need me. We have two bandits enroute to intercept them." Johnny and Shawn looked at each other as Major Silva paused for a moment. Both of them could clearly hear the stress in his voice as he continued. "Godspeed. Please be careful and bring her home."

The whining of the helicopter's engine lured me out of my semi coma. The side of my face was flat against the hard metal floor where I laid as though someone had tossed me carelessly behind a bench seat in the very back of the copter. I slowly opened one eye and looked across the dirty floor that stretched under the seat in front of me to a pair of shiny military boots. My eyes closed again under the weight of whatever drug it was they gave me and I wondered where we were and how long I had been out.

Jason's chattering popped my eyes back open. His voice was coming from the left side of the helicopter and I took notice of where he was seated. I scanned the floor trying to count the remaining pair of boots on board. There appeared to be four sets, two flying the copter and two in the jump seats.

A soft breeze flowed across my face blowing a loose curl in my eyes and I noticed the side door of the copter slightly ajar. "*Perfect,*" I thought and began my escape plan. If I could just get out of the door I could fly myself to safety, but I needed a weapon, anything I could use to protect myself and buy time. Below my feet sat the only object in sight, a small bright red fire extinguisher. It would take too much time to set it off, but I could definitely swing it.

A pain shot through my arm drawing my attention to the dull pinching around my wrists. My hands were behind my back and from what I could tell with my fingers, they were bound with zip ties. The special forces training I received in Hawaii kicked in and I was taken back to a day last fall when Zhao and I were sitting back to back on a cold cement floor trying to figure out how to shimmy our way out of these hard little, plastic demons.

"*Ok Claire,*" I thought to myself, trying to calm the

nerves I could feel pulsating through my body. *"You can do this. First- the plastic ties, second-the extinguisher, finally- a quick dash to the door."*

"ETA, 45 minutes," I heard the pilot call from the cockpit, in a thick accent I couldn't recognize.

At first I tried to shimmy my hands from the ties, but very soon discovered I couldn't do that without a lot of movement and I needed them to think I was out as long as possible. I spread my fingers wide and began a desperate search for something, anything that I could use to cut away at the plastic.

"Forty-five minutes Claire," I warned myself. Somehow I knew when we landed and I was under lock and key, my chances of escape were very minimal. I had to make my escape in the air. *"God, please help me,"* I prayed. *"Give me something."*

The helicopter jarred in the crosswinds outside and I slid backwards, my head hitting softly against the wall behind me.

"Just a little more turbulence," I heard the pilot call from the front.

"She ok?" The deep voice closer to Jason asked.

I calmed my breathing and lay very still, knowing he would be looking back to check on me. A seat belt clicked and then I felt his presence hovering over me.

"Still out," Jason said, leaning over and checking for a pulse on my neck with two fingers. "That stuff I gave her can knock a man three times her size out for at least 24 hours," he reassured the guy. "I'm not too worried

172

about it."

"Good, because from what I heard from Justin, she's a little spitfire," the other guy laughed.

"She is that," Jason agreed.

"What time do they want her at the airport tonight?"

"Eight," Jason replied. "If we don't have her in Singapore first thing in the morning, the deal's off."

I gasped silently. What did he just say? Singapore? My breathing increased drastically at the realization of what was happening. My worst nightmare. My family's worst nightmare. I was a hostage and I knew if I left this country, I would never see it again.

"*Slow breaths Claire,*" I warned myself. The helicopter shifted once again, sliding me closer down to the extinguisher. My fingers pressed against something metal and I felt a hot, stinging pain. I very carefully moved my body forward, putting distance between my hands and the metal and felt a tiny trickle of warm blood begin to flow from my fingertips. I felt around again for the sharp object, and soon realized it was leftover from an old jump seat that had been removed. Very quickly and without as much movement as possible, I began to slice away at the zip ties. To my surprise, it took just a few minutes to cut through and just like that I was free.

NINETEEN

JOHNNY AND SHAWN jetted through the air, while the US Air Force tracked my location on radar and guided them in the right direction. High above they watched as two fighter jets sliced through the sky enroute to my location, rumbling through the atmosphere.

"What exactly do those guys plan on doing when they find her copter?" Shawn asked. "I mean, it's not like they can engage with them."

"Intimidation," Johnny said, clenching his jaw in anger. "At least they'll know we're coming for them."

Shawn noticed the worry in his eyes. "We're going to get her back Johnny," he reassured him. Johnny nodded firmly in agreement, but Shawn could see right through his friend. He was worried.

"Hawk 770 from Campbell tower control," Major

Silva's voice cracked over the frequency.

"Go ahead tower control," Shawn answered.

"Be advised we have been switched to this emergency frequency. Also, the target has changed directions. It looks like they are headed for desert territory. Head directly west and we'll be contacting you with the exact numbers here soon."

"Roger that," replied Johnny.

"The desert?" Shawn asked.

Johnny reached up and flipped a couple of switches. "They're changing transportation modes."

"*You have to do it now Claire,*" I told myself as a cold bead of sweat dripped down my face. I clenched my fists together, going over one last time, each step I would take; first I'll take out Jason, then his friend and then make a mad dash to the door. I took a final deep breath and had just given myself the go, when a thunderous noise ripped across the sky. It became louder with each passing second and then in an instant enveloped the copter, vibrating through my ears and down my body.

"What was that?!" Jason's partner asked.

I heard Jason's seat belt click open and saw his boots walk towards the cockpit, kneeling between the front seats and staring out the front window.

"Air Force," Jason laughed. "Just an intimidation ploy, gentleman."

"But Jason…" the other guy began. I could hear the fear in his voice, despite the loud engine.

"Intimidation gentlemen," Jason said more sternly. "Do you really think they are going to engage us with her on board? Let's just get to the rendezvous point and you'll be free to go."

Suddenly a commanding voice boomed through the copter. "Bogey Copter 309, this is Captain Speicher with the United States Air Force. You must immediately land your helo at the airport 30 miles southwest of this location or we will be forced to engage."

Everyone grew quiet as Captain Speicher repeated his command and the jets began to circle back to the copter.

"What are they doing?" One of the pilots asked.

The scream of the jets echoed through the sky again, as both approached the copter head on, then split to either side at the last minute shaking us with force from the engine back draft.

"*This is it Claire,*" I told myself. I had to move while they were distracted. I grabbed the extinguisher and quietly flew over the seat, my plan quickly changing as I saw the guy who had held me down sitting closer now, his attention turned to the front with Jason.

I quietly swung both arms around and using the entire force of my body, launched myself into the air nailing the guy right in the center of his head. The cracking sound, followed by his loud grunt and slump onto the floor caught all three men's attention in the front.

"CLAIRE!" Jason yelled angrily, but it was too late.

I already had the extinguisher ready for a second blow and this one found Jason's cheek very quickly. I couldn't believe the power in my swing as Jason flew back violently against the control panel, his arm hitting the control wheel, sending the copter in a quick jolt to the left. I fell hard to the left side, my arm slamming against the wall. A hissing sound exploded and suddenly a bright cloud of white smoke from the extinguisher filled the cockpit, setting off a string of alarms.

I got as close to the ground as I could, as the pilot maneuvered the copter upright again, then crawled my way towards the cracked door. I grabbed the handle and pulled hard, sliding it a few inches, almost enough to get my body through. Around me a tint of pink illuminated off the white smoke as my Saturn tattoo glowed brightly. The copter made another sharp flip to the left again and I grasped the side of the door as the floor I was laying on, now became a wall almost parallel beside me.

"She's by the door Jason!" I heard one of the pilots yell.

I hung on tight, dangling in the air and looked up at the door above me where a sunny, clear blue sky was awaiting my escape, but still not wide enough to fly out of. I flew my body up against it and pulled with all my strength again. At last the door gave way, sliding all the way open with a loud bang. I had just got my head and shoulders through the door when I felt a strong clasp of a hand around my ankle.

"No!" I yelled, looking down at a bloody faced Jason who was pulling on my leg. Fumes from the extinguisher enveloped me as the fresh air sucked it out of the door, sending me into a coughing fit. My fingers slipped and I came tumbling back into the copter, kicking and punching all the way down.

The pilot maneuvered the copter upright again as Jason grabbed me from behind, wrapping his strong arm around my neck. We tumbled to the floor rolling to the back jumpseat and I landed on my back on top of him. I fought hard as he began to squeeze the oxygen from my body. In the past I had the advantage in ground defense, but like me, Jason was very trained in Jiu Jitsu so it was a battle of skill at this point. The lack of oxygen flow to my brain began to weaken my body and I started to lose consciousness.

Then, a small miracle. From somewhere inside, I heard Professor Corral's voice whisper in my head. *"Claire, you have to find that extra defense. That something as a woman you have that he doesn't. That one split second of distraction."*

I had no weapons, but I did know of one thing he had to worry about that I didn't. I pushed my feet through his legs and planted them firmly on the ground. I then clasped my hands behind me, lifted my torso in the air and used it to slam my fists back down into his groin.

Jason yelled out in pain, letting go of his grasp. I flew off of him and to the ceiling while my head continued to spin. The wind howled through the door pounding in my ears and pushing me hard against the ceiling. Jason suddenly popped up in front of me, but still slightly doubled over in pain as he clung onto the nylon straps hanging on the wall.

I looked just beyond him at the door. Freedom was so close. Just 10 feet away and I could fly into the open sky. Jason followed my gaze to the door, but kept one eye on me. We paused for a split second and stared into each other's eyes, his dark and cold. I didn't even recognize him anymore. His soul was gone.

"You're not ruining this for me Claire," he said through clenched teeth.

I returned his icy stare, but didn't see him at all. I saw Kass, Mom, Johnny, Zhao, Tessa, Danielle, Silva, Alicia, Lexi, Shawn, everyone that meant more to me than my own life. I had to make it back for them. I couldn't let them go through the pain I felt at the loss of Annessa.

From deep inside of me a cry of anger came out. I screamed over the wind and swung my legs in front, flying at Jason, feet first. My shoe hit his jaw, knocking him backwards, but not before he grabbed my leg and slammed my head into the wall. Pain pulsated from the back of my head to my eyes as I collapsed on the floor. I felt a stinging sensation and then the warm trickle of blood down the right side of my face and into my eye. The pilot tilted the copter to the right, in an obvious attempt to distract me and I watched in horror as the guy I had knocked out earlier rolled to the door and slipped out of the copter head first.

Jason watched him roll out, but didn't even wince. He grabbed my shirt with both hands and lifted me off the ground slamming my back into the seat, then we rolled across the floor, right up beside the door.

"Careful with her Jay!" The pilot yelled. "You have to get her there alive!"

Jason didn't seem to care as he attempted to body slam me again, but this time I managed to knee him in the side. Everything was happening so fast, as he swung at me in fury, knocking us off balance and we tumbled backwards into the door.

The copter began to rumble once again as the jets came streaking back across the sky. Jason glanced towards the pilot's seat and finally...there it was. That moment of distraction Prof. Corral had taught me to look for. In an instant I dove toward the door, this time almost completely out, when in a moment of desperation Jason grabbed my leg and came tumbling out with me. The air vacuum sucked us into a spiral fall as he pulled me down grabbing onto my waist and we began a freefall through the bright blue sky.

"Oh my god!" He yelled at me. "Stop us Claire!"

"I'm trying!" I yelled back, at his audacity to ask me to save his life at this point. But...then I looked down at the horror in his eyes. I decided no matter what and who he was, I had to at least try to save him. I knew who I was and I believed life was sacred and worth saving if possible.

I wrapped my legs around him as tight as I could as my mind went back to the first night I learned I could fly. I hadn't free fell like this since that night when I landed in the Ellis' pool. I had seen the ground below us and there was nothing but clay dirt with patches of green. No water to help break our fall anywhere.

I clasped Jason's hand. "Hold on!" I yelled down to him as the copter flew further away and the two jets were now making a large U-turn back toward us, piercing my ears as they grew closer. (I couldn't imagine what they thought as they looked out of their cockpit window in that moment. Jason and I dangling in the air must have been the craziest thing they had ever seen.)

I looked above me and with my other hand formed a fist and shoved it in the air above my head, focusing completely on flying. I breathed a sigh of relief as we slowed to almost a halt. I could feel the gravity seeping from my body, but not Jason's. I fought hard against his gravity, too scared to begin a light fall towards the ground in fear I would lose focus and what little strength I had. Whatever drug he had given me was making me lightheaded and dizzy.

I turned my eyes toward the warm sun, as its bright beams began to spin and stars and darkness began to cloud my eyes.

"Noooo," I yelled, knowing I couldn't hold on much longer.

"Claire!" I heard Jason yell back at me. "Stay with me!"

TWENTY

JOHNNY AND SHAWN stayed in contact with Major Silva as they approached the Arkansas airspace.

"We're gonna have to refuel soon Johnny," Shawn said looking down at the fuel level controls.

"Little Rock is not too far away," Johnny replied, referring to Little Rock Air Force base. "We'll head that way if we don't hear from them soon. Their copter will have to stop and refuel soon so we shouldn't lose too much time."

"Hawk 770 from Campbell tower control," Major Silva's voice called over the frequency.

"Go ahead Campbell," Shawn replied.

"We have our target on a stall just north and west of your location. Start heading that direction and I'll give you the exacts."

Johnny looked over at Shawn. "A stall?" he asked. "What does that even mean?"

Shawn shrugged his shoulders and turned the copter towards the northwest. "Campbell from 770, can you give a mile estimate from our location?"

"Approximately 30 from your location," came the reply.

"Can we make it?" Johnny asked, looking at the fuel level.

"Maybe there, but not back," Shawn said.

"Hawk 770 from Little Rock," came a female voice over the radio.

"Go ahead Little Rock."

"You are clear to land on runway 7. We have Black Hawk waiting for you."

"Clear, thank you," Johnny breathed a sigh of relief. "Let's head there. At least we won't have to wait to fill up."

Five minutes later they touched down at the end of runway 7. Just to the west sat a Black Hawk, its propellers spinning and ready for take off.

Shawn nodded his head in approval. "That's what I'm talking about!"

"Let's move!" Johnny yelled above the engines as they grabbed their belongings and ran towards the copter.

"Welcome aboard gentlemen," the co-pilot greeted them while they hopped aboard and secured themselves in the jump seats.

"Thank you sir," Johnny said. The Black Hawk lifted off the ground while they threw on their headphones. "I'm

Chief Warrant Officer Angel and this is Chief Warrant Officer Jackson. Do you know where we're headed?"

"Yes," came a voice from behind them both. "We know where we're headed, but we have no clue why we're headed there. Wanna fill us in?"

Johnny turned around to see an Airman with an iPad-looking mapping instrument in his hands. "Well, I can tell you so much, but I don't have clearance for everything."

"That's fine," said the pilot into their headphones. "Let's just get there."

"Well, your target is stationary," said the co-pilot, "whatever is causing that, we don't know."

"Little Rock traffic control to Helo 66."

"Go ahead Rock."

"Our jets have eyes on their target. They are in pursuit of the bird, but the target is stationary at approximately 500 feet above ground. For safety measures, we will be sending the location through the mapping program."

The pilot paused for a moment. "Clear," he said, skeptically.

"What could be staying stationary at 500, while they pursue the bird?" the co-pilot asked as they glanced back at Johnny, but Johnny was zoned out.

His mind went back to spring break the year before, as just he and I were out on his family's sail boat in the Gulf of Mexico. I had fallen off the boat in rough waters, not wearing a life jacket and had lost consciousness. Johnny told me he had frantically turned the boat around and was getting ready to jump in and find me, when for some weird reason my body rose out of the water. He said I was basically levitating above the water on my back, unconscious. *"Maybe that's what's happening now,"* he thought to himself.

"It's Claire," he said suddenly, looking over at Shawn.

Shawn's eyes grew wide. "What?" he asked in disbelief.

"Spring break…last year?" Johnny reminded him. "She's either unconscious or she's…she's…"

"Don't think that," Shawn interrupted him. "She probably just fell out and got the wind knocked out of her."

"We're closing in," the co-pilot warned everyone.

Johnny quickly slid into a harness hanging on the wall and attached it to a tether for safety. He slid open the door slightly and began to search the sky.

"Angel, we're going to circle whatever it is they're picking up on radar. Let me know when you see anything."

Johnny looked out into the horizon for a moment and suddenly, I was there.

"It's Claire! I see her!" Johnny yelled into the headphone mic. "Drop about 50 feet!"

The crew looked to where Johnny was pointing. Just below the helicopter and to the northwest I lay on my back suspended in the sky, with my legs and arms dangling in the warm air just like I had done over the gulf waters. The pilot took the bird down and to the south, directly across from where I was. Everyone on board gasped at the sight of me laying there with nothing but the vast bright blue sky around and tiny patchwork of fields far below.

"How is that…?" The co-pilot began to ask.

"Oh my god," the guy with the map almost whispered. "What..what is holding her up like that?"

Johnny turned to Shawn and the pilot. "We've got to get her out of the sky."

"Will you be able to do that?" The co-pilot asked. "Just pluck her away from whatever…whatever force is holding her there?"

"Yes."

"How do you know?" The mapping guy asked.

"Because I've done it before." Johnny said. "Shawn, hook me up." Shawn began to hook him into the cable as Johnny gave further instructions. "Sir, if you could get me directly above her, Shawn could guide me down."

"I'm sorry, but that's just too dangerous," the co-pilot replied.

"We do it all the time," Shawn said sternly, as he secured Johnny to the cable. "We're well trained. Now please sir, do as he requested."

The pilot paused for a moment and finally nodded his approval, then slowly maneuvered the copter 20 feet and directly above. Johnny gave his phone to the mapping guy. "Get this on video for me. I think they are going to need it for research later. Maybe it can help her someday."

"Ok," the mapping guy said hesitantly, a now blank stare of disbelief on his face.

Shawn tightened up Johnny's harness and triple checked it for safety just like he had been trained to do.

"Be careful," he warned, his brow creasing in worry.

"I've got this," said Johnny, as they high fived.

"You've got this," Shawn repeated back in assurance.

Johnny went out back first, just like he had been trained to do in Air Assault School, with Shawn guiding him carefully as the automatic cable slowly turned. Johnny breathed a sigh of relief as he cleared the copter and began the descent to my location. The winds kicked up slightly when he got nearer making him slowly pendulum swing. He was just above and to the south of my location, about 30 feet when he motioned up for the pilot to pull in closer. The pilot carefully guided him to me, the precision in his flight skills impressive.

Johnny gasped in the craziness of the moment. Seeing me suspended in the atmosphere, hundreds of feet above the face of the earth was overwhelming. He paused to catch his breath as the skies began to rumble again. The two fighter jets streaked above and across the sky to get a better look, but at a safe distance.

A voice boomed through Johnny's headphones. "Helo 66, this is Captain Speicher of the United States Air Force, be advised we'll be circling the perimeter to ensure your safety as you secure the target."

"Clear and thank you Captain," the pilot radioed back.

Johnny swung himself to me the final few feet, sliding both arms underneath my legs and lower back, holding me tight. His heart sank in his chest when he noticed a thick stream of blood flowing from above my right eye and down into my hairline.

"You're going to be ok, Claire Bear," he whispered into my ear, then gave Shawn the go ahead to lift us into the copter. Slowly the cable turned and Johnny felt a small jolt, popping me out of my airspace. Above us the mapping guy recorded our every move, occasionally whispering "*unbelievable*" into the camera.

Five minutes later the final five feet of cable cranked into the copter and Shawn reached out, pulling us both into safety.

"What are her vitals?" Shawn asked as they laid me on the floor, slamming the door closed.

"She's breathing at least," Johnny said, bending over and manually taking my blood pressure. "We need to get her to a hospital though."

"Little Rock from Helo 66," the pilot radioed immediately. "We'll be diverting to Baptist Medical with a patient in distress, make sure they have a doctor on standby." He then made an immediate sharp turn toward the south, choppering us to the hospital just a short ten minute flight away.

TWENTY-ONE

"SIR," SHAWN ADDRESSED the co-pilot. "Could you contact Campbell and let General Collins know where we will be?"

"I can do that," he replied as the copter set down carefully on the roof of the tall hospital. Outside a small team of nurses and three security guards stood by to greet us. I was quickly transferred from the copter to a gurney and rushed inside.

"Heard we have a VIP here," one of the male nurses said to Johnny as we entered a darkened hallway in stark contrast to the bright Arkansas sunshine. Johnny rubbed his eyes to adjust, ignoring the nurse's comment. "Where are you taking her?"

"Down to X-ray. We don't know what she's experienced physically, so that's where we'll start. We just want to make sure there's no internal bleeding." The nurse stopped us in front of an elevator and pushed the down button. "Where did you find her?" he asked, taking out a small medical flashlight and examining my head wound more carefully.

Johnny looked at Shawn and inconspicuously nodded his head no, warning him not to say a word. Instead both of them remained quiet and followed the nurse into the elevator. They watched as he pulled my hairline back revealing a laceration much deeper than originally thought.

"We definitely gotta get a CT here," he said, then looked up at the boys. "Where did you say you found her?" he asked again.

Johnny's jawline tightened. He wasn't giving anyone information about me after what happened today. "We didn't."

"Whoa," the nurse laughed, putting both of his hands up in defense. "Didn't mean to be nosey, it would just help the Doc with his diagnosis."

Shawn and Johnny gave him a hard stare as the elevator dinged and the door slid open. Once they wheeled me into the hallway, I was immediately whisked away through two doors directly in front of us. Johnny tried to follow, but was quickly turned away.

"No one is allowed in CT," another nurse said sternly, as she stood between him and the door.

"You don't understand," Johnny said. "I have to stay with her."

"It will just be a minute sir," she reassured him. "We

will come get you as soon as she is settled in a room. You both can wait over there."

Johnny sighed, reluctantly obeying her orders. "Yes ma'am. Come on Shawn," he said, heading towards the empty waiting room she pointed at. They settled in the soft, overstuffed chairs, catching their breath. Johnny looked at his watch and then leaned over placing his head in his hands, feeling overwhelmed with the day. It was now 3 pm. and they had been going since yesterday morning with no sleep.

"Who do you think did it?" Shawn whispered, interrupting his train of thought.

Johnny shrugged. "It has to be some foreign enemy."

Shawn shook his head in disbelief. "Johnny, they got a whole helicopter on our base and we had no idea."

"Oh it was definitely inside," Johnny said, as his phone rang through his front pocket. "Someone we know and trust. Silva," he said, glancing down at the number and then answered the phone. "Yes, sir. We had to get her to a hospital right away, sir. She was breathing, but unresponsive…they took her in for a ct scan. Yes sir… yes sir, we'll be waiting." He hung up the phone and rubbed his bloodshot eyes.

"He mad?" Shawn asked.

"Nope, but they don't want her here. Someone from the Air Force base is on their way." Johnny then lowered his voice to a whisper. "General is afraid they will draw blood and you know that can't happen."

Shawn nodded in agreement.

The double doors they had taken me through opened and a doctor in olive green surgery scrubs walked through. "Angel?" he asked, looking at the two guys.

"That's me," Johnny replied, standing up to greet him and shaking his hand firmly.

"Hello, I'm Dr. Nevins. She's in for a CT scan right now. Good news is all her vitals are stable and she is responding."

"Thank you sir," Johnny sighed relieved and shook his hand again.

"Well, you're welcome, but we're not out of the woods yet. We still need to look at the scan and I would like to keep her here for the night, but we've been ordered to turn her over to another medical team out of Little Rock Base. They are probably almost here, if not already. We'll let you know when they arrive."

Johnny and Shawn watched as the doctor disappeared through the double doors.

"Ok now we can relax," Shawn yawned, as he kicked back in the stuffed chairs and tried to get comfortable. Johnny soon joined him and stretched his long legs in front of him. Talking to the doctor had helped calm his worries and now the last 24 hours were beginning to catch up.

"Johnny…" a voice tunnel-echoed, stirring him awake. Johnny's drowsy eyes slowly opened to see a concerned

Shawn staring down at him. Immediately the crazy events of the last day flooded back. A feeling of dread punched to his core, knowing they had been sleeping longer than they should have.

He jumped from his seat. "What time is it Shawn?"

"Dude, it's already 5. Did Silva call you yet?"

Johnny looked down at his phone. There were no texts messages or missed calls from anyone in the last hour they had been asleep. "Nothing," Johnny sighed. "Let's go check on Claire."

S_N

"What do you mean there is no record of her?" Johnny demanded, slamming his fist on the hospital registration desk. "Who took her and where?"

"Sir please," the nurse tried to reason with him. "I'm not sure. I just came on the midnight shift."

"Then let us talk to someone who does know," Shawn said from behind him.

Johnny's eyes softened as he looked at the confused nurse who clearly had no idea what was going on and was typing as fast as she could into her database to figure it out. "I'm sorry ma'am. It's just...we've had a long day. Can we please talk to Dr. Nif...Niffans...Dr. Nevous?"

"Dr. Nevins?" she asked.

"Yes ma'am."

"Give me one second."

Johnny and Shawn watched as she walked through a

locked door behind her desk.

"I thought they were supposed to come get us when the medical team from Little Rock arrived," Shawn said.

Johnny sighed. "I don't know, but something's not right man."

The receptionist soon returned with a doctor in tow.

"Hi, I'm Dr. Bendetti," he said, reaching out to shake Johnny's hand. "I understand you're looking for a patient?"

"Yes sir, we brought her in today. Her name is Claire Haley," Johnny informed him.

"I understand," he said, his brow creasing in worry. "I'm showing no record of her here though. Are you sure you're in the right hospital?"

"Sure I'm in the right hospital?" Johnny asked in disbelief. "*Yes I'm sure!*"

Shawn put his hand on Johnny's shoulder to calm him down. "Doctor, we flew her here today." He pointed to the ceiling. "We landed her on this roof and we spoke with a Dr. Nevins about her care."

"We were told someone from the base was supposed to come for her because she is an Airman with the US Air Force," Johnny explained, more calmly now. "We were supposed to be notified when they arrived."

The doctor stared back at Johnny for a moment, obviously careful to select his words. "I understand...but like I said I have no record. But if you give me a moment I can try and contact Dr. Nevins."

Johnny sighed in frustration as his phone rang. "Yes

sir...yes sir. Yes sir," he said again looking toward the exit then hung up the phone. "Let's go Shawn."

Shawn followed his friend quickly out of the hospital, glancing back at the bewildered faces of the receptionist and doctor. A large black SUV was waiting for them under the carport. "What's going on?" Shawn asked as they jumped in the backseat.

"She's safe. We're going back to the base, then flying to Campbell. They have our bird ready to go."

"Who was that?"

Johnny's jaw tightened in frustration. "Silva."

"Where is she?" Shawn tried again.

"I don't know. He just said we need to get back."

TWENTY-TWO

"CLAIRE," I HEARD a soft voice, easing me out of my drowsy state. I slowly opened my eyes, then quickly closed them again as a bright beam of light came through a halfway opened window shade. I swallowed dry air and immediately began choking. My throat was so dry and burned with each deep cough. The pretty blonde lady in the room with me, grabbed a tall glass with a straw and came over to help me sit up. I took the ice water and began gulping it, not bothering to breathe, but cautiously keeping one eye on her the whole time.

"You ok?" she asked as she took the glass out of my hand. "Do you want more?"

"Who are you?" I asked firmly, tightening my fists in defense.

"I'm Dr. Mason…Meghan," she replied calmly. "I'm

an American and you're safe here Claire."

I sat up. "Where's here?" I asked, my voice dry and raspy.

She walked over to the sink and filled my glass again. "You're at a secure location so there's no need to worry. Do you remember what happened to you?"

I shifted on the bed, noticing for the first time a pain that throbbed from the top of my right temple. I slowly guided my fingertips over my skin to a pokey wire protruding out of my skin. They had given me stitches. My hands trembled as my mind flashed images of the helicopter and the white extinguisher smoke, Jason's cold eyes and the sense of urgency I felt to get out of that copter. I could still hear the sounds of the chopping blades and the strong wind blowing against my skin as we tumbled in the air.

"Jason," I whispered. "I trusted him."

"You don't have to worry about him anymore," she reassured me.

I winced, looking down at my bruised hips, I was aware of now. He had held them so tightly as he hung on to me for dear life.

Meghan sat on the edge of my bed, resting her hand on my knee on top of the thin blanket. I looked closely as her wide eyes stared back at mine. She looked so young. Very young. In fact, she looked younger than me.

"How old are you?" I asked, turning my head sideways and looking more intently at her.

"It's nice to finally meet you. We've all been waiting so long," she smiled shyly as someone knocked lightly on the door. Meghan got up to answer it and I heard a light conversation between the two as a tray was passed through the cracked door and then closed quickly.

"Here. I want you to eat this," she said, handing me the tray that consisted of some kind of barley soup and crackers. "I'll be back in 30 minutes to give you a check up and we'll talk more." She left the room quickly, the door snapping locked behind her. I turned my attention to the soup and quickly had it gone in minutes, then sat back against the pillow as my brain went into overdrive. I wondered where I was and who Meghan meant when she said *we've all* been waiting so long to meet you. Was this another compound? I wasn't safe at the last one obviously, so why should I trust her and whoever *we* are at this one.

A familiar sound brought me out of my thoughts and I turned my attention to the breeze that was blowing through the slightly cracked window behind the drawn, but open shades. I slowly slid myself out of bed, careful not to aggravate any unknown injuries I might have and shuffled my way to the window. My eyes popped open, surprised to see just beyond a well trimmed lawn, a pristine white beach with calm blue waves washing over it. I knew I was looking west as a beautiful sunset was glowing on the water. I pulled up on the window, but realized they wouldn't budge anymore. Of course they locked me in.

"*Am I in Hawaii again?*" I wondered, but somehow knew I wasn't. There was something different about this beach. Not as tropical and it had a different smell to it, if that makes any sense.

The chair I was leaning over slid out unexpectedly and I reached down to catch myself. There sitting in a neat pile were my training clothes I had been wearing, freshly washed. I quickly slipped off the uncomfortable hospital gown I was wearing and put them on, noticing a bulky object in the side pants pocket. "My phone!" I said, excited to have it available in case things went downhill for me here. I pushed the power button, but was disappointed to find it dead. "Figures," I sighed.

The door unlocked again and Meghan slipped back in. "Ahhh…I see you found your clothes," she smiled. "I meant to tell you about them before I left but I forgot."

"They look as good as new," I said looking down at them. "Thank you."

"Of course," she said, walking over to me. "How are you feeling?"

I sat down on the edge of the bed, still a bit dizzy. "I'm fine. Just a little tired."

"That's to be expected. We gave you something extra to help you sleep until you were better. The residual effects of that drug are wearing off now."

"How long was I asleep?"

"We've had you two days and it took them a day to get you here…so three."

"Where's here?" I asked, still not trusting Meghan, despite her kindness to me.

"In due time, Claire. I want you to rest tonight, because

tomorrow you have a busy day ahead. There's PJ's in that top drawer beside your bed, snacks and drinks in that little fridge, a bathroom behind that door and pretty much anything you could want to watch on that TV."

I looked to where she pointed as she mentioned each one. I hadn't noticed anything until now. My mind was fuzzy and I felt my eyes grow heavy again. I was so tired. "I need to go home," I said defiantly.

Meghan stopped on her way to the door. "Trust me Claire, you'll want to stick around one more day. Oh, one more thing. See that phone?" I looked at the desk beside the bed that held an old 80's phone, like the one my grandma had when I was little. This phone however, had no buttons, just a little light on the top. "Just pick it up. It will immediately call me and I'll be right here if you need me. Anything at all. Ok?"

"Sure," I sighed. "But when can I go home?"

"All in due time Claire," she repeated herself, giving me a big smile and closing the door behind her.

I reluctantly changed into the PJ's she had left for me and brushed my teeth in the small bathroom, then settled into bed and immediately fell back to sleep, too tired to even think about the next day.

I awoke the next morning to the sound of the door opening again. Meghan walked in smiling, wearing a bright white lab coat and carrying another tray. This time she had her blonde hair pulled back in a tight bun and a pair of smart reading glasses sat on the tip of her button nose. I could tell she was trying to make herself look older, but she wasn't fooling me. I had come to the conclusion she couldn't be anymore than 15 years old. A very mature 15 years and an old soul, but a 15 year old nonetheless.

"Good morning Claire. Did you sleep well?"

I sat up and looked at her slightly annoyed. I had actually barely slept at all. All night long I had nightmares and kept waking up to assure myself I wasn't with Jason back in the helicopter.

"Claire, I told you, you are safe here," she said, almost reading my mind.

"Really?" I asked, cautiously. "Well, let's see. I just survived a kidnapping off my own home base from a guy I've trusted and worked with for over two years now. I have no idea who you are or where I am or that I'm even safe, but I'm supposed to trust you even though we've only known each other hmm…" (I looked down at my non-existent wrist watch) 8 hours."

Meghan looked at me for a moment, then slowly set the tray on the table beside the bed. "That's fair," she said. "I don't think I'd trust me either, after all you've been through. But Claire, please just give us a chance."

"Who is *us*?" I asked emphatically. "I don't know you and I don't believe you." I was tired and when I was tired and upset, I would cry. I swallowed hard the lump in my throat and blinked back the tears. I didn't want to cry and I especially didn't want to cry in front of a teenager.

Meghan didn't say anything, but went over and picked up the old phone she had pointed out the night before. "Hey," she said casually. "Can you send him over please?...I know...I know, but I'll deal with that later. Ok...ok, thanks."

She hung up the phone and walked back to the door. "Claire, I have to go meet someone. You have an hour to eat breakfast and shower before I return. If you don't wish to wear the PT clothes you had on, there is a fresh flight suit in the bottom drawer."

I didn't even bother to respond or look her way. A few seconds later, I heard the door snap shut again. I sat crisscross on the bed and rubbed my temples that slightly throbbed under all the stress, then reached up to pull my thick curly brown hair out of the high bun I had it in. It fell around my face matted and dirty and on the side where my stitches were, dried blood was mixed in my hair and on my scalp. Suddenly I felt so gross.

The shower was small, but when I was done I felt so much better. After I threw back on my PT clothes, I sat on the bed letting my hair dry while I ate the fruit she had brought for breakfast. I looked at the clock. It was almost 8 and Meghan said I had an hour when she left at 7. I finished quickly, threw my hair into a high tight bun and gathered my belongings, eager to get out of the room. "*What would I do if she was lying and was actually working with Jason?*" I wondered, sitting in the chair with my bag ready to go. I looked around the room for the hundredth time, figuring out a plan of escape if need be.

At last the door opened again and Meghan entered. "Are you ready to go, Claire?"

I stood up and looked around making sure I had all my stuff. I had grabbed the tooth brush and personal items they had given me just in case I wouldn't have access to them later. I had no idea where I was going and what kind of situation I would be in.

I silently followed Meghan into a long, bright white hallway. We walked to the right and all the way down to a set of double doors. Once we reached the thick metal doors Meghan took out a set of keys and unlocked them. I took a deep breath, my body tensing up, unsure of what fate awaited me on the other side.

A blast of cooler air hit us as we walked through the doors and into what, to my surprise, looked like a small airport. On the right side of the wide walkway was a typical waiting room, complete with standard airport waiting room chairs and a round information desk in the corner. Just outside the tall windows three helicopters sat, one of them was an Apache like my Johnny flew. This was so weird. I could have sworn I was in a hospital.

No one else was in the room, except for a lone passenger who stood facing the desk and talking to someone on his phone. We walked closer and Meghan greeted him. "Hey, thanks for coming early," she sighed.

I looked warily at the back of the guy's head, curious

as to who he was, although something was eerily familiar about him. I had to catch my breath as he turned around.

I stared hard at him, not sure what to think. "Zhao," I whispered at last, completely stunned.

"Claire!" he smiled, quickly hanging up the phone and walking toward us. He scooped me up in one of our normal bear hugs and spun me around. I barely moved though, my body stiff with uncertainty. Zhao put me down immediately and backed off when he noticed my uneasiness. "Are you ok?" he asked, moving a small, loose curl from my face and eyeing my stitches. "This looks much better."

I didn't respond, but instead looked at him skeptically. I was not sure who I could trust anymore and though I would have never thought this in a million years, that included Zhao.

Meghan quickly joined us and put her arm around my shoulder. "Claire's been through a lot this week Z. She just needs some time."

Zhao took my hand and looked deep in my eyes. "But she knows me. Claire, it's ok. You're safe and I'm never going to let anyone hurt you." Then he put his arm around my waist and led us to a door that went outside. "Let's go. She needs to meet the others."

The door opened to a large carport and then into the bright sunshine. A warm tropical breeze zipped past us as we walked down a flower lined path that led to a two story earth toned concrete building, directly across a grassy knoll. To my right, I could see a taller building with windows open and Coldplay's song *A Sky Full Of Stars* streaming from one of them. To the left a shorter building, but all similar in color. As we walked, a long beeping noise came from behind and I looked up to see a tall air traffic control tower that doubled as a lighthouse. There were no roads, just sidewalks and grass and beyond that the ocean all around. That was it. We seemed to be completely surrounded by water.

"Where are we Zhao?' I asked.

"We're on a small island in the gulf, just south of Louisiana."

I breathed a sigh of relief. At least I was still in America, but if I was going to make my getaway, now would be the time. Zhao still had his hand around my waist, but Meghan walked slightly ahead of us so I could escape so easily. My body tensed at the thought of it and my Saturn tattoo shined even brighter.

"Claire, please don't fly away," Zhao said, squeezing me a little closer. "Please just trust me."

"I'm trying Zhao," I shrugged, as two men approached us on the sidewalk walking in the opposite direction.

They nodded toward us. "Meg...Z," one greeted them and then gave me a long, curious stare.

I stared back and watched them over mine and Zhao's

shoulders. They were both dressed in a black uniform and I gasped when the one who greeted us, glanced back for one final look. They had on the exact same uniform and black beret as my friend Annessa and the guys who had visited us at the compound had worn.

"Zhao, that's the same uniform…" I began.

"I know," he interrupted me.

"This way," Meghan said as she opened the glass door to the building.

Zhao reached down and grabbed my hand as we entered the two story lobby. My eyes grew wide at the sight of it. To our left, a large map of the world hung on the wall. Shiny metallic dots glowed all over the map that pointed out various locations. To the right small flags covered the wall in tidy black frames, some of them representing countries I recognized and some I had never seen before. Directly in front of us a wide staircase led downstairs to another lobby full of couches and chairs and what appeared to be a small snack shop.

We walked down the stairs and through the empty lobby, then followed a carpeted hallway. Along the hallway photos of men and women in the same black uniform rolled by. Some of the photos looked older in black and white at the beginning, with the more modern ones toward the end. I paused slightly when two familiar faces smiled down from the end pictures; Dr. Zhao and just below him Zhao, in shiny frames.

Zhao noticed my pause and gripped my hand even tighter, softly pulling me down the hall. "I'll explain soon enough," he said, before I could even ask.

The sound of sneakers squeaking and a ball bouncing drew my attention to my left and I caught a glimpse of a gym and several people playing basketball through a slender glass in the door. I paused for a moment and watched, before I felt a tug as Zhao led me across the hallway.

A sparkling glass door with the letters S and N painted in a circle in fancy lettering greeted us. Meghan paused and looked at Zhao before opening the door. Out of the corner of my eye, I saw Zhao nod at her to go in.

I followed them into a small lobby. Behind a half circle receptionist desk sat a girl who looked around my age. She had mocha colored skin and long dark hair and wore tribal jewelry that gave me the impression she was a Native American of some sort. She said nothing, but smiled sweetly as we walked by.

Zhao led us to a narrow hallway that descended slightly downward. My ears began to pop and I noticed the noise level begin to change as we walked down. Have you ever been in a soundproof music recording studio? That's what this felt like and it grew even more intense as he opened the door and we entered a small, but very modern dome ceiling movie theater.

The dozen or so people who were standing around the front and talking, stopped what they were doing to watch us walk down the aisle. Zhao led us about half way and chose the very middle aisle of seats. Meghan went in first and then me. Zhao made sure I was in the middle. We settled into the plush seats and I watched as a couple of the guys waved and nodded to him.

"These chairs recline back if you want Claire," he said, leaning over and whispering to me.

"I'm fine, thank you," I replied, as the lights slowly went down and everyone quickly found a seat. "What are we doing here?"

"Claire, you're so impatient," he lightly scolded me. "Just watch the movie and...and don't mind that it's mostly animated. It's designed to reach a broad range of ages."

I sighed way too loud and sat back in my seat, while Meghan waved to a heavily tattooed guy who looked like he could have just jumped out of a 80's rock music video. He came over quickly and joined her. Then suddenly the theater went completely black.

"Here we go," Zhao said, grabbing my hand in reassurance. "This never gets old." I held onto it tight this time, unsure of what was to come.

TWENTY-THREE

I SAT BACK in my chair and watched as the dome ceiling above slowly went from completely black to thousands of stars that began to appear and sparkle, an exact replica of the night sky. I immediately recognized the little and big dipper, Lynx, Arcturus, Draco, Polaris, and all the constellations I had learned on my many late night star gazing high above Clarksville and the Pacific ocean. I knew them all by name and was quick to share them with anyone who would lend me their ear.

From the left side of the dome a small green shimmering light appeared. It zigzagged across the sky leaving a tail-like comet streak behind it, slowly becoming larger until a big bug eyed, cartoon insect was hovering directly in front of us. It wore an old school silver space suit and boots and was a cross between a grasshopper and a fly.

I looked over at Zhao in a mixture of disbelief and slight irritation. *Was this a joke?* He just shrugged back at me, clearly amused.

"*Hello,*" the bug said in a cute little boy's voice. "*My name is Henry and welcome to my world… your new world. If you are here and watching this, it is because you are, as you have learned by now, a very special human. I'm sure you have already been told by the people in your life that you are unique and different. Today I want to help you understand your uniqueness and realize that you are not alone and maybe help you understand why you are the way you are.*"

Henry zipped backwards through space and disappeared, while to the right, the Milky Way galaxy began to emerge out of the darkness, making Earth front and center.

Henry continued, "*Today over 8 billion people live on planet Earth. Humans are the most unique of species, made up of many different races, but still only one human race. However, life on this planet has not always been this way. At one time, different types of human-like species lived on the Earth.*"

I sat up in my seat. What did he just say?

The earth shrank back into the Milky Way and the whole galaxy began spinning directly above us, sparkling, with all the planets shimmering in bright, brilliant colors. Henry once again came puttering into the picture in a small spaceship and buckling his seat belt as he spoke.

"*So now here comes the interesting part. Put on your seat belt, because you are in for a wild ride.*" He flew his ship up higher and pointed to the left and back of the theater where two faces appeared of a young girl with platinum blonde hair. One face was warm and pink in color with all the regular human features, including bright blue eyes. The second face was still her, only older. This one was white and very shiny, almost like porcelain and her eyes were completely blue and when I say completely blue, I mean no iris. All blue, except a darker blue circle that I assumed was the pupil. *"Like I mentioned before, thousands of years ago, planet Earth was occupied by numerous, different human-like species who were gifted with extra powerful human characteristics. Think- Goliath, the giant of the Bible, Samson and his super strength and David with his unmatched warrior combat abilities- just to name a few. These characteristics include extraordinary strength, hearing and sight, extremely high IQs, and non-human physical traits. They lived with and mixed with the human race producing a DNA that, although rare, can still be found in humans today. We have divided them into five groups. By name they are Lynx, Aquila, Delphinus, Perseus, and Hydra, after the constellations."* We watched each constellation light up as he spoke the name.

Henry then flew to the back of the room, where he stopped beside the girl's image. *"This little girl's name is Thaya. Thaya is of the Perseus and Delphinus lineage and was the first human ever recognized as part extra-terrestrial being."* (My mouth dropped open as I stared at her in disbelief. Did he just say this girl was part alien?) *"Thaya was born in 1924 and by the age of 3, she could play the piano better than some of the world's most gifted musicians."* Henry popped out of his spaceship quickly, then flew to the front again and looked down on us. *"Thaya was given numerous tests and harmless medical samples were taken from her to help understand the origin of her unique gifts at such a young age. After some time it was discovered that she had a different line of DNA that had never been discovered before and neither her parents, nor her two siblings had."*

Henry moved to the side as he continued. *"As time went on, more tests were run and more humans were discovered to be born with unusual and unique gifts in the arts, as well as super mortal IQs. Specially chosen NASA scientists determined five strands of DNA that seemed to be most prevalent. Humans like Thaya, who excelled at the arts at such young ages and were also graduating college in grade school were labeled Perseus. She also fell under the Delphinus strand because of her all blue eyes. All humans with unusual physical features are of the Delphinus lineage."*

Thaya's picture disappeared and another young teenage boy's face appeared on the screen. Soon after a short clip of him in a raging thunderstorm followed, his thick brown Beetle's style hair was sopping wet and stuck to his tan, chiseled face. I watched in amazement as he effortlessly moved a large tree that had fallen on a busy road, as if it were a small branch. This clip seemed to be from the 60's because the news lady covering the scene from the studio had her hair in the biggest beehive style I had ever seen.

"This is Robby," Henry said, flexing his arm muscles,

"*and as you can see, his strength is his super power. He and just four other boys and one girl have been found to be of the Hydra lineage that boasts super strength.*"

"*Next we have Adrian.*" Robby's face disappeared and Adrian, a young black man appeared to our right. He dove off a large yacht and into a clear blue ocean. I gasped in awe as the camera captured his every move, filling up the entire screen in an emerald blue and giving the feeling we were underwater, looking up at the surface from the deep.

"Beautiful," I whispered, as he swam directly over our heads.

"*Adrian is of the Aquila line. He can dive to unexplainable depths in the ocean in freezing temperatures, hold his breath for an inhuman amount of time and as you see, swim just as fast, if not faster than dolphins.*" I watched in amazement as he swam across the water so fast, that he appeared to be almost flying across it like me. "*Adrian is the only human alive today of this lineage that we are aware of, although we think his younger sister may have this same super gift, as she can hold her breath for prolonged amounts of time.*"

I felt Zhao's eyes on me as I slightly tilted my head and stared hard at Adrian's face which looked eerily familiar. I knew I had seen him before, but couldn't quite place him.

The theater went dark again for a moment, as I tried to process all I was taking in. Adrian had a sister who had the same superpower he did. I wondered if any of my family members had my same DNA line and even more, would my children have it?

A small ball of light that began to appear from the front grabbed my attention again. It steadily grew brighter and more colorful and soon became a beautiful sunrise filling up the entire front of the theater. Suddenly, two military jets came from the back and streaked across a now quickly forming, blue sky. Their engines rumbled through the theater seats and shook my body. Then came something familiar, chasing the sunrise; a beach scene with spectators, then firetrucks and finally Zhao.

"Z!" I heard someone yell, while several guys clapped and turned around as they recognized him. I glanced over at Zhao who slightly rolled his eyes and smiled bashfully at the attention.

Back on the screen the scene that I knew all too well, (as I had watched it probably a hundred times in the last few months) began to play out. I appeared from the clouds, flying down to the beach with Kirsten in my arms. We watched until the end with Mr. Lucas' dramatic rescue of me off the runway.

As the SUV we were in disappeared, Henry buzzed back into the picture. *"And finally, the newest addition to the family- Lynx,"* he said as he moved to the side and my picture from the Air Force Academy filled the screen.

Out of habit, I shrank down in my seat as if the people in the theater didn't already know who I was.

"Meet Claire, who through an accidental encounter with foreign space matter realized her supernatural gift. Lynx are brought to life because of a link that awakens their SuperNova DNA line. It transforms them from their

human capabilities to that of the supernatural and without this link, their unique gifts may never be born. As you can see here, Claire has the gift of flight. Lynx are also known to have a life changing blood plasma that can treat a rare blood disease, found mainly in newborns. Their bodies also have supernatural healing abilities."

Henry did not expound on what that link was, but Zhao and I looked at each other knowingly. The pink formula from the crate that night had ignited my flying power that I would have never known existed. It made me wonder how many other humans were walking around with the DNA strand I had that would produce the same power.

Henry once again flew to the middle and front of the screen until he was buzzing directly in front of us. *"Whether you fall under Lynx, Aquila, Delphinus, Perseus, or Hydra we want to welcome you to the most unique family in the world…pardon me, the universe; the SuperNova family. SuperNovas have existed for all of time and have thrived in the regular human world as they have become some of the top scientists, spies, astronauts, physicists, doctors, professors, soldiers, composers, entertainers and writers in history."*

I watched in wonder as many faces began to appear all around the theater screen with each occupation he mentioned. Some I recognized as famous, some I did not, but I gasped quietly at each famous person shown, especially the historical people I had read so much about. They had the same special DNA I did.

Henry flew back to the side as images of the island

we were on began to appear. *"Now that you are part of the SuperNova family, you are always welcome here on SuperNova Island. Please know you are not alone and that you always have someone who you can relate to or talk to. If you need time away, all it takes is a phone call and we will go to the ends of the earth to get you here."*

Henry flew to the other side of the screen as more images of the island began to appear. Each one showed people walking the island beach, playing volleyball in the sand, basketball in the gym, and hanging out on the lawn watching fireworks over the ocean at night. *"One more thing,"* he said, *"attend every retreat possible. It will connect you with other SuperNovas and help you learn more about yourself and your unique capabilities. Again, we welcome you, celebrate you and look forward to getting to know you!"*

I sat back in my seat stunned as Henry buzzed out of sight and the theater lights came up. Other people began to slowly stand and leave a few at a time, but not before waving or stealing a curious look in our direction. Pretty soon it was just me, Zhao, Meghan and her friend sitting in the theater all alone, none of us saying a word. At last her friend leaned over and whispered in her ear, then she turned to me.

"Claire, I would like to introduce Matty." Matty leaned over and eagerly shook my hand. "He's not only the greatest electric guitar player in the world, but is also the only human alive who can play every instrument that exists today. He's Perseus."

I nodded at Matty who blushed at Meghan's compliment. He couldn't have been much older than her. "Thanks Meg," he smiled and pointed at me, "But this girl is where it's at. Flying definitely trumps a musician any day of the week."

"Thank you," I said, trying to sound casual despite the numbness and shock I was feeling. "It's nice to meet you Matty…maybe someday I can hear you play."

"Definitely Claire! I would love that," he said, standing up and then looking down at Meghan. "You ready, sweetie?"

She looked at Zhao and I. "Are you guys ready?"

"Go ahead Meg, we'll catch up," Zhao smiled.

Meghan reached over and squeezed my hand. "I know Claire," she said, "But you get used to it…to us. Don't leave without saying goodbye to me ok?"

"Ok," I agreed.

Matty grabbed Meghan's hand and led her out of the theater. I looked over at Zhao who was staring straight ahead.

"How long have you known about me?" I asked at last.

Zhao cleared his throat and then looked down at the ground. "Since the…" he mumbled incoherently.

"Zhao," I said, knocking his arm off the armrest. "Stop mumbling."

He took a deep breath and then looked back at me. "Since the beginning," he said clearly this time. "This is my dad's island, Claire. I come from a long line of SuperNovas and because of that, my family are self made billionaires. My dad sent me to Hickam to make contact and try to get some info so we could help you. We had a feeling you were SuperNova."

I slowly shook my head in disbelief. "All this time?" I asked. "All this time Zhao? At Hickam and through the whole Kirsten thing and when I was hiding on my island? No wonder why they knew where I was! How could you lie to me *all this time?*"

"I had nothing to do with them finding your island. I honestly tried to hide you!" Zhao snapped back lightly. "And how was I supposed to know that we were gonna… that I was gonna…that we would become so close and I would care about you so much? You were just supposed to be another assignment Claire."

My scowl immediately melted away. "I'm sorry Zhao," I sighed, slightly irritated that he always seemed to know how to sweet talk his way out of trouble. "I just don't know what to do with all of this."

"I know," he said, lightly taking my hand. "I'm sorry to throw it all on you, but it was time you knew."

Zhao was so sweet to me and we sat in another moment of silence as I took it all in.

"I'm an …*alien* Zhao," I said at last, choking out the *A* word. I caught my breath and felt a little panic begin to set in. Immediately my face and neck grew hot and the red blotchies I broke out in when I was emotional, began to take over.

"Claire, you're not an alien. You just have a special DNA. This doesn't change anything. You're still 100%

normal and just as human as the next guy."

I rolled my eyes at him. "Oh really?"

"Well, you know what I mean," he explained. "Minus the whole flying thing."

My head spun with the reality I was facing. "I have so many questions Zhao." I looked back at him. "Do they still exist and if they do, do you think they will ever come here?"

"Who?"

"The beings Henry was talking about, that used to live on earth? The ones we share DNA with. I mean, do you think they will ever come for us?"

Zhao shrugged. "We don't know much about them, Claire. We believe they *may* still exist, but if they do, we don't believe they know SuperNovas exist and that we have any DNA ties to them."

"Who is we?" I asked. "Your dad and who?"

"My dad and three other scientists. Kearney's dad used to be one of them. Umm..plus a special unit of the military at NASA who specializes in UAP's. They work to keep us safe and wear the black uniform you saw. They adopted the pink Saturn rings as their logo after they mysteriously appeared on Brian Kearney-kind of paying homage to his life." He gazed past me, "Annessa was one of them."

"Annessa?" I asked.

"Come with me," he said, gently taking my hand and leading me out of the side exit door. I clasped my other hand over his, nervous for what else was to come.

The bright sunshine blinded me momentarily, as we walked up a small set of stairs and out onto the sidewalk. I held Zhao's hand tighter as he led me around the back of the building and through an ornate iron gate to a garden of flowers in full bloom. We followed a cobblestone path, passing several garden benches and a bubbling fountain that sat right in the middle of everything. We eventually stopped at a bright, white cherry blossom tree against the back gate. Zhao bent down and removed a small branch that covered a plaque at the trunk. I knelt beside him to get a closer look and was shocked by what I read.

Annessa Clarence
July 21, 1995- November 29, 2019
Beloved Family Member & Friend
Perseus Lynx
SuperNova

I began to sob as I read. "Zhao? You brought her here?"

"Of course," he said, wrapping an arm around me. "She was never alone, Claire. She may have had no blood family, but she had our family here and we miss her dearly. This is where she belongs."

I reached down and touched her name plaque with both of my hands, hoping she would somehow feel my pain and regret for what had happened to her.

"I'm so sorry Annessa," I whispered. "I wish I could have saved you. I wish you could have lived."

Zhao leaned down and squeezed me closer as I cried

into his shoulder. He patiently waited while I grieved for my sweet friend. With all the craziness that had happened after the accident, I felt guilty for not staying at the compound and properly saying my goodbyes.

"Claire, there's nothing you could have done," Zhao reassured me after a while. "This was not your fault. Annessa knew what she wanted and she went after it. From the first moment she saw you flying, she was obsessed with you. She begged for NASA to experiment with her and the pink juice and when they found out she was Lynx as well as Perseus, they agreed to give her a chance."

"Annessa was Lynx too?"

"Yep, just like you."

"So you knew Annessa before I ever came into the picture?" I asked, wiping my face with the handkerchief he had given me. "You just pretended like you didn't know her?"

His eyes creased with worry at my question. "No Claire, I didn't meet her until you introduced me. Honestly. I was in Hawaii when she was brought to the island. And my dad knew her, but didn't have anything to do with it. What Annessa decided to do was between her and her employers at NASA."

I slowly got up and he soon followed me. "I believe you, but it wasn't worth it, Zhao. Her *life* wasn't worth it."

He looked at me solemnly. "I agree, Claire. One hundred percent."

TWENTY-FOUR

WE WALKED QUIETLY out of the garden and down another path that led to a strip of beach. I followed his lead and sat on the grass to take off my shoes and roll up my pants.

"Leave your shoes," he instructed me. "We'll just end up back here anyway."

We strolled down by the water and followed the beach that led all the way around the little island. The first few minutes were quiet and we just listened to the waves crashing against the shore, as I tried to process everything. My brain was on overload, plus I was still a little sore from the beating I took with Jason. Finally Zhao picked up a rock and skipped it into the waves.

"Claire, isn't it so crazy to go your whole life thinking that our little world is it and then *bam,* you realize we're just a small part of it all?"

"It doesn't seem real," I mumbled back.

"You don't seem too impressed," he smiled slightly. "When I found out I was a SuperNova I was floored."

I stopped and looked up at him. "Trust me Zhao, I am. It's nice to finally know the source for my flying power. It's just…I guess after three years of flying, nothing surprises me anymore."

Zhao groaned and rolled his eyes. "Well excuse me your highness," he teased. "It is true that being able to play a lot of instruments certainly pales in comparison to flying."

I shoved him playfully and smiled for the first time in days. "You know what I mean."

Zhao wrapped his arm around my shoulder and pulled me closer to him as we continued our walk. "There's my Claire," he said, kissing the top of my head as I wrapped both arms around his waist and breathed a sigh of relief. I knew in my heart I was safe here, but I still had a lot of questions.

"Can I ask you something?"

"Go ahead, ask me anything."

I hesitated before I asked my first question, but I just had to know. "Have you ever had contact with *them*?"

"*Them?*" he smirked.

"You know what I mean," I smiled. "Our alien DNA ancestors who may or may not still exist."

Zhao paused and looked around for a moment to make sure we were still the only ones on the beach. I followed his glare to a man and his little boy who were flying a kite a little ways down. There was no way they could have heard him, but he lowered his voice anyway. "We haven't, but my dad and I think they have…they being a whole different and secret unit from us. One we don't have privy to…but believe me, we've heard stories."

I bit my bottom lip in frustration. "Zhao, why lie about it? I don't understand why they keep everything a secret. I think people deserve to know the truth, if another type of human possibly exists or did at one time."

Zhao shrugged his shoulders. "I think it's a fear of the unknown for them, maybe they are worried about how humans would react to it. I mean, you've seen how crazy humans can behave."

The more I thought about that, the more I agreed, especially with what I had just been through with Jason and whoever he was working with. "But how in the world have you guys been able to keep SuperNovas a secret? Surely by now someone would have let something slip out."

"I think most SuperNovas know their safety and the safety of their families are in play here, so it's been a pretty easy secret to keep. Only once have we had to disengage with someone because of their lack of confidentiality."

"What happened to them?"

"Let's just say the government has the means to shut someone up if they need to," he said stiffly as we approached the dad and his little boy.

"Hi Z," the little boy smiled brightly.

"Hey Collin! Nice kite!" Zhao said. "What is that?"

Collin pointed at it blowing back and forth across the sky. "It's a dragon! See its big tail?"

"What do you say Collin?" the dad asked.

"Thank you!" Collin smiled, as a gust of wind pulled the kite higher.

"Let more string go Collin," his dad instructed him.

Zhao and I smiled at each other as we continued to walk past. "He's Hydra..Super strength," Zhao said when we got a little farther away.

"His dad?" I asked, looking back.

"No Collin," Zhao laughed. "You should see him in the gym. It's crazy stuff for a 7 year old."

Collin's cry behind us startled me and we turned to see him pointing to the sky as his dragon spiraled into the clouds. "Nooo daddy. My dragon!"

My heart broke for him. I looked at Zhao and didn't even have to ask. He could read me so well.

"Go ahead," he laughed.

I ran down to the water and jumped into the air, keeping my eyes on the kite that was now just a tiny dot against the bright blue sky. I jetted through the winds that were even stronger at this height, while they shoved me back and forth, making it a little hard to stay on a single flight path. At last I was close enough to grab it, just before we were enveloped by a fluffy white cloud. I softly tucked the dragon under my arm and then looked back toward the island. I couldn't believe how far I had flown up. The island was now the little dot in the vast ocean of blue, with no land in sight. I paused for a moment to soak it all in. Being up here helped put the challenges of my life in perspective and made me feel closer to God. I felt peace and just knew that everything was going to be ok, weird DNA and all.

I dove down towards the island where Zhao was waiting with Collin and his dad. Collin's big blue eyes sparkled in wonder as I landed at the water's edge and approached him slowly, so I would not scare him. To my surprise he ran up and hugged me, almost bowling me over.

"That was the coolest!" he yelled. "What are you?"

"What?" I laughed, confused.

"I'm Hydra!" he exclaimed. "What are you?"

"Ohh," I smiled. "I'm Lynx..and I'm also Claire." Collin reached out his little hand for knuckles, which I gladly returned. "It's nice to meet you, Collin."

Collin's dad looked like he had seen a ghost, but he calmly thanked us, as Zhao patted him on the back and assured him everything would be ok. Then we quickly said our goodbyes and headed back down the beach.

"They're new to the SuperNova family, just this past week. I think his dad is still in the initial shock phase, so their family is staying with us for some adjustment time."

My mouth dropped open. "Zhao! Why didn't you tell me? I'm sure seeing me fly didn't help with his adjustment any!"

"Well, he's got to accept it sometime. We might as well be his first push into the crazy world of SuperNova. He'll get used to it Claire, and then it will become as normal as breathing."

"I wouldn't go that far," I laughed nervously, afraid to bring up the next subject. "Speaking of normalcy, you know I'm gonna have to tell Johnny, right?"

Zhao's face turned stern. "No Claire. You can't tell anyone. He can't know about the island, the DNA, nothing! Do you understand me?"

"What? Collin's dad gets to know," I argued.

"That's different Claire. He's a minor."

"But Zhao, I'm engaged to Johnny. How can I not tell him? Maybe he…maybe he won't want to be with someone with a messed up alien-DNA line. It's not fair for me to not give him that choice."

Zhao looked at the ground, purposely avoiding eye contact with me. "That's not going to happen, Claire. That guy is going to marry you no matter what. He would be a fool not to."

I smiled shyly at his compliment as the sound of a helicopter chopping through the air in the distance interrupted our discussion. Zhao and I watched as it approached the island and then flew directly over us toward the small landing strip I had seen earlier. I smiled when I saw the large American flag stamped on the bottom of it.

"That's my dad," Zhao yelled above the copter's noise. "Come on. Let's grab our stuff. He wants to see you."

"There she is!" Dr. Zhao said, as he greeted us with a one armed hug on the small tarmac. Swinging across his other arm was a laptop bag, while he balanced a big black leather folder in his hand. "Are you ok Claire? I know this is a lot to take in."

"Yeah, I'm fine Dr. Zhao," I said, trying to sound as casual as ever.

"She's lying," Zhao sighed, grabbing the laptop bag off his dad's shoulder.

I glared at Zhao as we followed his dad through the airport lobby we had been in earlier that morning and back outside to the large courtyard.

"Have you guys eaten today?' Dr. Zhao asked, "Because I'm starving."

"Not yet," Zhao replied and then looked over at me. "Are you hungry? It's almost dinner time."

"Let's head to the cafeteria," Dr. Zhao said before I could answer. "I don't want to send Claire home starving."

My eyes grew wide as they walked ahead of me. Did he just say I was going home?

"I just came from Campbell," Dr. Zhao said, as he took a sip of water. We sat beside a large window overlooking the ocean in a cozy, formal dining room that was anything but an ordinary cafeteria. The sun was beginning to set, casting a warm glow across our table and setting the crystal glassware a blaze.

I paused mid bite on my Caesar salad to make sure I had heard him correctly. "You were at Campbell... today?" I asked.

"Yes ma'am," Dr. Zhao smiled. "The base just came off lock down after four days. They were concerned some of Jason's crew still might be lurking around."

My tummy flipped inside. I had never thought of them sticking around. "Is my family ok? Did they get Justin?"

"They got him and everyone is ok," Dr. Zhao assured me, then paused for a moment. "But Claire, just so you know, Jason is dead and we shot down their bird. No survivors."

I breathed a sigh of relief that my family was ok, but my heart sank as I remembered my last moments with Jason. "I don't understand what would make Jason turn on me that way. He was my friend."

"Money, Claire," Dr. Zhao said matter of factly. "What people would do for money is astounding, even if it costs the most valuable thing they have. Their life."

"Who were they working for dad?" Zhao asked, looking around the sparsely populated dining room.

Dr. Zhao shrugged. "If the military knows, they're not telling us, son. But I suspect Mancuso and your guys from Hickam will handle the problem soon, if you know what I mean."

That made me breathe a little easier, but I knew somehow this was just the beginning. I could never feel truly safe.

"I don't know what to do now," I said quietly. "How can I ever live a normal life? If I go home, I put my family in danger and Johnny in danger and my whole base in danger. I don't want to be the reason someone gets hurt."

They both stared at me quietly for a moment, knowing I was right. No matter what, I would always be at risk of another kidnapping. This time I got very lucky, but next time it could totally go the wrong way.

Dr. Zhao folded his hands together on the table and leaned closer, locking eyes with me. "We were talking at Campbell this morning Claire and we all agree, it just comes down to this. You can live your life in fear and hide away or you can embrace the gift you've been given and let the military do what it's supposed to do and that is help protect you."

Zhao shook his head in agreement. "What happened this week was just a fluke, Claire. It's gonna take some time to get the bugs worked out, but give Campbell another chance." He softly enveloped his hand around mine on the table. "And you need to put on your brave face when you go back, because if they detect even the slightest bit of hesitancy or fear, they may second guess your freedom. You don't want to live your life in lock down mode after all you've worked for."

I squeezed Zhao's fingers that were intertwined with mine. "I know," I agreed. "I know. It's just Johnny will be living with me and if they are going to go after anyone, it will be him first. I just can't stand to think of anything happening to him."

Zhao chuckled under his breath. "Seriously Claire? Johnny handled himself just fine with these bad guys."

"What do you mean?"

"You don't remember?" Dr. Zhao asked, surprised. "Johnny is the reason you're sitting here right now. He rescued you Claire."

I gasped. "What?! How?"

Dr. Zhao calmly pulled out his laptop without saying a word and turned it gently towards me. I watched in anticipation as the screen filled with a runway and then a helicopter landing nearby. My heart leapt as I recognized Johnny and Shawn jump from the still running copter and down a short runway strip to a Blackhawk that was waiting to take off.

"That's Little Rock Air Force Base." Dr. Zhao explained. "Johnny and Shawn grabbed a copter as soon as they knew you were kidnapped and followed you guys. They stopped there low on fuel, where a new flight crew was waiting for them to go find you."

I held my breath as I watched them board the Blackhawk, then quickly lift off the ground. I had to remind myself to breathe as the video switched to an onboard scene from the Blackhawk. Johnny was hanging off the side, getting ready to repel through the wide open sky with Shawn guiding him as the cable slowly descended downward. The camera then panned below the blades and I was astounded to see myself laying mid air, hundreds of miles above the patchwork fields below.

"Oh wow," I gasped. This scene looked too familiar. It took me back to the time I had lost consciousness and almost drowned in the gulf. I had floated into the air, just like this and Johnny had managed to save me from that situation too.

The copter held steady in place as Johnny quickly glided down to my location. In one clean swoop, he plucked me out of the sky and before I knew it he was looking up at Shawn, as he carefully guided us back into the Blackhawk. I touched my stitches as I looked at the side of my face that was completely covered in blood, while he gently laid me on the copter floor.

"Is she ok?" I heard the cameraman ask.

Johnny said nothing, but began frantically checking for a pulse. He touched the side of my neck with two fingers, the concern in his face giving way to one of relief. "She has a pulse," he said back to the cameraman. "But we need to get her to a hospital, ASAP."

My eyes twinkled, as I watched him care for me with so much concern.

Once again, the scene changed and I was being lifted off the helicopter onto a gurney on the top of a high-rise building. Johnny and Sean jumped off and quickly followed the team of nurses as they wheeled me to an open roof door.

"Angel!" I heard the cameraman yell. Johnny turned around and ran back to the copter to grab the phone. He then nodded a thank you to the crew as the screen went black.

TWENTY-FIVE

"WHO ARE THOSE guards with?" I asked later that night as Zhao fumbled with the ring of keys, trying to find the right one to their apartment. We were on the very top floor of the residential building I had noticed earlier and it was heavily guarded at the front and back entrances.

"No worries. They're Marines out of Galveston," Zhao reassured me. "Normally there are not that many working, but you're here so…"

"How many of them are stationed here?"

Zhao tried a key that slid in but didn't work. "We usually only have about 20, but dad only keeps them here a month at a time so they don't get too suspicious."

This time the key he selected worked. Zhao opened the double doors and I gasped. This "apartment" was in fact more like a penthouse and was decorated in the traditional Japanese style that represented the Zhao family heritage.

"Oh wow Zhao," I said, looking around at all the beautiful brilliant colors. "This is beautiful."

"Thanks. My mom decorated it," he replied with a trace of sadness.

"Is she here?" I asked, looking past him. "I would love to meet her."

"Thanks Claire, but she passed away a few months before I met you."

"Oh," I said, my heart sinking. "I'm so sorry Zhao. How did I not know that?"

He picked up his backpack off the floor. "Because I never told you," he winked, smiling slightly at me.

"What else don't I know about you?" I asked, as I followed him from the foyer into a two story great room with a beautiful fireplace.

"Honestly Claire, that's it. Other than living on a secret government island and all the crazy foreign DNA stuff, my life is actually pretty boring."

I just stared at him.

"Come on," he laughed. "I'll show you where you're sleeping. Megs will be by in a bit to bring you some fresh clothes for the next few days."

I followed him up a winding staircase, wondering if I made the right decision to stay a few days. Dr. Zhao said Major Silva had encouraged me to stay put a little longer just to be safe so I decided to follow his advice. Plus I would feel incomplete if I left without knowing all

I could about myself.

Zhao opened the door to a pale yellow, beach themed room. Across the back wall behind the bamboo bed post, a pretty sunset had been painted in the most exquisite colors, complete with a small toucan bird that perched on top of a tropical red and orange plant. The patio doors that led to a small balcony were partially opened and a lace curtain blew lazily in the breeze.

"Oh wow Zhao," I said in awe. "This is beautiful."

"I tried to paint it the way you described it to me. You know…your island."

My eyes shot open. "You painted this? My island?'

"Yes ma'am."

I walked closer to the wall. "Another thing I didn't know about you. You're an artist? This is some Monet quality work, Zhao."

He smiled bashfully. "It's the Perseus in me."

"That explains it," I laughed, as I sat on the bed smelling the fresh ocean air filling the room. "Thank you Z. This room is perfect."

Zhao came over and kissed me lightly on the forehead, then took a closer look at my stitches. "Wow! These are healing quickly. Tomorrow we'll get you a check up with Meghan once more, but for now you should get some sleep." He walked over to the bamboo dresser and pulled out a PT short outfit. "Here's some jammies and everything you need is in the bathroom across the hall. Sweet dreams Claire and if you need me, I'm right downstairs."

The door shut quietly behind him. I walked over to the

little balcony to get a better view, leaning far over the rail to see down the beach. The sun was pretty much gone and twilight was taking its place. A sliver of the bright moon shined directly above the ocean in front of me, with a pretty diamond star sparkling brightly beside it. I was so tempted to go for an overnight flight, but was so tired. It had been a long day and what a day it had been. I was not the same person who woke up this morning in the airport building. Everything was different now. I felt so lost and also so found and the best part was not being alone in all of this anymore. There were others just like me, especially my sweet Zhao and that was the best feeling ever.

"Claire," I heard a voice whispering from the beach, that awoke me from my sleep that night. "Claire, help me, please."

I woke suddenly and sat up in bed. My patio door was cracked slightly and the room was eerily dark, except for a faint moon light coming through the sheer curtain. I looked over at the clock that read 2:34 am, then sat very still listening again. Outside the waves calmly washed against the sand, but other than that, the night was so still. I was just about to lay back down when I heard it again.

"Claire," a male voice whispered. I swallowed hard. The voice sounded distant and almost like it was in a cave. A deep, soft echo. I slowly slid out of bed and slipped on the PT shorts Zhao had given me, then crept over to the patio curtain. My hands shook and my soul trembled as I carefully pulled it back trying to peek into the night, listening for his voice again. A few minutes passed quietly, before I finally felt it was safe to sneak out on the deck. I slipped through the crack in the door, my body shivering slightly as my feet touched the cold concrete deck. I wrapped my arms around myself and walked to the rail. The damp air blew through my long curls, and I shivered once again, but this time from the creepiness I felt inside. Something wasn't right.

I looked over the edge and was reminded of how high we actually were. How in the world could I have heard a voice from the beach at this height? Maybe I should fly down, just to make sure everything was ok. I mean, what if someone was in trouble? What if it was Zhao?

I was just about to jump into the air, when I heard it again. Only this time he wasn't below and I knew it wasn't Zhao. "Hello Claire," he whispered, from behind me. Chills ran down my spine. He was close enough that I felt his breath in my hair. I turned around and froze in horror. I was staring into the cold blue face of Jason.

"No!" I silently screamed, as he plunged into me and wrapped his arms around my waist, sending us both over the rail and down headfirst towards the beach. I pushed with all my might, trying to free myself from his hard, frigid grasp but could not even budge him. My eyes looked toward the ground, as we cleared all nine floors in just a few seconds.

"Annessa noooo!" I screamed, then felt my body jolt.

I sat straight up in bed, in the warm morning sun and caught my breath, thankful it was all just a dream.

"So what we think happened, was that our ancestors had super abilities that slowly diminished over generations and only a lucky few of us were able to keep that DNA strand," Zhao said the following evening as we sat at a picnic bench, eating Chicago dogs and watching the sun go down. We had been here almost an hour, as I peppered him with questions trying to find out everything I could about my superpower. So far the only thing I knew for sure was that no one had a solid answer.

"So it's not alien DNA, it's just basically an almost extinct DNA?" I asked.

"Well…that's where we're stumped. We don't know exactly where it comes from. We can only guess."

"But Henry the bug said at that time the earth was occupied by a variety of different human species," I reminded him.

He paused for a moment to finish chewing his food, then wiped his mouth. "True, but our question is if they are partially human does that make them aliens? We don't know and we have no idea what happened to them."

"Yeah," I agreed, looking up into the beautiful blue sky. "And are they still out there just living somewhere else?"

"The thing that sucks for us, Claire, is that we may

never know. We just have to take it as it comes... but all that aside our main objective is to help newly discovered SuperNovas adjust to their new identities."

We paused for a moment and watched as a big pelican landed on the long dock that stretched out before us. Behind him the sunset pushed out hundreds of colors and I quickly grabbed my phone to get a picture of the pelican sitting on the wooden post.

"Look!" I said to Zhao, pleased at how perfect the picture had turned out.

"Beautiful," he smiled.

We continued to watch as he lazily stretched out his wings, jumped off the post and then flew directly over us to the other side of the island. The wind caught his wings lifting him higher into the air and I smiled to myself knowing the exhilaration that feeling brings.

In the distance a popping sound cut through the peaceful silence and a copter approached from the north side of the island. I noticed this one was deep blue in color, unlike the military ones I had seen flying in and out recently.

"That's our personal copter," Zhao explained, reading my mind. "We have a new family coming in today, a 13 year old girl. Her name is Camille and she's incredible, Claire. She can practically do whatever she wants and never gets hurt. My dad said she broke her arm playing volleyball and it healed itself completely in a day."

"Perseus, right?" I smiled, as we watched it hover for a moment behind the terminal building, then sink slowly out of sight.

"No," he winked at me. "She's a Lynx."

"Like me?"

"Yep. Remember? Her body quickly heals itself… Lynx."

I had to catch my breath as I remembered the day I got cut and infected with the pink liquid that gave me my superpower. My cut had been so deep that Johnny and I both thought I would need stitches. The next day though, the cut was completely healed and my Saturn tattoo took its place.

"Does she have the…?"

"The tatt?" He interrupted. "No. We're pretty sure that's just a side effect of the pink potion, but Claire…I think you might have a little Camille in you though."

I squinted my eyes in confusion.

"Think about it," he said, his excitement building as though he was discovering something for the first time. "Your Lynx DNA naturally protects you. I mean, when you were knocked unconscious the other day, your body totally suspended itself in the air and kept you from falling."

"I thought it was just a fluke," I said.

"Yeah, it's like your body has its own auto-pilot. You're hurt? It heals itself quickly. You go unconscious mid-flight? It keeps you from falling out of the sky."

"So, I'll probably never have to worry about falling out of the sky?"

"It's looking that way to us, but of course we want to test it in a controlled environment just to be sure."

"I'm definitely no stranger to testing," I smiled, then grabbed his hand. "Zhao, I want to help you guys. I remember how nervous and scared I was when I first got my superpower. I felt so all alone and if I can help another young person going through the same thing, that would mean the world to me."

Zhao wrapped his strong arm around me. " Oh trust me," he laughed. "We will definitely be calling you back to the island a lot. You're a SuperNova now and we look out for our own."

"Good deal," I smiled.

"So what do you want to do on your last full day here tomorrow?"

I shrugged. "I don't care. Just hang out with you…but I definitely know what I want to do tomorrow night."

He cocked one eyebrow up quizzically at me. "What's that?"

"A night flight," I laughed.

"Of course," he smiled mischievously. "That's exactly what I was thinking."

TWENTY-SIX

THERE WAS A knock on my door at 8 am sharp the next morning. I rolled over in bed, not ready to get up yet. Zhao and I had stayed up late watching our usual 80's movie marathon, including *Ferris Bueller* which I was excited to introduce him to.

"Claire?" he said, softly knocking again.

I felt the PJs I had put on to make sure I was decent before I invited him in. Black velvet shorts and a SuperNova tee. I was good to go. My long curls fell all around me as I set up in bed. "Come in!"

"Good morning sunshine," he smiled, peeking around the door.

"Morning," I yawned and rubbed my sleepy eyes, as he came and sat on the edge of the bed.

"So were you serious about helping other SuperNovas

242

out?"

"Of course," I replied, looking at him inquisitively.

"You remember the girl from yesterday?"

"Miss Miracle?" I grinned.

"Yes. Well she had a rough first night."

My smile faded. "Oh no."

"Yeah," Zhao sighed. "We're scheduled to do the movie with her at 10, so dad and I thought it might go a little better for her if you were there."

"Of course. Anything I can do to help."

"Well, like a lot of girls her age, she's been following your fan page.."

"My what?"

"You know… your fan page," he looked at me amused.

"Zhao, what are you talking about?"

"Seriously Claire?" He picked up his phone and searched on it for a minute, then handed it to me. "You don't know?"

"Ummm…no," I choked looking down at it. Zhao had opened an app called *"Your Biggest Fan,"* where people would post the latest news, photos and videos of their favorite celebrity. I did a double take at my page that boasted an insane 222 million followers. "What in the world?" I gasped as I quickly scrolled through the photos and videos that dated all the way back to my high school days. My big brown eyes looked up at Zhao in disbelief.

"Yep," he smirked. "So anyways, about Camille.."

I looked back at the phone again. "Camille?"

"The girl from yesterday," he reminded me.

"Oh yes," I remembered. "I'll definitely be there."

"Ok, meet me in the dining room in an hour?"

"Of course," I mumbled, not looking up from the phone. How was this even my life?

S̶N̶

"Claire, I would like for you to meet Camille," Zhao said, at 9:45 that morning in the lobby of the theater.

I reached out my hand and gently shook hers. Camille looked at me wide eyed, like she was seeing a ghost, a look I had grown quite accustomed to.

"Hi Camille," I smiled. "It's so nice to meet you."

"You too," she smiled back. I noticed the braces on her smile, reminding me so much of my Kass when she was in Jr. High. She even had the brown eyes and a light scattering of freckles across her cute little nose. The only difference was her deep brown skin. My heart was immediately drawn to her. Poor girl.

"Do you mind if I sit with you?" I asked.

Her eyes popped open. "No, of course not!" she said excitedly.

We found our seats, pretty much the same place where Zhao and I had sat just a couple of days before.

"Have you seen this movie yet?" She asked me so innocently, obviously unaware of what was to come.

"Actually… yes I have. Just the other day as a matter of fact. I'm new to the island too. I've only been here three days."

"At least I'm not the only one," she sighed.

The lights in the theater dimmed. "Camille, if you have any questions about this, let us know," I whispered. "I still have a lot of questions myself, but just know everything's gonna be OK and you're not alone."

I couldn't see her reaction in the dark theater, but her soft "OK" was enough for me to know how scared she was feeling.

The movie soon began with Henry the bug back on the screen. I was actually pretty ok with watching it again just in case there was something I missed. This time I paid closer attention, making sure I remembered each strain of DNA and what it represented. From time to time I snuck a peek over at Camille and her mom, Julissa, just to see their reactions.

"How do you think they're doing?" Zhao whispered to me at one point during the movie.

I shrugged. "At least they're still here."

I hung onto Henry's every word. When I watched it the other day, my mind was in a complete daze and I was sure I had missed something important. I was thankful to hear more clearly that SuperNovas were not considered alien beings and Henry pretty much confirmed the whole DNA thing to me like Zhao had said. I felt like I had a better grasp on it now and I would be able to help Camille or any other young SuperNova in the future understand.

The movie flew by much quicker than the first time I watched it. When it was over, the dozen or so people in the theater stood up and began talking amongst themselves. I looked over at Camille and Julissa who sat in silence, neither of them moving.

"Say something," I mouthed to Zhao.

He immediately leaned over me. "Mrs. Johnson, Camille, would you like to go get something to eat? Maybe Claire and I might be able to answer any questions you might have."

"Actually mom, I just want to go back to the room," Camille said.

"Of course Camille," she said. "Zhao, Claire, thank you but I think she needs to rest."

"That's ok. We definitely understand," I assured them. "But if you need anything just let us know, ok?"

Camille smiled at me and her mom nodded her head in agreement, then they got up and left.

"What do you think?" I asked Zhao, when I heard the theater door shut.

"She'll be ok, Claire. Everyone reacts differently."

"Maybe I should see if she wants to hang out this afternoon for a bit?"

He slowly stood up and stretched. "No, she just needs time. Trust me. We've been through this before. Wanna grab some lunch?"

"Sure," I replied, a little surprised by Zhao's nonchalant response. He was usually a little more sympathetic. My heart was so sad for Camille. I could see the fear in her eyes I was all too familiar with. It immediately took me back to the first night I realized I could fly just a few short years ago. Memories flashed through my mind as we walked to the cafeteria. I recalled the first day, skyrocketing off the ground, flying over my neighborhood, and being suspended upside down high above the roof tops of my quiet subdivision. Those memories sent chills down my spine to this day, but mostly, I remembered the loneliness. Even through all the craziness of that night and those first few months, the loneliness is what was the hardest and I recognized that same loneliness today in Camille's eyes. I knew I could not leave tomorrow without helping her and I would somehow make sure that I did.

My phone text dinged around midnight as I was throwing on the new SuperNova sweatshirt Zhao had bought for me earlier that day in the gift shop. I looked down, hopeful it was Johnny, but soon realized it was not possible. Zhao had explained to me as he handed back my phone, the island was off limits to outside communication. In fact, as soon as the helicopters land on the island, all outside communications are immediately turned off to personal cell phones. I could understand the reasoning behind this, but it was not easy going days without talking to my family or Johnny.

"*Please be careful up there tonight,*" Zhao repeated for the 20th time today.

"*I promise. I will,*" I reassured him. I had made no

plans of staying out too late as I wanted to be well rested when I returned home tomorrow. I couldn't wait to see my family and Johnny.

I slipped out of the sliding glass door and onto the balcony carefully checking out everything before I took off into the night. The breeze was blowing steadily, and although it was pretty warm, there was still a slight chill in the air.

I listened to the waves crashing below and closed my eyes as I soaked in the fresh salty air. I was so eager to get out into the night sky and explore what this side of the gulf had to offer.

I was securing my pouch that was strapped across me when I heard it. Though ever so slight, the soft sobs of a young girl carried on the wind. I popped over the rail and followed the cries three floors down, to the west side of the building, then leaned up against the wall and peeked around the corner. I wasn't surprised to see Camille, sitting out on one of her deck chairs, wiping her tears with a well used tissue.

"*What to do,*" I thought to myself, not wanting to startle her and or be nosey, but quickly decided to just go for it before she went in and I missed an opportunity to talk to her.

I flew off the side of the building and slightly above her deck watching for the right moment. Inside I could see a dim lamp light on and her mom asleep on the bed.

"Camille," I said softly, but loud enough so she could hear me. She slowly lifted her head from her hands and looked behind her. "Camille, up here." I said again. This time she followed my voice and walked quickly to the rail, looking down into the darkness. This time I took out my phone and turned the flash light on, waving it in front of me. "Up here," I tried again.

Camille's eyes widened in surprise. "Claire?" her voice shook.

"Yeah, it's me. Can I come down?"

"Sure," she agreed, but I could tell she had her guard up as I approached.

I slipped out of my position in the air, landing effortlessly on the deck. "Thanks," I smiled.

"What are you doing here?" she asked, pulling a fresh tissue out of her pocket and blowing into it. Her eyes were so swollen. She must have been crying for a while.

"To be honest, I heard you crying and I couldn't just leave you."

She nodded in agreement and then sat back down on the chair. "I'm sorry. It's just been a little overwhelming, all of this."

I sat in the chair beside her. "I understand Camille. I remember when I first found out I could fly, it was so overwhelming for me too. I felt very alone and very scared."

She looked at me skeptically. "That's surprising. You don't seem like you're scared of much."

"Well trust me, I was. I think having to face my superpower and all the uncertainty that comes with it has toughened me up a little. It's been a bumpy road getting here though."

She shrugged and looked into the room at her mom who was still sleeping soundly. "Well, I'm not so worried about myself, but all I have is my mom and I can see the worry is taking its toll on her."

"The rest of your family don't know?" I asked, surprised.

"We're all the family we have. My dad drowned in a boating accident when I was three and both of my parents were the only kids. I have a grandma and she lives with us, but she has dementia so…"

"Oh," I whispered. "I'm sorry Camille. I don't know what I'd do without the support of my family."

I looked over at her but she didn't notice. She was staring off into space somewhere. She reminded me so much of Annessa and not just because she didn't have a solid family unit, but there was something else I just couldn't put my finger on. Something in her soul. Maybe it was the SuperNova connection, I wasn't sure, but I felt really protective of her even though we had just met.

"Do you ever wonder why us Claire?" she asked, turning her attention back to me. "Why out of the billions of people on the planet we randomly got this special DNA?"

I paused for a moment, already knowing how I felt about this one, because I had turned it over in my head a million times too. "Yes," I said quietly, "but I don't think we were randomly chosen, Camille. You're here for a reason and you are who you are for a reason. God designed every bit of you for a purpose and now you have to find that purpose. Nothing about you is random."

I watched as her face relaxed from a light scowl and she nodded in agreement with me. Maybe I said something right.

"My grandma used to tell me that before dementia got her," she sighed.

I took her hand in mine. "Well it's true and you have family now Camille." She raised her eyebrows at me in question. "Me," I smiled. "We have the same Lynx DNA you know."

"You're a Lynx?" she smiled slightly, her eyes turning warmer.

"Yes ma'am."

"Is flying your only SuperNova power?"

"Sort of..as far as I know…but can you keep a secret?"

"Sure!" she exclaimed.

I took a deep breath, while she held hers in suspense. "I think I may have a little of you in me."

"What do you mean?"

"I mean…you know how your body can heal itself?" She nodded, not taking her wide eyes off me. "Well, my body protects me when I can't protect myself."

"Like a force field?"

"Well, almost. Like the other day, I was in a situation where I was knocked unconscious and my body kept me suspended in the air until someone could rescue me."

Camille sat up in her chair. "No way! You were stuck in the air? How high?"

I laughed at her excitement. "You wanna see?"

"Absolutely yes!"

I took my phone out of my pouch and pulled up the video Dr. Zhao had sent me of the rescue.

"I thought our phones don't work on the island," Camille said.

"No internet or outside contacts, but they still give us access to our photos. Remember, SuperNova secret, right?" I said holding up my pinky finger.

She smiled and hooked hers in mine. "Right!"

We scooted closer and watched the video together. Camille soaked it all in and would hold her breath and then partially cover her eyes in all the scary parts.

"Wow! Who is that?" she asked, clearly impressed as Johnny descended down the cable to rescue me.

"Believe it or not, that's my fiance," I smiled, proudly.

"Your *fiance*?" she asked in disbelief.

"Yes. Isn't he a hottie?"

"Ummm…yes!" she laughed.

When it was over she stared at me starry eyed. She had so many questions. I began to tell her my story and even though I had told it so many times, I did my best to tell it as if it were the first time. She listened intently and I showed her pics of my family and different videos I had of all my flights.

"I think we are a lot alike Claire," she smiled. "It's good to not feel so alone."

"You're not alone," I said, wrapping an arm around her. "Maybe you don't have a lot of blood family around, but you do have DNA family with us now. I'm going to give you my number and if you ever need me, I'm here for you no matter what."

Camille hugged me back and I breathed a sigh of relief as I watched her mood change. Suddenly she was more eager to talk. "Do you want to see what I can do?" She asked, jumping up and walking to the balcony rail. She turned and smiled, then before I could stop her, jumped over the rail.

"Camille!" I yelled and ran over to grab her. We were about 9 floors up and by the time I hit the rail and tumbled over to grab her, she was already half way down.

I plunged after her, trying desperately to catch up, but it was too late. She hit the ground and to my astonishment bounced off the lawn like a rubber ball. I reached the ground just as she was landing like Cat Woman on a picnic table in between a concrete patio and the side of the building.

"Camille!" I gasped, running over to her. "What are you, crazy? You scared me to death!"

"A little," she winked. "Like you haven't scared someone with your superpower."

I cracked a little smile and shrugged in agreement. "Are you ok?"

"Oh yeah," she laughed at my concern. "See? Not even a bruise."

I jumped up on the bench and looked her over closely, in awe of her ability to not even break a bone. "I'm not even going to ask how you figured out you could do *that*," I laughed.

"I was in the boating accident with my dad when he died," she said matter of factly. "I was three and was underwater for a good half hour. I shouldn't have survived, but I was breathing normally within minutes of being pulled out. No side effects, no brain damage."

"Oh Camille I'm so sorry," I said, but she just shrugged it off. "Then you're Aquila too?" I asked quickly, trying to change the subject.

"What?"

"You know…Aquila? The H2O DNA line?" I reminded her.

"Nooo," she said confused, "they just told me I'm Lynx."

"Hmm," I said thoughtfully. "That's something I'll have to ask Zhao about. You have the characteristics of Aquila too and if you're gonna be a part of this SuperNova thing, they might as well get your bloodline right. It sounds like you're both and that's super cool."

Camille's eyes sparkled in excitement. "Wow, that would be so awesome!"

"Well, I'll ask tomorrow," I laughed, jumping off the chair.

"Claire, do you think you could fly me back up?" She asked, looking up at her balcony high above us.

"I think I can do that," I laughed, then before she could even blink, I scooped her up and we shot into the sky.

TWENTY-SEVEN

AFTER I DROPPED off Camille, I was too wide awake to go back to my room. I took off into the air and jetted over the gulf, eager to get some night flying in. It had been a while since I was able to take a flight out exploring over the ocean. The night was so dark, that I had to pull out my compass on my phone to keep from getting lost. Not much was happening on the ocean's surface so once I got to a comfortable altitude, I laid on my back in the sky for what seemed like forever to watch the stars pass over. This was definitely one of my favorite parts of flying. I quizzed myself on the different constellations and when I got to Lynx, which was a series of 8 stars spread out sporadically, I paused and did my best to snap a picture. Lynx was mine now.

The distant sound of music caught my attention. I

looked below to see a small bright dot on the ocean's black surface. I quickly dropped altitude to get a better view of what was clearly becoming a giant cruise ship as I got closer. I hovered just above the ship, high enough to be out of sight. Up on the top deck, a large crowd had gathered for a concert on the main stage. I watched in amusement as they danced and loudly belted out the lyrics of Bon Jovi's "*Living On A Prayer.*" No doubt this was definitely an American cruise ship.

The smell of something grilling filled the air, making my tummy growl in protest and reminded me that I didn't have time to eat dinner.

"*Hmmm..*" I thought to myself. "*Maybe I'll go down to get a closer look.*"

I found the darkest part of the ship I could touch down on and after hiding behind one of the large steel beams as a couple walked by, I landed safely out of sight. I followed the music to the large deck that was packed to the brim with people dressed in their island best, laughing and yelling for an encore after the last song finished. In the back of the crowd, I found a little stool at the bar in the corner and did my best to blend in, as the band played the beginning bars of Journey's "*Don't Stop Believing,*" sending the crowd into another frenzy. I smiled to myself when I remembered Shawn telling me once this song was the white girl's anthem. I think I would have to agree with him. I love this song.

"Can I get you something Miss?" The bartender asked in a thick Jamaican accent, plopping a menu down in front of me.

"Ummm...sure," I said, looking over the menu, but I knew immediately what I wanted. "I'll have a cheeseburger and a water please."

"Can I make you a drink?"

" No thanks. I'm flying back home and I don't want to drink and fly," I smiled sweetly, not caring at this point that anyone knew who I was.

"Flying huh?" He laughed. "Ok, miss. It sounds like you've already had one too many anyways."

I laughed and shrugged at him, then turned my attention back to the concert, where the lead singer was now doing his best imitation of Steve Perry. I had to give him props, because although there will never be anyone who can touch Steve Perry's voice, this guy was doing it justice.

I leaned back against the wall, soaking in the party around me for a few minutes. How could this even be real? This was my life though and it was very real. My flying power had brought me a lot of tears, but even more it had brought me joy and moments like these that I would have never experienced had I not crashed onto that crate that night.

"Here ya go. One cheeseburger cooked to perfection and only the top shelf bottle of water for you Miss Claire," the bartender winked at me.

My face froze. "How did you...?"

He laughed. "Everyone knows you, my friend. It's all good. No worries here."

I relaxed and looked down at my food. He had added

a generous helping of fries and they looked amazing. "Thank you…friend," I smiled.

"Khenan," he said, reaching his hand across the bar for a fist bump.

I returned his bump. "Nice to meet you Khenan."

"You didn't walk on this ship did you?" he smirked.

I cracked a guilty smile. "No Sir."

"What are you doing way out here then?"

"I just needed to get away for a bit. You know?"

He nodded in agreement. "You're a lucky girl," he said, as he turned to help another patron. "I wish I had that ability. Just to fly away from my troubles. But anyway, for whatever reason brought you here… welcome aboard!"

$$\mathsf{S\!N}$$

It was well past 3 am when I finally arrived back on SuperNova island. I landed on my little balcony and slipped back in to grab a quick shower. The ship had been so much fun and before I flew off I had to hit the dance floor with all the other college kids my age. When Abba's *Dancing Queen* boomed loudly over the speakers, I found myself surrounded by 200 plus of them, dancing and singing as loud as we possibly could.

But now, reality loomed ahead. I had to be at the airport building at 9 am for a short meeting with Dr. Zhao before I flew back to Campbell. I laid in bed that night, exhausted, but too excited to sleep. I couldn't wait to see Johnny and my family. It had been a very exciting, but long week and a half.

At 8:45 the next morning Zhao and I walked to the hangar for what he said would be a small debriefing before I left. Dr. Zhao was waiting in the hangar lobby for us and to my surprise Mr. Lucas stood beside him, just as cool and calm as always.

"Mr. Lucas!" I said surprised. "What are you doing here?"

"You're traveling, I'm traveling," he smiled.

I smiled back in approval as Dr. Zhao guided us to a small sitting area in the corner of the room. His mood was immediately serious as we all took a seat and Mr. Lucas left us to do his usual preflight security check.

"Claire, I want to go over a few things before you go. First and most importantly I want to remind you that this island and everything you have learned here is top secret. Under *no circumstances* are you permitted to tell anyone about our SuperNova community. I know Zhao said you were concerned about not telling Johnny, but please just trust us on this one."

Always one to wear my emotions on my sleeve, my face clearly reflected my displeasure with that one. Dr. Zhao must have noticed, because he quickly added, "In due time, letting him know can be a possibility, but for right now you are not married and we must choose carefully who we allow into our world."

"You don't have to agree with us Claire," Zhao added, "but you do have to respect our decision. Help us protect our people please."

I sighed in surrender. As much as it hurt me to keep more secrets from Johnny, I knew that the safety of the SuperNova community was the bigger concern. "I promise," I agreed, reluctantly. "May I ask who will know?"

"No one," Dr. Zhao said firmly. "At least no one in your circle. We will call you back for training and updates, but that will all be done under the guise of the military."

"Training? For what?" I asked.

Dr. Zhao looked at Zhao, who in turn looked at me. "Claire, dad and I are wanting to send you back with something to think about. You don't have to answer now, but just something to think about."

"Ok," I said, nervously looking back and forth at them.

Zhao leaned in closer. "We have a team here…um, it's called SuperNova Elite. Basically, it's just the best of the best of us and we step in and help the military or the FBI on special assignments that they may not be able to work out on their own."

I was intrigued. "What kind of assignments?"

"Well, nothing that's going to put you in danger," Dr. Zhao assured me.

"No, I would *never* allow that to happen," Zhao said firmly. "Just situations that need a little extra help, where our SuperNova powers could be of assistance."

Dr. Zhao lowered his voice, although we were the only ones in the entire hangar. "For example, do you remember Adrian, our human fish from the Aquila line?" I nodded my head yes. "Well, he just helped the Navy on an undersea mission."

My mind went back to the movie as Henry's voice echoed through my thoughts explaining the SuperNova power of Adrian; he could swim at super speeds, hold his breath for prolonged periods of time and withstand the freezing temperatures of the deep.

"What did he do?" I whispered.

"Two words," Zhao said slyly, holding up two fingers. "Enemy and submarine."

My face froze and I had to catch my breath knowing what he was implying.

"Again, nothing that put him in danger," Dr. Zhao assured me. "But Adrian has had specialized training under us and the Navy, plus he was compensated very well for his mission."

"Was he successful?" I asked.

"Oh yes," Dr. Zhao smiled. "He's actually gearing up for another one next week. He's not here or we would have introduced the two of you."

"Well, you guys have kind of already met, at least as far as he goes," Zhao smiled.

I looked at him surprised. "Really? When?"

"The USS Chafee. He brought your food and belongings to you that morning you were on the ship."

My mind went back to that day. Everything was so crazy with the rescue off the island and the hurricane, I had barely given him a second glance, but I remembered him. I had given him autographs on two photos he had brought with him.

"I knew he looked familiar!" I said excitedly. "That was

Adrian the Aquila?"

"Yeah," Zhao continued. "I guess he's the biggest reason why they were able to keep such good tabs on you when you were on the island."

"He was the secret weapon? The underwater navy spy?"

"Yep," Zhao smiled. "Remember when you almost got eaten by those sharks? Adrian distracted them."

I was dumbfounded. "Zhao, why didn't you tell me?" I said, lightly punching him in the arm.

"Ow," he teased. "Claire, I didn't put two and two together until after you left and even then, how was I supposed to tell you? We were still trying to figure you out and if you were even a SuperNova. Lynx is a fairly new category for us."

I still had so many questions. "Who all knows I'm a SuperNova?"

"No one, but our SuperNova family." Dr. Zhao assured me. "We have one tie to the military and he's a SuperNova and only I know his identity."

"I don't even know him," Zhao chimed in.

"But he's getting up in years…actually he should already be retired," Dr. Zhao continued. "And that's where Zhao comes in."

"I'm staying in the Air Force, so I can be the next SuperNova link to the military," he explained. "No matter what, it's important that we stay connected, since most of us end up in some sort of military service anyway."

I paused for a moment to gather my thoughts and they both sat quietly to allow me some time. I thought about the past few years of my life and how I had found that the greatest joy in flying has been being able to help others who were in trouble. I remembered the robbery I was able to help the Clarksville Police Department with, the little girl Lucy I had saved from the apartment fire, Maci, I had saved from the car wreck at the bridge and Cody I had rescued from the forest not too long ago. Not to mention Kirsten. So, in a way I have been doing this SuperNova/superhero thing most of the time anyway.

As if he read my mind, Zhao added, "You know Claire you've already been a SuperNova Elite in your own right anyway.

"Yeah," I agreed with him. " Being able to help others has definitely been the highlight in all of this."

"Well, you have certainly proven you're more than capable," Dr. Zhao smiled.

Zhao lightly took my hand. "So what do you think Claire?" he asked.

I looked at them both, their eyes flashing in anticipation. "Ok guys," I said at last. "I'm in."

TWENTY-EIGHT

LATER THAT DAY I sat with Mr. Lucas on a private military jet that took off from some small obscure military base in Louisiana. The helicopter flight off the island took just under two hours to the airport, so I had an idea of how long a flight I would have should the need ever arise for me to fly there myself. It was a possibility, after all I had flown all the way to California from Texas.

"You ok?" Mr. Lucas asked, when we were alone at last, in the quiet of the jet's cabin.

"Yeah," I sighed and lightly touched my forehead where the stitches had been. "I healed up pretty quickly."

"I see that," he said, taking a closer look. "But I meant mentally, you know, where it really counts."

I nodded my head in agreement. "Right…but somehow I'm ok Mr. Lucas. Like I'm getting used to the chaos of it all."

Mr. Lucas shrugged, reluctantly agreeing with me. "Maybe. I'm not saying you can't get thicker skin through all of this, but just don't let it quietly drown you Claire."

Quietly drown me. Those words were familiar. I remembered my mom telling me the same thing after my dad had died.

"I won't, Mr. Lucas. I promise."

"Well, unfortunately for you, I'll be able to hold you to that," he smirked at me. "I'm being reassigned to Campbell."

"What?" I gasped. "Why?"

"Why?" he laughed, pulling out a toothpick and popping it in his mouth. "Why do you think? They are pulling in the big guns after this little stunt."

I dropped my head in shame. I felt terrible that Mr. Lucas had to uproot his entire life because of me. "I'm so sorry Mr. Lucas."

"For what?"

"Just because…because you have to move now. I'm sure Clarksville doesn't hold a candle to the action in DC and the Pentagon."

"Don't feel sorry for me Claire. It was time," he laughed. "Actually, they should have done this a long time ago. Besides, do you know how many guys in my circle were begging for your assignment?"

I slowly shook my head no. Why would anyone want to deal with my crazy life? I was fully ready to admit my stubborn self could be a handful. I wouldn't wish it on anyone.

"A lot," he said simply. "No, Tennessee is a great fit for me. It's all good."

"Tennessee is a great fit for everyone," I laughed. That made me feel a little better, but I was very curious as to what he knew about SuperNova island. "So...what did you think of that island?"

"Nice place to recover?" he shrugged, then winked. "They didn't tell me anything, if that's what you're asking. I figure if I need to know, I will in due time."

"Don't feel alone in that. They won't let me share anything with Johnny and he's going to be my husband."

"Again Claire, he'll know when the time is right."

I sat up straighter in my seat. "But how is that fair to him?" I asked. "What if I have...there are things about me that might change his mind if he knew?"

"You think he's gonna change his mind about marrying you?" he sighed. "Like his feelings for you are a light switch he can just flip off? Claire, you're smarter than that." He sat back and kicked his feet up on the seat in front of him. "That guy knows exactly what he's getting into and he's ok with it. You don't give him enough credit."

I sat back in mine again and relaxed. I had learned not to push too much conversation at Mr. Lucas when he kicked back. I knew he would be asleep any minute now, but he surprisingly threw one more thing at me.

"Be thankful you have someone to hide information from."

My heart skipped a beat as the ground grew closer and the runway lights of the Fort Campbell Army Airfield glowed brighter. The airfield seemed busier than usual with copters flying in the distance around the perimeter and military vehicles zooming back and forth. I counted five Blackhawks just in my window view alone. "*They must be doing some special kind of training today,*" I assumed.

"Alright Claire, windows closed up. You know the drill," Lucas said, taking his usual spot at the door of the plane as we touched down. "Out of the plane and into the car."

I nodded my head in agreement, then grabbed my stuff and patiently waited in my seat. "*I wonder if I got regular phone service back yet?*" I thought to myself as I pulled it out of my bag. Zhao had told me it should be programmed back to normal as soon as I left the island, but I had no service during both flights and I just chalked that up to extra security on a military flight.

My face beamed in excitement as I powered the phone on and found everything back to normal. 63 missed messages and over half of those were from Johnny. I scrolled quickly over the last few.

"*Claire Bear, I'm missing you so much. They still won't give us any information. Just that you're ok and you'll be home soon. I hope so. I love you.*"

"*Claire Bear, just checking in on you before bed. I'm lying here missing you so much. I'm so worried about you. I love you.*"

"Hey Claire, please let me know you're ok ASAP. I'm so worried. I wish I could have got to you sooner. I should have never let you out of my sight. I love you."

Oh my heart. Just a few more minutes and I would be with him.

"Well, this is not happening Sir," I heard Lucas say into his sleek silver cell phone. That caught my attention. Who was he talking to like that? "She's not deboarding this plane until all these people are gone, except the one delivering the vehicle."

I looked toward the window, forgetting that I could not see out anymore.

"I am her driver. It's her and I in the car alone, that's it!" he huffed, then paused to listen. "Well, we saw how that worked out last time…I'm in charge of her security from now on and if you have a problem with that, I have a number you can call. Now, do as I asked. Clear this area out." He snapped his phone shut. "It's gonna be a while," he said, looking down at me with steely eyes. I had never seen him so angry before.

"Who was that?" I asked, calmly.

"Some Airfield Commander," he answered, going back to the door window and looking out. "Look at this," he motioned me over. I immediately joined him, standing on my tiptoes to try and see out. "Looks like a circus out there. One, two, three, four, five, SUVs…got helicopters flying around and 30 or more people just standing around. For what?! How am I supposed to screen thirty plus people?"

His phone rang again interrupting his rant.

"Lucas. Hello Major…it's ok, but if I'm in charge of Claire's safety, this is going down my way from now on."

I went back to the door window to look out once again and see what was happening while Mr. Lucas listened to whoever was talking to on the phone. My eyes peeked over the top, but I could still barely see. Just the sky and the roof of the hangar. Easy fix. I slowly levitated 2 feet off the plane floor, much to the amusement of Mr. Lucas. I looked over at him and returned his bemused smile, then turned my attention to the activity happening outside the plane. The line of SUVs were quickly reduced to just one and the people began to scatter. I watched as they filed into the hangar as one lone person walked out. My face lit up as I recognized Major Silva confidently stride past them and up to the plane steps. I hadn't seen him since he was in the hospital and had been so worried about him.

"Major Silva!" I exclaimed to Lucas.

"Just wait," Lucas warned me. "He's going to give us the all clear when it's safe."

Major Silva turned around, surveying the area while Lucas grabbed his shades off the small hook they were hanging on.

"Ok Claire, out of sight until I give you the all clear," he commanded, opening the door.

I dropped to the floor and stepped behind the small wall that divided the galley from the passenger area. I heard the door pop open and then a warm breeze ripped through the galley and down the middle aisle of the plane. I took a deep breath. It smelled so clean and fresh after breathing in the stale jet air.

I listened carefully as Lucas and Silva talked at the bottom of the stairs but all I could make out was something about General Collins.

"Claire, let's go!" I heard Lucas yell up to me at last.

I bounced down the stairs as quickly possible, just as Lucas had directed me to do. Major Silva was waiting with the car door open and a big smile.

"Hey Major," I smiled at him giving him a little salute. "I'm so glad you're ok."

"Me?" he laughed and gave me a quick hug. "We've been worried to death about you. Come on, your momma is waiting to see you."

Major Silva climbed in the back with me as Mr. Lucas took over the driving. We drove straight to my mom's new house on the base. I noticed Major Silva didn't ask too much about what had happened to me, so I assumed Johnny had already given him the details.

My heart flipped as we turned down my mom's picturesque oak tree lined neighborhood. I was so thankful she had adjusted here so well. With Kass in college now and her living alone, I knew she was safe and Silva made sure of that.

We hadn't even pulled into the driveway when I saw her bounce out to meet us.

Much to my surprise and delight, Kass was right behind her. I jumped out of the car and made my way quickly down the sidewalk where they both wrapped their arms around me. None of us said a word, but I could feel Kass' body tremble as she began to cry softly. My mom whispered, *"thank you God for keeping her safe"* as her voice trembled. With that, I broke too. I had been so wrapped up the past week with SuperNova busyness, that I hadn't fully taken in what had happened to me or even more concerning how it affected my family.

"I'm so sorry Mom," I sniffed, after a long moment.

"It's ok Claire. It wasn't anything you did wrong. We've just been so worried about you," she reassured me.

It broke my heart to see her cry. For someone who was so kind and vulnerable, one thing she rarely did was cry in front of us. While I'm sure there had been many occasions where she had cried alone, she has always been so protective of our feelings and would put on a brave face no matter what was happening around us.

At last Silva interrupted us. "Ladies, for everyone's safety we better take this inside." He wrapped his arms around all three of us and ushered us inside. I noticed mom's eyes go from sorrow to a slight sparkle. I know she was grateful to have Silva in her life, watching over her and protecting her and he seemed more than happy to oblige.

Mr. Lucas pushed past us and immediately walked through the house opening doors and checking behind curtains. My mom didn't even bat an eye and even gave him a tour to make sure he covered every inch of the house.

"Where's Johnny?" I asked when Mr. Lucas had finished his check.

"He's on his way," Silva answered. "He was at the airfield, but he had to leave with everyone else."

My face dropped and I looked over at Mr. Lucas. How could he have made Johnny leave? He just shrugged back. "We need better communication Claire."

"We'll get the kinks worked out," Silva reassured us.

Outside the sound of a car screeching to a halt, stopped our conversation. I immediately ran to the door. Johnny had pulled his truck halfway on the driveway and the grass and was already up the walkway when I bolted off the front porch and into his arms.

"Seriously girl," he said, squeezing me tightly. "I was so worried...I was so worried."

I hugged him hard and kissed his cheeks a thousand times. "You saved me," I whispered in his ear. "I saw you. I saw the video."

Johnny smiled and didn't say anything, but looked cautiously around. "Let's get back inside," he said, as he kissed my forehead and wrapped his arm around me, guiding us to the door.

Late that night Johnny and I sat face to face on my bed holding hands and discussing the past week. I was careful not to expose my new found world, while trying to figure him out. I wanted to know how he was feeling about everything, particularly marrying someone as complicated as me.

"Claire, what kind of question is that? Of course I still want to marry you. Why would you even ask me that?"

"Because…" I took a deep breath, "because I obviously don't have a normal human anatomy anymore…and aren't you scared? I mean, look at what happened this past week. You literally had to pluck me out of the sky Johnny."

"Claire, I would have gone to the ends of the earth to save you…"

"I know you would," I interrupted. "But don't you worry about our kids? How this will affect them? How they might turn out to be like…like *me*?"

Johnny sighed and let go of my hands. "I *want* them to be just like you. Why are you trying to talk me out of marrying you?"

I gently grabbed both of his hands with mine again. "Johnny, I'm not. I just really want you to know for sure that you're ready for all of this with me."

"I am ready and in fact," Johnny said sternly and then took a deep breath. "In fact, we are getting married in 3 weeks."

I froze. "What?" I asked, dumbfounded.

"You heard me. I already discussed it with your mom and she gave me her blessing. I'm tired of not knowing where you are and when you're coming back and what's really happening in your life. I'm an outsider, Claire."

"Really?" I whispered. "That's what you think? You're not an outsider Johnny. You are the center of my world."

He sat quietly, while my heart sank. He was right in

a way. He had no idea what was really happening in my life and I wasn't allowed to tell him.

"Johnny, we can't plan a wedding in three weeks…"

"The girls are already on it. Alicia will be here in the morning to take you to Nashville to find a dress. Lucas will go with you."

"I… I thought I had to meet with General Collins," I stammered.

"No, they're giving you the weekend. You'll see him Monday." Johnny stared at me for a moment, his eyes full of anticipation. "So…what do you think?"

I paused for a moment, trying to process everything. "*Three weeks.*" I thought to myself. "*Three weeks to plan a wedding. Three weeks to pull our families together from all over the country…but three weeks until I could finally change my last name to Angel and never have to be away from Johnny again.*" It was a no brainer.

"Yes," I smiled. "Three weeks. Let's do it."

TWENTY-NINE

"ALRIGHT CLAIRE," LUCAS said, later that week as we stood in front of a large warehouse on the south side of the base. "I'm going to teach you how to use a new line of weapons to protect yourself. Some of these you may be familiar with, some you probably have never heard of because they are not available to the public, but you're going to learn how to use them."

"What do you mean by 'new kind of weapons'?" I asked, cautiously.

Mr. Lucas smiled to himself looking straight ahead as the warehouse door slid open. I followed Mr. Lucas into the darkness, making sure to stay right behind him while the door closed behind us.

"Lucas," I heard someone say coolly. Another door opened directly in front of us, flooding the hallway with light.

"Ake," Mr. Lucas laughed, obviously glad to see him. "Thanks for coming down man."

"Not a problem. I'm looking forward to working with you again." He looked at me. "So this must be Claire."

"Yep," Lucas answered. "Claire, this is Mr. Akana. He specializes in weapons training for my division."

I looked up at Mr. Akana, then reached out to shake his hand. This guy was big and intimidating, dressed in dark tactical gear with at least three gun holsters strapped to him that I could see. His black tee rippled over his toned muscles and looked to be two sizes too small.

"Nice to meet you finally," Mr. Akana said kindly, in a thick Hawaiian accent. "Lucas here, talks about you all the time."

I looked sideways at Mr Lucas who mumbled, "Not all the time."

"It's nice to meet you too. You guys worked together?"

"We did for a while," Mr. Akana said.

Mr. Lucas opened the door and led us into the next room. "Claire, Mr. Akana is going to be a part of my security detail here. He's experienced, very well trained, and there's no one I trust more on this planet than him."

"You're gonna have a security team?" I asked, looking around the large industrial room that contained a small sitting area and a large indoor shooting range. Behind us the metal door slammed shut, making me jump slightly, followed by the snap of the door bolt. No one said a word as I followed them both to a long table that held 5 shiny metal suitcases. Mr. Akana took a small set of keys out of his pocket and unlocked one, while Mr. Lucas and I squeezed in on either side to see what was inside. The case made a small hissing noise and clicked three times, then slowly opened automatically.

"Wow," I gasped, as I looked at the strange weapons laying in the blue velvet lined case. Mr. Lucas was right. I had never seen any kind of weapons like these.

Akana picked up the largest one of the three and when I say largest, that's not saying much. It was barely the size of my tiny hand spread out and was the shape of a handgun, but much sleeker. The color was weird too, a matted gold and silver mixed together. I looked at it closer. The barrel was so tiny, I wondered how any ammunition could escape it.

"Claire, allow me to introduce you to the C-474 and her sisters the C-1113 and the C-711," he said. I glanced at the other two, as Mr. Lucas picked up the C-1113 that was the same color, but had a more round hand grip. "The C-474 is what we will be training you on."

"So they're guns?" I asked, still trying to figure them out.

He nodded toward the last booth and I followed them there, grabbing a pair of ear protection headphones and slipping them around my neck.

Mr. Lucas smirked and quickly took them back. "You won't be needing those."

"Stand right here, please," Mr. Akana instructed me. I did as he asked, facing the target that seemed further away than usual. Then he stood directly in front of me.

"Claire, just so you know, you are the first person outside of our agency to ever be trained on our weaponry. I know you hear this a lot, but this is classified information and you are not to share the existence of these weapons nor your knowledge of them with anyone. Understood?"

"Yes Sir."

"Before you even ask," Mr. Lucas interrupted, "Once you and Johnny are married, he will be trained as well. We can't expect you to keep everything from him."

I smiled in appreciation at him. "Finally something I can share. Thank you."

"Ok," Akana said. "Same as a regular firearm, Claire. Always treat it as if it were loaded." He held it up in front of me and placed his index finger on a small pad at the bottom of the grip. "Fingerprint identification," he explained. "We will reprogram it to yours tonight. It's useless without your fingerprint, so we never have to worry about anyone else using it."

He placed it gently in my hands and I immediately pointed it toward the target.

I couldn't believe how light weight it was. Almost as light as a toy gun. "So you have the safety on the left… go ahead and slide that to the off position." I moved it with my index finger with ease. "Look down your optic." I focused on the red dot directly on the top of the skinny barrel. "So now-the shot," he said quietly as if someone was listening. "There are no bullets by the way." I gave him a side glance, taking my eyes temporarily off the dot. What did he mean there are no bullets? "You're going to feel a slight pulse, followed by a light zapping noise. Just keep the gun pointed at your target. Ok, now on the count of three, pull the trigger. One...two...(I took a deep breath)...three."

S̗N

Mr. Lucas and I stood in front of the dummy I had just hit. A perfect little pin hole sat directly between the eyes. All around the hole was burnt residue.

"Well, we don't have to worry about your aim," Mr. Lucas said, rubbing his finger over the hole. "Hmm... still hot."

"The hole or my aim?" I teased.

"Both," he smirked.

I looked closer. "What was that?" I whispered, looking over at Mr. Akana, who was back at the table, opening another case. "There's no way that was a bullet."

"It's a laser, Claire. A high intensity laser that shoots faster than the speed of light. It discharges a beam that is about the size of your pinky finger and is always lethal no matter where on the body it hits. Each laser is DOA and will not penetrate any person or thing beyond your target. Of course we only use it under the most extreme of circumstances."

I looked down at the tiny laser gun. When I had pulled the trigger, there was no kickback, no jolting, nothing to even let me know I had discharged it, other than a small zapping noise, just like Mr. Akana had said.

Mr. Lucas took it out of my hand and held it up. "Another thing. See your safety?" I nodded yes. He flipped it over. If you need a taser instead, safety off and just a touch of this button. Understand?""

I nodded my head yes again. "Can I try again? Now that I know it's a laser."

"Of course. Take as many shots as you need to feel more comfortable, but do be conservative with your lasers. They are not cheap."

I walked back to the line. Safety off. Right button pressed and Zap! I couldn't believe this thing. How could something so small and seemingly insignificant be so powerful? I took two more shots, careful to not waste them. Both were a direct hit to the target and I tried not to gloat too much.

"Ok Claire, one more thing we have for you," Mr. Akana said, as I followed them both to a long thin suitcase on the last table.

"*What kind of weapon could possibly fit in that?*" I thought to myself.

Mr. Akana lifted up the handle on the side and punched in a code that beeped different tones with each number hit. At last, it made a hissing noise that sounded like air leaving a tire and lifted slowly open.

They stood behind me as I cautiously approached the table. My eyes glimmered in wonder at the navy blue bodysuit it contained. It reminded me of a wet suit and every curve was outlined with sleek aqua blue tubing that ran up and down the legs and arms, front and back and even outlined the bottom. I turned and looked at the guys, questioning with my eyes if I could even touch it.

"Go ahead," Mr. Lucas smiled. "It's yours."

I gently lifted the soft, but sturdy suit from the case. It wasn't until I held it up that I noticed the unusual collar; a slender turtle neck that looked like it would cover not only my neck, but half of my face. To my delight I also discovered an exact replica of my Saturn tattoo on the left sleeve.

"I'm sure you have a lot of questions," Mr. Akana smiled as they came and stood beside me.

"Yeah," I laughed nervously. "It looks like a…a…"

"Superhero costume?" Mr. Lucas said, while I nodded in agreement. "It is kind of. Claire, you've always told me you wish you could reach new heights with your flying power right?"

My face froze, scared, yet excited about what I knew he was going to tell me. "You mean this…?"

"Yep," he said, as cool as ever, but I could see a twinkle of excitement in his eyes too.

"How high?" I gasped.

He shrugged. "As high as you want."

"And as fast as you need," Mr. Akana interjected. "See these tubes? They convert air to usable oxygen."

"The suit is also designed to withstand any temperature, any amount of pressure necessary and is bullet proof," Mr. Lucas added.

"Bullet proof?" I said as I held the suit up to get a closer look, completely flabbergasted. "Who designed it?" I asked. "And is it safe?"

"Our people, but that's all you need to know. And yes, it's safe and ready to go."

I held it against me. "When will I be testing it?"

"No testing. It's ready to go," Mr. Lucas assured me. "It's already been approved by NASA. Now if you want to test it on your own, we'll have to make a plan for that. Understand?" He asked with a little wink.

I understood perfectly and my heart leapt inside my chest. I would be flying in this little baby on my own time, free of heart monitors and oxygen checks and I wouldn't wait another day. I was flying tonight.

THIRTY

THAT NIGHT, AFTER everyone was in bed, I stood in front of my full length mirror at my mom's house. Time couldn't have gone any slower as I waited all day to try on my new flying suit. I pulled the black duffle that Mr. Akana had given me from under my bed. Inside, my suit was folded neatly and my laser gun tucked away in a small zip compartment. The bag was unlocked by my own personal code and came complete with a device tracker. The material was made from something otherworldly and unbreachable and Lucas assured me there was no way anyone could get in the bag without the code.

I slowly pulled the suit up my body and put both arms through the slender long sleeves that also covered my hands in a snug glove. It fit so perfectly and though the material outside was tough, inside it was so smooth and soft. Now for the turtle neck part. I carefully unrolled it up my neck and my chin, completely covering the whole bottom of my face, right up and over my nose, where two small tubes tucked just inside of my nostrils. Only a sheer material covered my mouth, making it possible for me to talk without sounding muffled.

I held my left wrist up and looked at the small Saturn planet patch that laid directly over my real Saturn tattoo. Mr. Akana told me rubbing my right wrist over it would activate the suit. I took a deep breath, then did exactly as he instructed. Immediately the suit went into operation, tightening around me and sounding like it took a deep breath, almost as if it were breathing. The aqua colored tubes glowed slightly, as well as the Saturn patch and I felt my whole body go warm as air began to flow into my nose. I quickly threw on my black combat boots and then looked at myself in the mirror again. My long curls hung softly down my shoulders and my bright eyes gleamed in contrast to the dark suit. I put my hands on my hips and did my best superhero pose.

"Looking good, Claire," I said to myself. I looked at least three feet taller and much more intimidating. Ok, now to give this thing a little ride.

I checked the clock on my phone. It was already one am. I carefully slid open my window quietly to not wake my mom, because although Mr. Lucas knew I would be flying tonight, my mom had no idea and I didn't want to worry her. I climbed out of my second story window and sat on the edge looking carefully around our little military neighborhood. I felt like I was back in highschool, when I would sneak out of my bedroom window for a midnight flight and stay out until the last gleam of moonlight faded.

Mom's house was set back off the road with a few trees around it, but still not enough for me to go unnoticed. I flew to the top of a large oak tree that stood on the west side of the house and found a large branch at the top to perch on. Just across the street a blacked out Charger sat guarding our house and I breathed a sigh of relief knowing Mr. Lucas and his team were in charge of my security now.

When everything was clear, I stood on the branch and bounced off it, rocketing like a bullet into the stars. Up and up I went, higher and higher until at last I looked to the west. A couple of miles away a commercial airplane was flying directly into my flight path. I paused in the air and looked at my left wrist where the Saturn rings had disappeared and in its place flashed 35,000 feet. The scream of the jet's engines came closer and I quickly flew another 50 feet up as it rocketed underneath, the force of its wind spinning me in the air. What a rush!

I caught my breath and watched it quickly shrink away into the night, then looked above. I had never seen the stars clearer or the moon brighter. I couldn't believe how high I was and still felt totally normal. My breathing was fine and despite the deep chill in the air, I was so warm. Could I possibly go any higher? There was only one way to find out.

An hour and a half later, I landed safely back into my window as rain began to hit the pane softly. I slid it closed behind me then collapsed on my bed. "Oh my gosh Claire!" I whispered to myself, as I rolled the oxygen tubes off my face. "60,000 feet! 60,000 feet and I didn't feel a thing!"

I sat up on my bed and checked myself. Usually after a flight, I was pretty wiped, but not tonight. I was wide awake. I slipped my shoes off and carefully slid the suit off my body, noticing it immediately shut down as soon as my last leg was out. I folded it carefully, placing it back in the duffle that locked on its own, then threw on some jammies and pulled out my phone to look at some of the footage I took. Kass was going to love this. The shots were incredible and my favorite in particular was a whole body shot selfie I took at 35,000 feet, with the bright lights of mid west America shining below. The video looked like something out of a movie and for the next 30 minutes, I worked on making the raddest tiktok I could with Coldplay's *Sky Full of Stars,* playing in the background. Of course I would need to get it approved by Mr. Lucas, but I was sure it would be ok. I had people begging me for more footage and since I had come this far with them, I didn't see the point in stopping now.

"Claire, your tik tok has over 7 million views," Alicia said later that week as we sat in a booth with Shawn and Johnny at our favorite pizza dive on base.

I smiled shyly, while Johnny rolled his eyes. "Oh Alicia, don't make her head any bigger than it already is."

"Whatever," I laughed and playfully pushed him away, as he tried to squeeze me back close to him.

"How high did you go up?" Shawn asked, almost in a whisper.

"60,000 feet," Johnny answered for me. "I told her she's crazy…but she does look really hot in that superhero suit, so…"

I laughed, "But I was totally fine and it was so incredible you guys. I could actually *see* the curve of the earth!" I took a breath in my excitement. "I can't wait to go back up."

"These past 4 years have been a trip, huh Claire?" Shawn smiled.

"You're not even kidding Shawn," I agreed.

"And now only six days until you guys are married!" Alicia gushed. "I can't believe you're getting married in Hawaii!"

"I know!" I agreed. "I can't wait to go back! You guys are going to love it there."

"Do you feel like we covered everything Claire?" She asked, pulling out her ever present list from the past three weeks. "You know, Corrin has been so great in helping us get everything together on the Hawaii end."

"She is awesome," I sighed. "I can't believe she arranged

the entire reception!"

Alicia scribbled something at the bottom of the now very wrinkled paper. "Well, I have to say it hasn't been easy pulling a wedding together in three weeks, but I think we should be good to go."

"Look *Mony,*" Johnny teased. "If you want me to say I'm sorry for rushing this, I just can't, because I can't wait to marry this girl."

"Aww," Alicia smiled. "I guess it was worth it then."

"All I can say is, it's about time," Shawn said, as the waiter arrived with our pizza and set it on the table.

"Excuse me, Claire," the waiter said hesitantly, handing me his order pad. "Could you sign this for me, please? It's for my girlfriend."

"Sure," I smiled at him. "What's her name?"

"Annessa."

I paused for a moment, unsure that I had heard him right. "Annessa?" I repeated slowly.

"Yes ma'am." He looked curiously around the table that had suddenly become really quiet.

"A-n-n-e-s-s-a?" I choked a little, while he nodded yes. I took the order pad and wrote the first thing that came to my heart.

"*To Annessa, the most beautiful name in the universe. The stars are yours. Reach for them. Love-Claire.*"

He looked down at what I wrote and smiled his approval. "Thank you. This will mean the world to her."

"That was a weird coincidence," Shawn whispered after the waiter was out of earshot.

Alicia reached her hand across the table and grabbed mine. "You ok Clairey?"

"I'm fine," I smiled at her.

"That wasn't a coincidence," Johnny said, pulling me closer. "That was Annessa reassuring you everything is going to be ok."

THIRTY-ONE

THREE DAYS LATER, our military plane touched down safely at Hickam. My heart leapt inside to be back here, especially with my family, friends, and Johnny in tow. General Collins at Ft. Campbell had gone out of his way to make sure everyone who wanted to come was on this flight today, while Lt. General Gray at Hickam arranged for us all to stay at the guest housing on the base.

I was thrilled to see Lt. General Gray and Corrin waiting for us as we deboarded the plane. My mom hugged Corrin tightly after I introduced them and thanked her for taking care of me and I heard Johnny telling Lt. General Gray the same.

"Not a problem," Lt. General Gray said. "It's nice to finally meet you too. What you did to save her was just extraordinary."

Johnny wrapped his arm around me as we walked with my family off the tarmac and toward two vans that awaited us. The sun was so warm and I looked around almost in tears at all my family that were with us. Mom, Major Silva, Kass and Kyle, Tessa and Ryan, Darcy, Alicia and Shawn, Lexi and Tater and of course Mr. Lucas. Johnny's family would be joining us tomorrow to make it all perfect. Well, almost all perfect. I had yet to get an RSVP from Zhao.

The next morning we were all busy preparing for the wedding that was now just twenty four hours away. I had chosen the beautiful foyer of the Shack for our wedding and General Gray was not only going to officiate it, (who knew he was also a chaplain?) but also allowed us to use the Officer's club for our reception that conveniently sat right across the street from the ocean.

"The Shack?" Johnny had teased me when I told him where I wanted to get married. "I think we can do better than that."

"Wait till you see it," I laughed. "It's far from a shack."

My family oohed and ahhed as we entered the back foyer to the Shack compound for the rehearsal. It was even more elegant than I remembered. The tall two story glass windows allowed the sun to trickle in between the palm trees that stood majestically outside. Beautiful beige and gold covered chairs were lined in perfect rows that led up to a large round wedding arch covered in white tropical flowers, while small white lights twinkled everywhere.

"Corrin, this is unbelievable," I said, catching my breath and looking around. It couldn't have been more perfect.

"I tried to match everything to your wedding colors," she smiled. "Plus I feel like you and I share a lot of the same taste as far as style goes."

My sisters, plus Lexi, Alicia and Janey soon gathered around me while the guys followed Johnny outside to check out the Shack and Lucas did a walk thru of the perimeter with Lt. General. Johnny's mom Nora, Corrin, and my mom sat in the last row chatting endlessly like they had known each other forever, while Mario, (Johnny's dad) and Major Silva worked on a small string of lights that had gone out.

Lexi's eyes lit up in excitement. "How are you feeling about tomorrow Claire?"

"I'm nervous, but I'm just so excited," I smiled, looking down at my sparkling engagement ring.

"Nervous about..?" Kass winked at me.

"Really Kass?" I laughed. "Nooo. I'm excited about the honeymoon, if that's what you mean… not nervous."

Lexi tilted her head and gave me an inquisitive stare. "Wait a minute. You mean you guys haven't..."

"Lexi, quit being so nosey!" Alicia smiled and quickly added, "But no, they haven't."

Everyone laughed, as I blushed and glanced at Janey

to make sure she wasn't feeling uncomfortable with our conversation. After all, she was Johnny's sister. But she seemed fine. I really liked Janey. She was so laid back, just like Johnny and she hit it off really well with us all, but especially my sister Tessa. Janey and her husband Josh had made fast friends with Tessa and her husband Ryan.

"Nothing wrong with that Claire," Darcy winked at me.

"So Janey, how was your family when Johnny told you about Claire's little secret?" Tessa asked, changing the subject.

"Wellll…" Janey smiled. "Johnny didn't tell us. My dad saw it on the evening news."

There was something about the way she said it so matter of fact, that made us all pause and then laugh.

"The news? As in the actual six o'clock evening news?" Kass giggled.

"Yep," Janey smiled. "And it was the national one! My dad called my mom and I from the kitchen and pointed at the screen calmly and said, "I think that's Claire on the TV, flying." We all laughed even harder at her mimicking her dad's thick Italian accent.

I couldn't imagine what that day had to be like in their house. When Johnny told me they knew, I worried if they would want him to break everything off. But they were so gracious and when he proposed, they were genuinely excited for us.

"Excuse me ladies, can you tell me where Lt. General is please?" We turned our attention to the gate guard, who appeared out of nowhere and seemed in a hurry.

I pointed to the double doors that led outside. "He's in the shack."

"Thanks," he said, quickly heading out back while the girls continued talking. I halfway tuned into their conversation while watching the guard out of the corner of my eye and Mr. Lucas who casually followed him out.

The guys soon joined us and we began rehearsals. "Where's Lt. General?" I asked Corrin as we stood in the back waiting for my cue to walk down the aisle.

"He's going to join us for the rehearsal lunch. Some kind of emergency came up," she replied calmly, while my eyes filled with worry. "Claire, don't worry. I know exactly how everything will go and Adam knows how to officiate in his sleep. Don't worry please. It will be just fine."

Corrin was right. Rehearsals went off without a hitch and before I knew it we were at the Officers' club for the rehearsal lunch. I hadn't been here since I had come to the Officers' ball last year with Zhao. That night seemed like an eternity ago and despite my deep happiness in the moment, my heart sank momentarily as we walked past the dark empty ballroom we had been in. I couldn't believe Zhao was not coming to my wedding.

Later that afternoon, the girls and I gathered our things together for a quick trip to the beach. It was only two and we wanted to get back in time to watch the sunset at our favorite ocean side restaurant while the guys went golfing.

We were just on our way out when my phone rang.

"Claire?" I heard Lt. General's voice.

"Yes?"

"I'm so sorry to bother you today of all days, but could you come over to my office? Lucas is waiting in the lobby to escort you."

"Sure. Is everything ok?"

"Yes...well, I'll brief you when you get here."

I hung up and looked at my girls. "I have to go see Lt. General real quick. I'll meet up with you guys soon."

Kass' smile quickly faded. "Is everything ok?"

"Yeah," I said, linking my arm in hers as we walked down to the lobby. "Everything's fine. I'll be back soon. Just save me a beach chair please."

THIRTY-TWO

LUCAS AND I walked into Lt. General's office. My eyes lit up when I saw Johnny there, but my heart sank at the same time. He was supposed to be golfing with the guys so why was he here? He squeezed me close as I began to notice everyone else in the room. Shawn, who was sitting in the corner, gave me a halfway smile as my eyes met his. Captain Crew was also there, along with Sgt. Mancuso and Major Wang, the doctor in charge of my health at Hickam. I suddenly became self conscious in my black see through cover up dress and my favorite neon pink bikini that was so obvious underneath. Why didn't anyone tell me this was an actual *meeting*, meeting?

Lt. General pointed at the middle chair in a semicircle of chairs directly in front of his desk. I quickly took that seat and everyone else joined me while he opted to lean on the front of his desk.

"Claire, you know I would never want to bother you, especially the day before your wedding, but we have a real situation on our hands." He took his phone out of his pocket and handed it to me. Immediately a message began playing as the view of the inside of a commercial airplane appeared.

"*Lt. General, this is Agent Fellows of the Australian Security Intelligence Organization (ASIO). This afternoon we had a situation happen at the Sydney airport in Sydney, Australia. Flight 114 was out on the tarmac, preparing for departure when it was hijacked by three armed terrorists.*"

I watched the airport security footage that showed a line of passengers walking up a portable staircase to a 747 plane that was parked out in the middle of the tarmac. The footage then sped up to the last person boarding and then to a stewardess walking to the door, who grabbed a bag from one of the ground crew men who was wearing a reflective vest. My body jumped as the man suddenly dropped the bag and grabbed the stewardess from behind holding what appeared to be a knife to her throat. Very quickly a different camera angle popped up and two other men jumped from a baggage cart and followed them into the plane, with one of them scooping up the bag before slamming the door shut. The footage then jumped to the inside of the plane.

The ASIO agent continued. "*The plane was hijacked and is now en route to L.A. As you can see, this is inside of that plane. We have one of the members of the World*"

Championship 14u baseball team feeding us footage, whenever he can do so safely. This team is based out of the Nashville area and are returning to the US after having just won the 14u championship. We are expecting them to be flying over your area around 10 pm Pacific Coast time and will notify you for further assistance. In the meantime, please put your base on high alert and we will be updating you soon.

The phone went black and I glanced up at Lt. General who stared back at me, matching my worried expression. The room was eerily quiet, until I asked the questions I knew everyone else was thinking.

"What are their demands and what are they threatening to do?"

"Well, they have none," Lt. General said. "And that's the problem. Their only goal is to destroy as much as they can." He paused for a moment before he continued. "We're worried about what will happen as they fly into LA, Claire. They are a splinter from a terror cell who want notoriety outside of their old group. We're pretty sure they have no intentions of letting anyone survive."

My heart dropped. "How old are the boys?"

"Ninth graders, so 13 or 14 maybe. Plus their families and an additional 140 souls on board."

Just kids. I couldn't imagine how scared they were right at this very moment and it hit even closer to home because they were Tennesseans just like me.

"What do you need me to do?" I asked, sitting up straighter in my chair.

I felt Johnny's eyes on me. "What do you mean what do they need you to do?" He asked, softly. "Claire, there's nothing you can do. You can't magically appear in that plane."

I turned to him. "Maybe I can. Maybe…maybe somehow I can get up there and get in the plane. I know I can fly that high…"

"Well..it is a possibility," Lt. General interrupted. "We can get you in the plane, but it would take a lot of planning and I'm worried we just don't have the time. We are mainly just requesting that you be on alert and ready to fly out over the ocean in the event of…of a recovery operation."

"How would you get me into the plane?" I asked, ignoring option B.

"Claire, I don't think…" Lt. General began.

"How?" I asked again.

A knock on the office door grabbed our attention and my heart skipped a beat when I saw who followed the guard into the room.

Zhao's eyes immediately found mine as Lt. General quickly left the front of his desk to greet him and Dr. Zhao.

"Hello Zhaos," he said, breathing a sigh of relief. "Just in time."

I stood up to greet Zhao who walked toward me. "Hey

Claire," he smiled and hugged me tightly.

I squeezed him back. "I knew you'd come," I whispered.

"Of course I came," he said. "I didn't want you to have to deal with this alone."

My smile faded and I backed away from him. "So you're not here for my wedding?" I gulped.

"Of…of course," he stammered. "For both."

"Why didn't you answer my invitation then?" I asked, not caring that all eyes were on us now.

Zhao stared back at me, obviously having no good answer. "I'm here now," he said quietly. "I wouldn't miss it for the world, Claire. Please believe me."

"Claire," Lt. General said calmly. "Let's focus here for a minute, ok?"

"I'm sorry Sir," I said, sitting down beside Johnny again, while Zhao grabbed the other seat beside me and pulled his laptop out of his backpack. "Just tell me what I need to do to get in the plane."

"Claire…" Johnny tried to reason with me.

"Please Johnny," I pleaded. "They're only kids. I have to at least try."

I saw Johnny's jaw line tighten and I knew he was not happy. I had only seen him upset twice since we've been together and both times were because of me.

Lt. General Gray cleared his throat, turning our attention back to him. "We have been talking with the Zhaos to see if there's something we can do to intercept the plane and bring it down safely. Dr. Zhao, would you like to share any thoughts with us?"

I peeked over at Zhao's laptop that showed the architectural structure of the airplane from the bottom up. He punched in a few numbers and the wheels came down. Zhao stole a side glance at me and raised an eyebrow. I knew exactly what he was asking. I discreetly nodded a yes.

Dr. Zhao joined Lt. General up front. "Just a few new details we can share with you. We do know who this terrorist group is. My son was able to pick up a little of their dialect and pinpoint their origin. They have no demands, like Lt. General Gray has said, therefore it's a life and death situation. We do have a plan and it is a risky, but doable plan that involves all of you. It's also a plan that we can abort should we need to do so, because at the end of the day, Claire's safety is our main concern."

We all listened intently to Dr. Zhao as he explained it from A to Z. It sounded pretty simple to me;

1. The plane would approach Hawaiian air space around 10 pm tonight.

2. I would go up in an UH-60 (helicopter) with Zhao approximately 30 minutes beforehand to get us at 19,000 feet and directly under the plane's flight path. This would save my energy for the rescue and give Zhao a better chance of getting me in the plane.

3. Zhao would intercept the plane's Flight Management System (FMS), opening the landing gear, which would allow me passage into the plane through the nose wheel.

4. I would follow Zhao's directions through the cargo area and up into the rear cabin to take out the enemy

using a firearm with a suppressor. (I stole a glance at Mr. Lucas who gave me a slight wink, his affirmation that this was my chance to use my new laser 474.)

5. Once the plane was secure, we would return to Hickam.

"Any questions?" Dr. Zhao asked, looking around the room.

Shawn cleared his throat. "What about the pilots of this plane? Are they ok and aware of what we are planning?" he asked.

"Well, one of them are," Lt. General answered, solemnly.

The room grew quiet again.

"Excuse me Sir, but can I have a couple of minutes alone with Claire please?" Johnny asked, standing up suddenly.

"Of course."

Johnny nodded for me to follow him and as always Mr. Lucas came out right behind him. "I'll be right down the hall," Lucas said, closing the office door and patting Johnny on the back.

"Thanks," Johnny said, then turned to me. "Claire, you know you don't have to do this."

"I know…"

"I mean…seriously?" he interrupted. "Climbing through the wheel well of a 747? That's their big plan?"

"I know it sounds absurd Johnny, but it's actually really doable." I paused before I shared my next thought. "I've been in worse situations," I shrugged, trying to make light of the situation.

He was not amused. "Well, there was nothing I could do about those situations, but this one I have say-so in."

"You do," I reassured him. "And if you are 100% against me going, I won't." I moved closer to him and wrapped both my arms around his waist and pulled him close. "But I think we both know there is no out for me on this one. If anything happens to those boys, I would never forgive myself. I have to at least say I tried."

Johnny reached down and kissed my forehead. "Claire, you can't save everyone."

"I know and I promise I won't always try...but I think us being here at this exact moment is not just a coincidence Johnny. I promise you, if I feel unsafe at all, I will terminate the mission...but I know I can do this."

I wanted so much to introduce him to the SuperNova side of me, because maybe somehow it would calm his nerves, but I also knew this was neither the place nor time. Instead, I just kissed his cheek and whispered in his ear, "There's more in me than you know."

Johnny wrapped both arms around me in a warm bear hug. I breathed in his sweet smell that I loved so dearly. He gave the best hugs and I never wanted to lose them.

I heard him breathe a sigh of surrender. I know he knew I had no choice really, but it was his job to object and do everything he could to keep me safe and I loved him for it. "Ok," he said at last. "But I'm going with you. Shawn and I will fly the 60."

"Johnny..." I began to protest.

"I'm going," he said sternly. "Let's go tell them."

THIRTY-THREE

LT. GENERAL GRAY didn't mind Johnny and Shawn piloting the helicopter that was going to take us up. In fact, he smiled his approval when Johnny "demanded" it, in order for me to participate. "That can be arranged," he had said, throwing a little side glance at Captain Crew. I learned later that had been their plan all along, especially with the way Johnny and Shawn had saved me from Jason and his evil henchmen.

After the meeting, everyone went into the hallway and left Johnny, Zhao and I alone in the office. Johnny and Zhao stood up face to face.

"Zhao, it's nice to finally meet you," Johnny said, extending his hand. "Claire talks endlessly about you so I feel like I know you already."

I smiled when Zhao shook his hand firmly. I had been

waiting for this moment for the last two years. My two favorite guys, finally together. "I can say the same. She's definitely a fan of yours."

"Look, I hope you understand my hesitancy in letting her do this," Johnny sighed. "I know she can fly, but at the end of the day, she's still just a 20 year old girl. I can't let anything ever happen to her."

"I get it man," Zhao agreed. "I would never forgive myself if anything happened to Claire."

I stood up, joining their conversation. "Well the good thing is, if I'm in danger I can terminate the mission like Lt. General said. And I will."

Shawn waited for us at the door and introduced himself to Zhao, then we grabbed our stuff and headed out of the office. Johnny and Shawn walked ahead of us discussing the copter they would be piloting.

"Nice dress," Zhao smirked as we paused at the door.

I rolled my eyes. "I was on my way to the beach, Zhao."

He laughed, then lowered his voice. "Just so you know Claire, we have other SuperNovas here. Adrian the Aquila is going to be stationed on a boat directly under our rendezvous point just in case he is needed in the water and my buddy Caspar, who is a lead tech at NASA, will be assisting me from the ground in the event we need to put the plane on autopilot. But we don't anticipate that happening. Caspar is a Perseus just like me. Also, Camille is here just for personal reasons only."

My heart skipped a beat. "Is everything ok? Is Camille ok?"

"Personal as in your wedding personal," he laughed. "She's fine. She said you invited her."

"Of course," I smiled. "I didn't think she could come though. Unlike some people, she actually RSVP'd."

Zhao stopped and looked at me. "You know I could never miss your wedding Claire. It's just, as you know, we never know what can come up as a SuperNova. I didn't want to say I was coming and then not show up."

I folded my arms in protest. "Like I wouldn't understand that Zhao. I'm SuperNova too, you know."

"Oh I know," he smiled, wrapping his arm around my shoulder and leading me down the hallway. "So can we just let it go now? I don't care what happens, I will be at that wedding tomorrow and so will you. Let's just get this done."

I went from headquarters to the beach to meet up with my girls. Despite the meeting seeming to drag on forever, we were only there an hour so I still had time to enjoy the sun for a bit, plus I didn't want anyone to be suspicious of my absence.

I sat under my big beach umbrella, with Darcy napping beside me, watching the girls who were floating on their boogie boards. I had been out with them for a bit, but decided to save my energy and get out of the sun. I would need all the strength I had for tonight.

I smiled to myself as I watched them ride the waves

back to the beach then float out and do it over and over again without a care in the world. It was so crazy how unaware they were of the insane task I had ahead of me tonight. I wouldn't dare tell them either. My sisters would have a meltdown and I definitely wasn't going to tell my mom either. She had enough to worry about with the wedding tomorrow.

I spent the next half hour at the beach fending off the bad thoughts. What if I didn't make it back? What if I survived, but failed my mission? All of those souls on board, each life unique and innocent in all the madness of this. Their lives depended on our whole team, but at the end of the day most of the weight would be on me. Very quickly my nerves turned to anger though. I so much wanted time to speed up so I could avenge these people, especially the young boys on the plane. At this very moment they were rocketing towards us, uncertain and scared of what was to come.

I looked at my phone. It was already 5:30. I had been given enough time to eat dinner with my family and then be at the hangar on Hickam at 8:30. Johnny had made up the excuse of having a last minute surprise planned for me while our friends and family attended a late night luau. If everything went as planned and I prayed it would, I would be back and in my bed by midnight.

"Ok Claire, see this?" Zhao asked, as Johnny, Shawn,

Mr. Lucas and I squeezed in close with him to see the inside of the cargo area of the plane on his laptop. "That's where you'll enter the nose wheel of the plane, right between the back two wheels. Now when you approach the plane, you're going to come up from the west, but do not approach the plane until you are in front of the engines." He turned and looked at me sternly. "Do *not* get near the engines. You understand? I don't have to tell you all the things that could go wrong there."

I rolled my eyes slightly. "Zhao, I think I'm a little smarter than what you're giving me credit for."

"Excuse me for doing my job," he smirked.

The hangar office door opened and Captain Crew poked his head in. "Gentlemen, we have your bird ready," he motioned to Johnny and Shawn.

Shawn jumped up. "Let's do this," he said, rubbing his hands together in anticipation and heading to the door.

Johnny leaned down and kissed my forehead. "I'll see you out there ok?"

"Ok," I said, as cheery as I could, trying to hide the nervous knots that were beginning to tie up in my tummy.

I watched him walk out the door and then turned my attention back to Zhao. He carefully went over each step I would need to take to get to the galley. Mr. Lucas even threw in a few pointers, giving me the feeling he had done something like this before.

When we were done, Mr. Lucas handed me my duffle bag. "There's a bathroom over there you can change in," he said pointing me in the right direction.

I grabbed the duffle and headed quickly to change. It was already 9 pm, just one hour until the plane entered our airspace. I went into the single occupancy bathroom and shut the door. Luckily this bathroom had a bench and a full length mirror. I set the bag on the bench with a loud clunk. That was weird. I opened it and looked in to see a helmet sitting on top of my neatly folded flying suit. "Oh wow," I said to myself as I pulled it out and tried it on. This was probably the coolest looking helmet I had ever seen. It was so lightweight and made out of some weird shiny material. It was navy blue, the same color as my body suit and even had matching Saturn rings in pink on the side. I tried it on, looking for a strap that would secure it underneath my chin, but instead felt the cushion inside expand, fitting the shape of my head snug. No straps needed!

I quickly slid on my body suit and boots, zipped my laser 474 in its pocket on the side of my pants and took a final look in the mirror. Not to brag, but I looked pretty intimidating. I inhaled one deep final breath and gave myself a quick pep talk. "Ok Claire, you know you got this. You are not the product of an accident. You were chosen for this. You are brave, you are strong, you are smart and you were born for such a time as this." *Born for such a time as this.* That little scripture was a staple of my childhood. Esther 4:14. My mom had repeated it to me and my sisters over and over since the day we were born. So small, but so powerful and tonight it gave me great confidence.

"Wow," Johnny mouthed to me, as I approached the copter with Lucas and Zhao. I blushed at his compliment, grateful he liked my flight suit. He held out his hand to lift me gently aboard, immediately wrapping me in his arms and kissing me softly.

Shawn was at the controls and was assigned to co-pilot in the event I ended up stranded in the air like the last time. We quickly took our seats and buckled up, preparing for take off. Outside the engines whined loudly and I looked out the window where Lt. General, Captain Crew, and Major Wang stood watching us lift off. I smiled and waved to give them some reassurance, because they all looked really worried. Just before we boarded, Lt. General had given me a hug and whispered "Godspeed" into my ear.

"Claire, do you copy?" Zhao said into my headphones that were built into my cool helmet.

"Roger that," I replied.

"Everyone check in please," Zhao said.

"Lucas here."

"Clear," Johnny replied, flipping switches over his head, getting us ready for lift off.

I watched him intently. I had never had the opportunity to see him in action, doing his job that he loved so much. He was so smart and had worked so hard to get in that pilot seat. My mind briefly went back to the first summer we had met and our first date at the hangar, when we sat together in a helicopter. He had shared with me his dreams of being a pilot and now he was. I was so proud of him.

"Claire, test your shades please," Lucas said, bringing me back to the present.

I pressed the bottom right side of my helmet with my gloved hand and immediately a pair of sleek goggles slid down from inside the helmet covering my eyes.

"Night vision," I commanded, watching in amazement as everything became more clear and precise in the dark. "Day vision," I instructed them and they magically switched to regular sun glass mode. "I'm good," I said, giving a thumbs up to Lucas and then Zhao who was looking back at me clearly impressed.

The UH-60 began to vibrate as the chopping of the blades grew louder. We began to roll down the runway and then slowly lift off, nose down first and then rising quickly. I breathed in deeply. This is it.

THIRTY-FOUR

I CHECKED THE time on my phone. It was 9:15. Thirty minutes before we had to be at the rendezvous point over the Pacific. Higher and higher we climbed until at last we reached our cruising altitude. Tonight the sky was so clear and looked so calm and enchanting. The moon was full and bright and it cast a warm glow over the waves of clouds below. Everything out there seemed so peaceful, a stark contrast to what we were all feeling inside the copter.

"Four minutes until go time," Zhao announced, grabbing my hand and squeezing it.

I squeezed his back in reassurance and winked at him. I was going to be ok.

Johnny unbuckled his harness and joined us in the back, attaching himself to a safety tether by the door. "Ok

Claire, we'll be pausing for your exit in two minutes."

I nodded and began a last minute check to make sure everything was in order and all my equipment was a go, then unbuckled myself to join Johnny at the door.

"Claire," Mr. Lucas said, grabbing my arm and turning me toward him. "Laser, not taser." His eyes were steely and hard.

"Yes Sir," I said, my determination pushing away my nerves.

Johnny held out his hand to me and I joined him at the door. "Remember, you can abort at any time you feel you need to. It doesn't make you any less a hero."

I reached up and kissed him quickly. "I'll be back Johnny. I promise. Remember? We're getting married tomorrow."

Johnny gave me a half smile and kissed my forehead. "Yes, we are."

"Go time!" Zhao said into my headphones.

Johnny reached past me to open the door. Suddenly I felt the air sucked out around me and my whole body shifted toward the door. I kissed him one more time on the cheek and rolled the mask part of my suit up and over my nose, then rubbed my right wrist over my left to activate it. Immediately the oxygen began to flow and my body grew 10 degrees warmer.

"The plane is on schedule," Zhao announced over my headset. "In five, Claire. Five. Four. Three. Two. One."

My eyes met with Johnny's one last time and I dove out into the night.

I allowed myself to free fall for a few seconds, to safely clear the blades of the copter, then shot up in the sky. I watched below as Shawn made a large U-turn to head away from the point of contact and get far from the plane to avoid any chance of the copter showing up on the plane's radar.

Levitating mid air, I listened to the popping of the copter blades that eventually faded away and then-nothing. Dead silence enveloped me as I looked up at the millions of stars sparkling in the sky. I paused for a moment to gather myself and focus. "God, I need you tonight," I whispered. "Please be with me."

My headset's staticky reception suddenly echoed through my ears, then Zhao's smooth voice came in loud and clear. "Claire, do you copy?'

"Roger that," I replied.

"Ok, we are clear on your audio and visual. Target is 10 air miles due east, coming in from the southwest. Get your start."

"Clear."

I dropped my safety glasses down and rocketed the rest of the way up and to the east, keeping my eyes to the west. Mr. Lucas had told me when the plane came into view they would do all the work, zeroing in on the target and guiding me to the plane's front wheels.

Right on cue, a small alarm began to sound and a bright green laser light shot across my glasses, forming a little square around the aircraft that was now a small white dot in the distance. I did as Zhao instructed me and began flying ahead of the plane, knowing it would catch up quickly.

"Target spotted," I informed them. "I'll be in flight."

"Clear," Zhao said. "Nose wheels dropping."

I fired up my speed, my hands clasped together in front of me, superman style. "*Faster!*"my mind instructed my body. The roar of the jet grew closer as I flew as fast as possible, focusing on my breathing. I looked down at my wrist where the saturn rings had disappeared and was now flashing an unbelievable 450 miles an hour. The sky began to rumble louder as the jet soon overtook me and I looked up to see the nose, just above.

"*Whatever you do, don't get behind the engines,*" I heard Zhao repeat in my mind.

I flew directly beneath it, my body rocking back and forth and twisting in a spiral as the plane was now right above. Even with a helmet on, the sound was deafening. I cautiously pushed myself closer to the underside of the nose, trying to get out of the strong jetstream left behind as the plane cut through the air. I glanced quickly behind me. The wheels were just below. All I had to do was fly down the side of the plane to get to them, while being careful to not lose speed and end up behind the engines.

"Steady Claire. You got this," I encouraged myself as I inched down the side of the plane. 20 feet away...now 10... I carefully reached for the large metal thing the tires were attached to and soon both hands were clasped firmly around it. I swung my body up and locked my left leg around a smaller bar above it, then looked up for the hole Zhao told me to enter through. Thankfully I found it pretty easily.

I was just starting to climb in when the engines let out a frightening scream and the large plane tipped slightly on its side. I gasped as the inertia flung my body upside down and slammed my head against the plane wall, but I didn't dare let go. If I did, there was a very good chance I would never catch up again, but thankfully we leveled off and I began my climb up the wheel well.

"Good job Claire," I heard Zhao gasp in my ear, then breathe a huge sigh of relief. "We're not sure what caused that. Ok, see the hole to the right? Climb through it and move as fast as you can. I don't want you in the well for very long."

I had no problem obeying that order. It was so small and scary in here and I very quickly remembered I was claustrophobic. I grabbed the top of the hole and shimmied my way through the small opening and into a little compartment that wasn't much bigger.

"Ok, now what?" I asked, catching my breath.

"The ceiling above you, just lift up and slide it to the left."

I pushed both hands against the metal plate above my head, that lifted easily off and slid it to the left as he instructed. I poked my head up slowly and looked around a cargo area, which was stuffed with suitcases and various parcel packages. I flew up onto the floor and into the middle of a long narrow aisle that glowed dimly.

"Good job Claire," Zhao said. "Make sure you slide it closed again."

"Ok, give me a minute," I whispered, laying on my back and folding the oxygen mask onto my neck. Fighting against the powerful wind and flying had done a number on my energy level. I allowed myself just a minute, then did as he instructed, sliding the metal plate back in place. I looked around the vast cargo space. It was much bigger than I had imagined it would be.

"Ok, follow the lights to the very back of the plane," Zhao said.

I paused for a moment. How did he know my every move?

"Zhao, can you see me?" I whispered.

"Affirmative," came his response.

"What? How?"

"The GoPro in your helmet. Now, get moving Claire."

I followed the lights down the aisle, careful to grab onto the metal beams for balance. The plane shifted slightly to the left again and I knelt to the floor for a moment to keep from falling. A slight bump and rolling sound came from my right and a bright white baseball eerily rolled across the floor coming to a stop at my foot. I picked it up and rose slowly while noticing a bunch of baseball bags stacked on the side of the wall. I walked over to the bags and began reading the names to myself. V. York, C. McLean, C. Bergstrom, G. Strauss, C. Woestman, Z. Foust. All of these bags represent a promising, young life.

Tears brimmed my eyes. What if I failed?

"Claire, you got this," Zhao said softly into my ears.

"Right," I said firmly, trying to refocus. My determination returned, thankfully drowning out that fleeting moment of doubt and I moved quickly down the aisle. "Ok, I'm at the end."

"Go to your left. There's an elevator door. Slide it open and stay inside until I instruct you further."

I found the door, slid it open and stepped inside a compartment that was no bigger than a small hallway closet. I took a deep breath. This was it. I had no choice but to succeed, because the point of aborting this mission had passed. There was no way off the plane now.

"Claire, when I tell you to, hit the button to go up. Now listen carefully, we have a flight attendant we are in communication with and he's going to give us the all clear. We have three targets. One is in the cockpit, one in first class and one in coach, who occasionally walks to the back of the plane. This elevator will lead you to the galley at the back of the plane. Do just as we discussed. One at a time."

"I got this Zhao," I said with confidence.

"I know you do." His voice was sweet, but I could still hear the uneasiness in it. "I'll be back with you soon."

I reached down and unzipped my laser gun out of my built-in holder on the side of my hip, then double checked to make sure the safety was on and I was ready to go.

I closed my eyes for a moment and imagined myself

tomorrow, standing at the altar with Johnny with all of our family and friends around. I could see his smiling face right in front of me and hear the waves crashing in the background. I felt the excitement of finally changing my last name to Angel. I had dreamed of it for so long. There was no way I wasn't going home tonight.

"Claire, we're a go. Press the button now," he said, bringing me back to reality.

I took a deep breath and pushed the button. The lift shifted slightly, almost knocking me off balance, then slowly began to ascend. Luckily it made little noise as it climbed 10 feet to the next level.

"Alright I'm here," I whispered.

"Wait," Zhao said as I reached out to open the door. "Wait."

I paused, then reached down clasping both hands securely around my gun, going over Mr. Akana's instructions in my head. I wish I had more practice time under my belt, but I would just have to trust that I knew what I was doing.

"Ok, go into the galley," Zhao directed.

The door slid quietly open and I glanced across the galley. My eyes went immediately to a male in a pilot's uniform, laying against the back wall.

"I have a male subject down in the galley," I whispered to Zhao, then walked quickly over to him to check for a pulse. "No pulse," I said, sadly. "It looks like the pilot."

"Co-pilot," Zhao corrected me. "You have to move on Claire."

The sound of someone clearing their throat drew my attention to a wide eyed, red headed flight attendant sitting in a jump seat not far from me. His name badge read "Andy" and he had a direct view of the front of the plane. He glanced quickly at me from his jump seat, then back down the aisle. He looked genuinely puzzled to see me (maybe he wasn't expecting a girl) and motioned for me to stop while looking straight ahead. I assumed this was the guy Zhao had been communicating with, since it seemed like he was waiting for me.

I watched as he gave the ok for me to move forward a little with his pinky finger. I did as he instructed, getting closer to the aisle, my laser up and ready to go. I used two fingers to point to my eyes and then to the aisle, asking if it was ok for me to steal a peek. He chomped nervously on his gum and looked ahead again and then nodded yes.

I slowly peeked my head around the corner. Two boys sitting on the very last row whispered loudly to each other, alerting the last three rows around them of my presence. I realized the whole back section was occupied by the baseball team.

"Shhh," I mouthed quietly and pointed for them to look forward. Just down the aisle I could see target one turned in the opposite direction of me, looking toward target two at the front of the plane. I didn't realize how long the plane actually was. It looked like it went on forever and I was going to have to inconspicuously make my way down the aisle without them noticing.

Andy coughed lightly, getting my attention. His blue eyes were wide again and he nodded down the aisle. "He's coming," he mouthed.

I quietly ducked into a small open closet and behind several Captain's jackets and a large hoodie that hung neatly in a row, taser up and ready.

"Target 1 heading my way," I whispered quietly.

"Stay still and if you have to eliminate him now, then so be it."

"Clear." I swallowed hard and my hands shook. Training to take a life was one thing, but actually taking it was a whole different level. Breaking a bad guy's arm or leg (I had done both) to save a life was bearable, but I couldn't even kill an insect without feeling a tremendous amount of guilt.

"Get up!" I heard a voice command angrily in a thick accent.

I was able to see slightly through two of the jackets, but just the cabinets and a small sink that were directly across from the closet. Suddenly Andy was flung up against the cabinet, his head smacking loudly against the panel surface.

"Make coffee and whatever food you have for me and my brothers, but that's it," the guy growled, before slamming Andy's head again. "Understand?"

"Yes," Andy gasped.

I clenched my teeth together, anger rising from the depths of my soul and ripping through every part of my body down to my fingertips that were now wrapped securely around the trigger on my laser gun.

"Where's the bathroom?" Target 1 asked, holding a very large knife to Andy's throat.

"There," Andy said, pointing behind the guy and then turned slightly, glancing at me. My heart sank when I saw the large amount of blood spilling down his face and onto his crisp white uniform shirt. With that, all my hesitation went right out the plane window.

I watched as the man walked down the tiny hallway to the bathroom. When I heard the door shut, I slid out and without saying a word, grabbed a towel off the counter and held it to Andy's head.

"I'll be right back," I whispered, then made my way to the bathroom. There was no place to hide, so I made sure to stand where the door would open in front of me, at least giving some kind of cover.

"Claire you got this," I heard Mr. Lucas' calm voice say into my earphones. "Remember, this is a laser, not taser mission."

I took a deep breath, making sure my gun was in laser mode. "I remember."

THIRTY-FIVE

TIME SEEMED TO move in slow motion as I waited outside the restroom. Each breath I took was long and deep and echoed louder and louder inside me. Breathe in, breathe out. Every moment from the time I was first injected with the flying potion until now flashed through my mind. Every rescue, every flight over the ocean, mountains, and the hills of Tennessee. Every beautiful sunset, every stormy sky and every person who meant so much to me. I waited patiently.

The snap of the bathroom lock was like a punch in my stomach. I glanced down the little hallway, where Andy stood, his mouth open and his face frozen in fear. Our eyes met in that moment of uncertainty and I gave him a little smile of reassurance.

Target 1 walked confidently out, making the terrible

mistake of not checking behind him. As quickly and quietly as possible, I was on him. My hand covered his mouth, just as Prof. Corral had taught me to do when we worked on a smothering technique. The laser gun went directly to his temple and without hesitation I pulled the trigger, my military training taking over my civilian insecurities. His body immediately went limp and fell backwards, knocking me off balance and pinning me against the wall. In a flash Andy was at my side, helping to lift his heavy body off of me.

"Target 1 eliminated," I said into my helmet.

"Good job Claire," Zhao reassured me.

"Omg seriously?" Andy whispered, loudly. "Are you ok?"

"Quick, help me get him to the closet," I huffed, pulling with all my strength.

We dragged his body to the closet and hid him the best we could, but finally had to settle with covering his feet with a small blanket.

"Ok, I gotta move before they notice him gone," I whispered, throwing the sweatshirt that was hanging in the closet over my head and covering my helmet. "Go back to your seat. I need you to let me know when I'm clear again, ok?"

Andy nodded, then obediently returned to his seat and put on a light jacket to cover his blood stained shirt. I waited for his cue that seemed to take forever.

"Are you the flying girl?" One of the boys from the last row mumbled out of the side of his mouth, looking back at me.

I nodded my head yes and silently reminded him to be quiet and look straight ahead. He did just as I asked, but not before I noticed his look of worry melt away to a smile of relief. These guys were counting on me. I was their final lifeline.

At last Andy gave me the all clear and I peeked around the corner. Way down at the front of the plane, I could see Target 2 talking through a cracked door with someone in the cockpit. This was my chance to get as far down the aisle as I could.

I pulled the hoodie down further and yanked on the strings to somewhat close it around my helmet, then bent down and walked halfway down to row 14 where an aisle seat was vacant. I slid in quickly, just as target 2 was turning around. All the loud whispering and excitement that swirled around the back of the plane at my arrival was quickly shut down as Target 2 looked suspiciously at the passengers.

"Shhh," someone whispered.

The door to the cockpit slammed shut as he began to slowly walk the aisle, a large automatic pistol tucked firmly in his hand. I looked down at the ground, careful not to make eye contact, praying he wouldn't notice the new face in the crowd.

The teenage Asian girl beside me breathed a sigh of relief as he passed our row. I glanced quickly at her inquisitive stare as she looked me up and down, then poked my head out into the aisle to see how far back in the plane he was going to go.

"He has a gun," I whispered to Zhao.

"I saw," Zhao said. "Just remember, make sure his hand is off the trigger before you take your shot. We don't want him shooting into the plane."

"Clear." I said, as I watched him walk closer to Andy, occasionally turning to check behind him.

"Where is he?" I heard him growl at Andy when he reached the back.

Andy nodded down the hall. "Bathroom," he said, staring at the ground, trying to hide the left side of his bloody face.

Target 2 turned to the left and disappeared behind the galley wall.

I stood up and rushed back down the aisle. "This is it," I said to Zhao. "I have to take him out now."

Every eye on the plane turned to watch as I hurried to the back and stood behind the last row of seats, my back against the wall. I took my laser gun out and listened as he called towards the bathroom door.

"Zayhn!" his voice echoed through the galley. "Zayhn! Open the door!"

"Andy!" I hissed. Then motioned for him to move to the front.

Andy quickly left his seat and joined some of the boys a few rows up.

"Where is he?" Target 2 yelled, stomping back towards us.

In a split second decision, I flew to the ceiling, staying

glued against the wall.

Below me, dozens of eyeballs stared wide eyed and some even gasped aloud.

Target 2 never knew what hit him. He came out of the back like a crazed psycho looking for Andy. He put both of his hands around the throat of the first boy he came to and demanded to know where Andy went. That was the only invitation I needed. I jumped on him from behind and put my laser to the back of his head. In an instant he was gone. He fell forward onto the ground, while I hung midair, a blank stare on my face.

The plane was quiet for a long moment, then suddenly came alive with a chorus of voices buzzing in excitement as a wave of hope swept across the plane.

Andy stood up and motioned for the crowd to quiet down. "Ok, shhh...shhh! We're not in the clear yet people." He turned to me. "One more in the cockpit," he said.

I joined him on the ground. "I know."

"How are you going to get in?"

I shrugged. "Knock on the door."

Andy's eyes lit up. "Let me do it Claire."

"Andy, I don't want to..."

I heard a deep voice behind me. "I'll kick the door open once he cracks it and then back you up." I turned to see one of the baseball coaches standing behind me.

I started to shake my head no. I didn't want any civilian help on a military operation.

"I'm trained in grappling and I'm a cop," he said to

further convince me.

"Claire, Johnny says let them help you," Zhao said. "We're running out of time."

"Johnny said to?" I asked.

"Yes."

"...Ok then," I agreed, but reluctantly. I trusted Johnny with every decision. He always chose what was best for me.

The coach looked around for a moment, clearly puzzled. "Where's the rest of your team?"

I shrugged. "I'm it."

He looked me up and down. "You're here alone?"

"Yep." I gave my gun a quick once over to make sure it was a go and then looked at both of the guys. "It's a simple one, two, three operation," I explained and pointed at Andy. "One, go grab his food and then knock on the door." I looked at the coach. "Two, as soon as the door cracks, give it one swift kick, just under the handle...and three is all me. If something happens to me, just keep him away from the pilot. Understand?" They both nodded anxiously. "Ok, let's do it."

Andy went to the galley and quickly returned with a tray, while the coach and another man moved Target 2's body to the galley. "You ready?" Andy asked when he returned, his tray rattling slightly. The poor guy was scared to death, but I had to admire his bravery, in spite of it.

I nodded yes and then quickly shed my sweatshirt, following Andy and the coach up the narrow aisle. When we reached the cockpit door Andy paused for a moment while we got into position- the coach behind the door and myself just behind Andy and around the galley wall.

Andy closed his eyes for a moment, took in a big breath of determination, squared his shoulders back and knocked.

I looked back across the plane at 150 plus pairs of eyeballs frozen on me. Minus the hum of the engines it was totally quiet in the plane and we all held a collective breath waiting for the door to open. Andy looked over at me.

"Knock again. Harder," I instructed him.

He nodded his head and knocked more firmly. Again, no answer. We waited.

"No answer," I whispered in my mic to Zhao.

"Ok, well you're going to have to…"

Suddenly the door unlocked and slowly opened, interrupting Zhao and sending my heart dropping to my stomach.

"Your food…" Andy began to explain, holding it out to Target 3. Soon after a loud crack echoed through the plane when the coach kicked the door, followed by a crashing of the tray and a thud. That was my cue. I immediately flew around the corner, shoving Andy safely to the side, who then landed on the coach, sending them both into a heap on the floor. I had one goal at this point and that was to disarm him and keep him from shooting the pilot or into the plane.

I bolted helmet first into his stomach, knocking him back against the co-pilot controls. The plane dipped forward on his impact, pushing us both violently into the front window of the plane as the pilot attempted to gain control. To make matters worse he landed on my right hand that held my laser gun, sending it somewhere under a control panel. Laptops, backpacks, books, and objects of all kinds began flying into the cockpit from the passenger section as we continued to fly nose down toward the Pacific.

Target 3 swung his elbow, luckily connecting with my helmet instead of my face. I freed my hand and flew into the air, hovering above, my gun still not visible to me. I watched as he froze, his eyes unsure of what he was seeing, then I delivered a hard kick mid air to his face. He let out an angry scream and grabbed my ankle. I kicked again with all my might and grasped the side of a door that was now above my head as the plane descended. I desperately needed to find my gun before he grabbed his.

"Hey!" I heard someone yell from behind us. I looked up to see Andy inching his way into the cockpit. "Let her go!"

I kicked again, harder. Target 3 rolled to his left and against the window to avoid the hard tip of my boot, revealing a large automatic rifle slung to his back. I knew I had to get control of it and now.

THIRTY-SIX

THE PLANE BEGAN to quickly level off now that Target 3 was away from the controls. He stumbled his way toward us and grabbed my throat with both hands, trying to lift me off the ground.

"Kick Claire!" Zhao yelled, his voice desperate.

I knew a defense move to this kind of choke, but had only done it on my back in my early days of training. No reason I couldn't do it in the air. I pulled my knees up and towards his chest and put my legs over his shoulders, half inverted. I thrusted my hips upwards, locking both of his arms straight and in between my legs, then grabbed his hands and squeezed his arms tight with my thighs, while he desperately tried to release the grip on my neck. He was able to free his right arm, alleviating the pressure, but I had a firm grip on his left arm and kept raising my hips until I heard it pop. His face turned bright red as his elbow snapped and he screamed in pain, while calling me every name in the book.

Target 3 reached for his rifle and tried to get it into a firing position, once he realized this kind of fight was not working in his favor. My heart pounded hard in my chest as I swung at him, in a desperate attempt to keep him away from the weapon.

"Kick Claire!" I heard Zhao yelling again in my ear.

I obediently pulled my right leg close to my face, while still hovering in the air and kicked it toward him as hard as I could, but the tip of my boot barely grazed his chin.

"I got him!" I heard a voice growl.

I breathed a sigh of relief as the coach came from behind. He put Target 3's right arm in an escort position with a wrist lock, while I flew around him and applied a rear choke. He tried desperately to headbutt me, but I easily avoided that by tucking my head down into his left shoulder blade. There was no way I would be showing up for my wedding with a black eye.

In a final attempt to escape, he leaned forward and we fell to the ground, but I supported his weight and continued to choke him. I could feel his body slowly going limp. The coach looked at him and then looked up at me. I knew what he was asking- will I let him live or end it all? I didn't know what to do. I just held the choke, scared of him coming to.

My mind raced back to my training with Prof. Corral. He had made it clear to me that if my life or someone else's depended on it, to hold the choke after they go unconscious, that it would take time to finish the job permanently. He always reiterated the fact that someone trying to hurt or kill you can't be given a second chance. It was in that 60 seconds that I considered letting go and letting him live.

The time went so slow and even though I struggled with it, I knew that I had to hold on. If given the chance Target 3 would wipe out everyone on board, with no second thought.

Two minutes later I released the choke. The coach saw the uncertainty on my face and reassured me. "You did what you had to do Claire."

S̶N

Target 3 fell to the ground with a thud that vibrated through the floor of the plane. Everyone went silent, except for a few terrified gasps. I stood frozen at the front of the plane, my mind numb and still questioning my decision. I breathed deeply, my body exhausted from the trauma of the past 30 minutes.

Then from the back of the plane came a loud cheer. I looked up to see the boys from the baseball team jumping out of their seats, high fiving and hugging each other. Like a wave, everyone from the back of the plane to the front stood up and started clapping and cheering. Some of them cried and hugged each other tight, knowing they were safe.

My heart grew ten pounds lighter as I watched them. These innocent people were safe and that's all that mattered to me.

Zhao's voice interrupted my thoughts. "Good job girl. I knew you could do it," he said, breathing an audible sigh of relief. "Now get in that cockpit and lock the door just in case there's a sleeper," he warned me.

"A sleeper?" I asked above the cheers. No one had mentioned, nor had I thought of a sleeper being a possibility. I grabbed the rifle and quickly went into the cockpit and secured the door, which included a safety bar that locked down in place. I finally found my gun, well underneath a control panel, then grabbed the first aid kit that hung just inside the cockpit on the wall and began attending to the pilot.

"Are you ok?" I asked, slipping off my protective gloves and replacing them with the medical gloves in the kit. The medical training from my Special Forces days kicked in and I was so grateful for it.

"I've lost a lot of blood," he gasped. "I'm feeling a little dizzy."

"It's ok," I reassured him, while I cut a makeshift butterfly bandage. "You're going to be ok, I just need to stop the blood flow."

"Claire, have him head back to Oahu," Zhao instructed me. "Hickam is going to be the closest and we have the whole hospital on standby."

"Clear," I replied. "How far off course are we?"

"45 minutes back."

I carefully applied the butterfly bandage to the open cut on his forehead. "We have to head back to Hawaii, Sir. Do you think you can make it?"

"Yes," he said, looking at me confused. "What's going on...where's the other bad guys?"

"They've all been eliminated."

His eyes grew wide in shock. "Who's with you? How?"

"It's just me," I said, avoiding his intense stare and securing the first aid kit back to the wall. "And God... and the coach...and Andy."

"Who...who are you?"

I jumped back into the co-pilot seat and looked over at him. "I'm Claire. Now please Sir, can we get this plane headed back to Oahu? I have a wedding I have to be at tomorrow."

"Of course," he said, still unsure about me.

He slowly glided the plane into a big U turn and headed back towards Hawaii, amidst a loud roar of cheers from the back. I looked out the window into the silent night at the thousands of stars that seemed to be all around us and for the first time in what seemed like forever, was able to catch my breath.

"*God, thank you for your hand of protection on my life and the lives of all the people on this plane,*" I whispered to myself. Even with a superpower, I knew I couldn't have done this one without the true source of power in my life.

Suddenly the plane began to shake and a loud engine scream ripped through the still night. I looked outside to see two Air Force fighter jets fly past us.

"Z, I have two F14's flying by. They know the plane is secure, right?"

There was a long pause before he finally answered. "Affirmative. They'll be escorting you back to Hickam."

I breathed a sigh of relief. "Clear."

$$S_N$$

The runway lights at Hickam glowed brightly in front of us, as we approached Oahu. At the end of the runway a large fleet of emergency vehicles awaited our landing, lights flashing brightly.

I looked over at the pilot, who I now knew as Howie and who looked like he was on his last ounce of energy.

"Zhao, I'm going to need medics in the cockpit. Our pilot needs medical attention immediately." I squeezed his hand. "You've done good Howie."

"Thanks Claire," he smiled, then looked back at me. "But please, I have to know…who are you and just how did you get on this plane?"

I looked at his pleading eyes. I guess it wouldn't hurt to let him know a little bit about me.

"*Well, here goes nothing,*" I thought. "Ok…so, I am in the United States Air Force and I have a super power. I can fly, which is how I got on this plane."

"Careful Claire," Zhao said in my ear.

"You're the flying girl?" Howie gasped.

"Yes, but that's all I'll tell you, ok?"

"Ok," he smiled as we began our descent. "Thank you Claire and to whoever is in your ear, thank you. Because of you, I get to hug my family again."

I stood outside an SUV with Lt. General Gray and watched as passengers were being processed off the plane. Howie and the Coach were taken off first and whisked away to the hospital, then one by one, passengers were matched with their passports and lined up under the bright lights of the plane.

Lt. General gave me an ice pack to hold on my arm that was slightly swollen under my super suit.

"Thank you," I said with a yawn, then looked at my phone. It was almost 1:30 in the morning.

"You're welcome," he smiled, then let out a big sigh. "Claire, I hate putting you in danger like that. Just so you know, tonight was not a decision I wanted any part of."

"I know that," I quickly reassured him. "But Lt. General, I know it's what I had to do." I looked over at the passengers who were buzzing in relief. "I wouldn't have traded tonight for anything. Seeing those people on the ground and safe, it's all worth it."

"Well, it's not that I didn't have faith in you. I mean I knew you could do it…I just wanted you to be ok."

I shrugged. "I know and I appreciate that so much, but I think we all have to get used to it. This is my life now and I want you guys to know I'm always willing to help. What good is a superpower if you don't use it to help others?"

"Claire!" I heard a guy's voice yell from the crowd. "There she is!"

Suddenly we were swarmed by the crowd, patting me and Lt. General Gray on the back and shaking our hands. Andy and one of the taller baseball boys grabbed and lifted me up on their shoulders, while the rest of the team and passengers gathered around us. Baseball bats clanked on the ground and the crowd began to jump up and down.

"Claire! Claire! Claire!" They yelled in unison.

I looked down at all their faces and smiled. "Wow! Thank you guys!" I yelled at the top of my lungs. I had never felt so much love and gratitude. I reached down and shook their hands as tears began streaming down my cheeks. This was so surreal.

THIRTY-SEVEN

THE NEXT AFTERNOON Johnny and I stood in the beautiful foyer of the Shack, surrounded by thousands of glowing lights and all our close friends and family. My timeless, but simple princess wedding gown sparkled in the lights, while Johnny looked the role of my prince in his navy blue tux. My heart fluttered in excitement as we exchanged vows and I became Mrs. Angel.

Johnny took both my hands as he began his vows. "My sweetest Claire Bear, Saturday night, July 15th, 2017 I had plans to stay in my barracks and study for a flight test I had coming up, but thankfully my good friend Shawn here, talked me into going out for a while. I think about that day and I thank God with every breath I take that I agreed to go with him, because I just can't imagine having never met you. You have made my life complete and are my every happiness." He smiled mischievously at me. "I know our life together is going to be far from normal, but at least you're not boring (he winked) and I look forward to every twist and turn. I want you to know I'll always be there to catch you and protect you and cheer you on no matter what we may face. I love you and I'm so grateful you love me too."

I gasped at how sweet that was. The perfect wedding vows. And now it was my turn. My eyes were brimming with tears. How could I even speak after that? I took a deep breath and squeezed his hands tighter. The room was so quiet and I closed my eyes quickly to focus and chase the tears away.

"Johnny…I can't imagine this life without you. You are truly the most admirable and kindest man I have ever known. You have become my best friend, my confidant, my protector, my calm in the storm and believe it or not, the best thing that has *ever* happened to me. Because of you my life has changed for the better in every way imaginable and has become something only dreams are made of. I can't wait to come home to you everyday and take care of you and love you for the rest of my life."

"Thank you," he whispered.

The rest of the ceremony flew so fast. Before I knew it, Lt. General was saying "I present to you Mr. and Mrs. Johnny Angel. Johnny, you may kiss your bride."

Johnny leaned down and kissed me for the thousandth time, but the first time as Mrs. Angel. I was on top of the world.

S̸N̸

Somehow none of my family and friends were aware of what happened the night before and neither Johnny nor I showed any signs of fatigue. We were both riding high on adrenaline for today and after what had happened last night.

Later that night at the officer's club, as we danced and celebrated with our family, Janey approached me while I talked with Johnny's parents.

"Excuse me dad and mom," she interrupted us, grabbing my arm. "But can we borrow Claire for a second?"

"Sure," they laughed, as she pulled me away and across the dance floor where my sister's and friend's were waiting, all huddled together. Janey stuck me right in the middle and they enclosed a circle around me.

Tessa pushed her phone in my face to show me a photo of myself on Instagram, sitting on the shoulders of the baseball players surrounded by the crowd, with the plane in the background. I immediately recognized the profile photo of the coach that helped me on the plane last night. This was his Instagram post and I was impressed. He was a very talented photographer. I knew mom would want this one for her scrapbook of my adventures.

"Wow...that's a great pic," I said nervously, then was quiet for a moment while they all gave me the death stare.

Alicia put her hands on her hips. "Is this where you went last night? You're 'late night meet up' with Johnny?"

I couldn't help but crack a guilty smile in her direction.

My mind went back to the day at the mall when she first discovered my tatt on my arm and the motherly scolding she gave me. I knew what was coming. She was so dramatic, but protective and I loved her for it.

"I didn't *lie*. It was late and Johnny was there," I defended myself.

No one said anything, but stared intently at me waiting for more info.

"They needed help," I tried again, meekly.

Tessa ignored me and began reading the post. "Tonight myself and the passengers of flight 114 were given a second chance of life, thanks to the heroic bravery of this girl. Thank you Claire, for risking your life to save the lives of 202 total strangers. What a crazy night we had together. I feel like I've been raised from the dead."

"You got tangled up in a hostage situation?" Darcy asked, looking over Tessa's shoulder and reading the rest of it.

I shrugged. "You guys, I'm fine. Everyone's fine and safe on the ground and that's all that matters."

"Claire, you could have been killed!" Kass gasped. "And the night before your wedding?"

"But I'm here and I'm fine," I said calmly. "Seriously, they're not going to throw me into something I can't get myself out of." I cleared my throat and spoke more firmly. "This is my life and who I am now…and I love you guys, but you just have to accept it."

Alicia let out an over exaggerated sigh and then squeezed me tight. "We're just glad you're ok Claire, but

I don't think it's something we can ever get used to, if that's what you're saying."

I hugged her back. "I appreciate that and I understand, but I had to help."

All the girls squeezed in for a big group hug as the DJ's voice boomed over the speaker.

"Okay everyone! If you could clear the floor, it's time for the Father of the Bride dance!"

My heart sank as I looked at the shocked faces of my sisters.

"Someone must have forgotten to tell him," Lexi whispered in the awkwardness of the moment.

"It's ok," I gulped and looked around the room for my mom. I worried that might hurt her, but we soon locked eyes and she smiled at me sympathetically. Suddenly I felt a soft tap on my shoulder.

"Is it ok if I fill in?" Zhao asked, reaching out his hand for mine.

I smiled in relief, as he took my hand and led me to the middle of the dance floor. "Always to my rescue," I said, as he softly wrapped me with his right arm and took my right hand with his left.

"Of course," he smiled back as Louis Armstrong's 'What A Wonderful World' filled the ballroom. "I'll always be here for you Claire. We're SuperNova, remember?"

"I remember," I said, trying not to cry. We danced in silence for a moment, then I asked, "You know what the best part of being a SuperNova is Z?"

"Ummm…free vacations on the island?" He smirked.

"Close," I laughed. "But no, it's knowing how much I'll get to see of you now. I was afraid of never getting to see you and I can't imagine not having you in my life all the time."

This time Zhao was the one to blink back tears. "Same here," he gulped. "And Claire, I just want you to know how happy I am for you. I got to know Johnny well yesterday and he really is a nice guy."

"Thanks," I said, looking over at Johnny who smiled back at us. "But when did you get alone time with Johnny?"

"Oh, we had to go over some last minute stuff," he said, nonchalantly.

We danced quietly again for a moment, while Zhao led me in a couple of twirls and guided us in a small circle inside the dance floor. I breathed a sigh of relief knowing what I said was true. He and Dr. Zhao were going to remain a huge part of my life, as I would be going to SuperNova island at least every other month now.

As the song came to an end, Zhao paused our dance and looked down at me. "I know I never met your dad Claire, but I know what he would say to you on this night. He would tell you first of all how much he loves you and secondly how very proud of you he is. What you did last night was just…just incredible Claire."

I squeezed his hand tighter. He was so sweet to me. "Thank you Zhao, but you know I couldn't have done it without you."

He nodded and smiled his appreciation. "Well, I know I'm not even a close second to your dad, but it was an honor to dance this one with you."

I hugged him tightly. "Thank you Z."

Johnny and I changed into more casual, comfy clothes like Corrin instructed us to do and then joined our friends and family outside who had formed two lines with big, bright sparklers that led to a waiting black SUV. At the end of the sparkling tunnel Johnny's parents, my mom and Major Silva were all waiting with big smiles.

I immediately wrapped my arms around my mom. "Thank you mom," I whispered in her ear. "Thank you for just always being here for me. I don't know what I would have done without you guys." I looked over at Major Silva who was smiling at us both.

My mom blinked back tears. "I'm always here and will always be here for you."

"We both are," Major Silva said, wrapping an arm around us.

Johnny reached his hand out to shake Major Silva's hand, while I kissed my mom's cheek and then gave a quick hug to Johnny's parents.

Everyone cheered as we turned around to wave goodbye, then climbed in back of the SUV. I couldn't have asked for a more perfect and magical night, but now the moment I had been waiting for was here-Johnny all to myself for the next five days.

"Where's Mr. Lucas?" I asked, looking around as the

door closed and locked behind us.

"He's taking a few days off," Johnny smiled and pulled me close to him. "Where we're going, he won't be needed."

"Where are we going?" I asked for the hundredth time.

He laughed. "You'll see Miss Impatient."

I leaned over and kissed his cheek. "That's Mrs. Angel to you Sir."

$$\mathbf{S_N}$$

Fifteen minutes later, the SUV pulled up to the port at Pearl Harbor. I looked around at the two large ships docked in for the night, one of them being coincidentally, the USS Chafee.

"What are we doing here?" I gasped as Johnny helped me out of the SUV and then grabbed our bags in back.

"This way Mrs. Angel," he said, heading toward the last dock where a mid-sized yacht lit up the dark water around it. I paused and caught my breath as I read the name of the yacht printed in bold navy blue letters.

"Welcome aboard the *SuperNova!*" the young man at the end of the ramp greeted us. "I'm Adrian and I'll be around if you guys need me ok?"

"Thank you so much," Johnny said and went ahead of me up the ramp.

I paused for a moment and stared at the young man. "Adrian the Aquila?" I whispered.

"Yes Ma'am," he chuckled. "And you are Claire the

Lynx."

"Yes I am," I smiled. "Thank you for your help last night. It put me at ease knowing you were in the water in case something went wrong."

"My pleasure and may I say you did an incredible job. I was able to follow everything on my radio."

"You may," I laughed and then looked up at the yacht behind us. "Does this belong to the island?"

"Kind of," he shrugged. "It's actually the Zhaos but you didn't hear that from me," he winked.

My eyes lit up in surprise. "You mean the Zhaos are letting us borrow this?"

"Yes. That's why we were a little late in arriving. Z wanted to get here at the beginning of the week but we hit some pretty rough storms and it threw us behind a couple of days."

"Oh," I said quietly, regretting how I treated Zhao yesterday for being late. Sometimes my impatience got the best of me. "Thank you Adrian. It's so nice to finally meet you."

"You're welcome…and Claire, welcome to the SuperNova family."

"Thank you for having me. I'm so excited to be a part."

Johnny was waiting for me at the top of the ramp. He reached for my hand and gently helped me aboard. "Isn't this incredible Claire?" he said.

"It's unreal," I gasped, as he took me in his arms and kissed me sweetly.

"This way," he said, grabbing my hand and leading me

around the deck to the back of the yacht and down a small flight of stairs to a narrow hallway.

"How do you know your way around already?" I laughed.

"I had to pop in yesterday with Zhao for clearance."

The horn softly blared outside as the engines began to roar to life. Johnny opened the door to a spacious, elegant suite complete with a master bath. The beautiful two tone colors of sea blue and pale sand blended perfectly together to match the sailor decor.

"We're staying here?" I asked, dropping my stuff and jumping on the soft bed. I melted into it and Johnny soon joined me.

"Yeah, but don't unpack."

My heart sank. "You mean we're not staying here?"

Johnny rolled over and wrapped me in his arms. "Well, just for tonight," he whispered. "But trust me on this one, Claire Bear."

"Ok, I trust you," I sighed.

"This is the most comfortable bed I've ever laid on. I'll be asleep before you know it," Johnny said, winking at me.

THIRTY-EIGHT

I WOKE EARLY the next morning, too excited to sleep any longer. My heart skipped a beat as I looked over at my husband (I still couldn't get used to that) who was sound asleep, laying on his tummy. I stared at his sweet face, in disbelief that we were married. My flying power was a complete blessing, but it didn't even compare to the excitement and joy that Johnny brought to my life.

I slid over closer to him, making sure to touch every inch of my skin with his. He in return, wrapped his arm around me and pulled me closer, half asleep. I couldn't blame him. We didn't get much sleep last night and while my SuperNova body seemed to get by with very little sleep, Johnny always made sure to get his full 8 hours.

"I love you Claire," he said quietly.

My heart melted. "I love you too Johnny, so much," I

whispered.

I lay quietly beside him for a while as he dozed back to sleep. We were both wiped out from the last two nights, but the excitement in my heart far outweighed my exhaustion.

Outside the winding down of the engines caught my attention. I slipped out of bed and tiptoed to the porthole window to see where we were, but unfortunately there was just water all around.

"What are you looking at?" Johnny asked, rolling over slowly in bed.

I pointed outside. "The engines slowed down. I was just trying to see where we are."

"Ok Snoop Dogg," Johnny laughed, pulling his arms high above his head for a long stretch. "Come here."

I jumped back in bed with him and snuggled up close. "Are you tired?" I asked.

"Well, you almost killed me last two nights, but no I'm fine," he smiled and kissed my forehead, as my cheeks blushed a bright red.

"I would say sorry... but I'm not," I smirked, then sat up beside him. "So, are you going to tell me where we are now?"

"Nope," he yawned, his eyes heavy. "You'll see when we get there."

"But Johnny..."

"No Claire. I'm sorry, but you're going to learn to be more patient," he teased.

"Starting today."

I picked up my pillow and knocked him softly on the head. "Fine," I huffed. "I'm going to jump in the shower."

I took a quick shower, then towel dried my curls and let them dry naturally the rest of the way. I put on some sunscreen and just a little lip gloss and mascara, then slipped on my favorite yellow short romper.

Johnny was still sleeping soundly on the bed when I came out of the bathroom. The sun was just rising and it was only 6.

I decided to go up on deck and do a little investigating. I slipped out the door, down the dimly lit hallway and up the stairs to the galley door that led to the deck. I opened it slowly and a bright warm sunbeam quickly pierced the dimness, warming my body 10 degrees instantly. Outside the thick salty air filled my lungs and I took a long deep breath soaking it all in.

I stepped onto a bright white deck. Above us a dozen seagulls circled the boat squawking loudly. Land must be somewhere near, I assumed. I followed the narrow open walkway to the front of the SuperNova, where a large deck opened up to a sitting area and several dining tables covered by large beautiful bamboo umbrellas. This yacht was so classy and beautiful, I couldn't imagine how much it cost.

"Good morning Ma'am," I heard a voice behind me.

"May I get you something to drink?" A waiter dressed in a crisp white uniform with the letters *SN* embroidered on the lapel, smiled brightly at me.

"Sure," I said. "May I have a water please?"

"Of course."

I watched as he disappeared through a door behind a small bar tucked under the covered portion of the deck.

The sound of water splashing caught my attention and I went to the bow of the yacht. Down below a pod of dolphins circled, playfully jumping in and out of the Pacific. My mind went back to my island and how much fun I had swimming with the dolphins. Every night for the past few months, I had fallen asleep imagining myself there. What I wouldn't do to go back.

The dolphins chirped loudly again, closing my island thoughts.

"Oh, so you're going to be like that?" A male voice laughed from below the deck.

I stood up and leaned over the rail to see where it was coming from. To my surprise Adrian the Aquila shot out of the water and back in, mimicking the dive of the dolphins with perfect precision. I eagerly waited a few minutes for him to resurface and when he finally came up it was with one of the dolphins. I smiled as he gently held the dolphin's face in his hands and kissed him on the cheek.

"Alright, I'll see you guys later," he said, swimming toward the yacht.

I sat down on the deck chair quickly, not wanting to

look like a gawker, since I knew what it was like to be gawked at myself. Adrian quickly scaled the ladder on the side of the yacht and bounced up on the deck grabbing his towel.

"Claire!" he smiled, surprised to see me. "You caught me!"

"Yeah," I giggled. "I didn't want to interrupt your love fest with the dolphins."

Adrian came over and joined me at the table. "Oh you saw that!"

"It's ok," I winked. "I've had a few love fests with them myself. I would be in the water all the time if I could. I can't imagine the view from below."

"The ocean is truly one of the most beautiful places on the earth," he agreed, "but I can't imagine your view from the sky."

"Oh, the view from up there is breathtaking," I sighed, as the waiter returned with my water. "How long can you stay under?"

"So far, I'm up to an hour, but I just swam in from the mainland this morning and that was all surface swimming."

I did a double take. "You just swam here from Oahu?"

"Yep. I would have left last night with you guys, but I had to meet with the Zhaos before they headed back to the island. I'm kind of like the captain of the SuperNova. I'm in charge of getting it safely back to the island and pretty much anything that goes on with it."

I was stunned. "So…you just swam all night?"

Adrian smiled at me, clearly amused. "Yeah. I prefer swimming at night. Less eyes watching, as I'm sure you can relate."

I nodded my head silently, imagining him casually walking into the ocean and swimming off into the night to catch up with us.

His eyebrows shot up in surprise. "Oh, that impresses you? I impressed the girl who can fly. That's some feat!"

"I am impressed," I laughed, "Plus it's nice to meet someone who shares my…my…weirdness?" I couldn't think of a word to describe us.

"Gift Claire," he corrected me. "It's not weird and it's not a curse. It's a gift and we are lucky enough to own it."

I nodded in agreement. "Touche'."

Adrian and I talked for the next half hour about our gifts, as we now called them and how we discovered them. Like me, he was only in high school when he realized he was different, but it wasn't until he hit his mid twenties that he was linked to the SuperNova family.

"You're lucky to have their support early," he told me. "It can be pretty lonely trying to fit a square life into a round world, especially when you're young. You never quite fit in but you adjust accordingly."

"I'm definitely a square all the way around," I laughed. "Adrian, can I ask you something?"

"Sure."

"How did you tell your family? I mean, I'm going to tell Johnny all about being a SuperNova this week and I want to explain it right."

Adrian smiled at me sympathetically as if he knew exactly what I was feeling. "Claire, there is no wrong way. No matter how you tell him, he loves you unconditionally and he's going to stand by you no matter what."

I don't think Adrian will ever understand how his words encouraged me on this day. From that moment on all my fears of what Johnny thought of me being other worldly melted away. In fact, now I couldn't wait for alone time so I could finally get it off my chest.

"Good morning." I immediately recognized his deep voice behind us.

"Good morning," Adrian said, standing up to greet him. "How did you sleep my friend?"

"So good," Johnny said, stealing a wink at me while I smiled bashfully.

"Hello husband," I smiled, getting up to hug him.

Johnny reached down and kissed my forehead. "Hello my wifey." He then turned to Adrian and reached out to shake his hand. "How's it goin' Adrian?"

"It's all good. Congratulations man. I'm so happy for you guys."

"Thank you," we both said in unison.

"We must be getting close," Johnny said, looking over my head and to the south.

"Close to what?" I asked, following his gaze and then up on my tiptoes to see over the side deck. I gasped and ran to the bow of the deck as a small island came into view. I recognized it immediately as the island I was forced to hide on the night the helicopter had chased me back to my island from Oahu.

I turned to Johnny, tears brimming my eyes. "Johnny, are we going to," I paused to catch my breath "to my island?"

"You mean Claire Island?" He smiled at me and pulled an envelope from his back pocket.

"Claire Island?" I repeated. I took the envelope and opened it. In it was an Air Force map of the entire Pacific Island region, with my little island clearly marked off by itself. "Claire Island," I whispered again as I read the name stamped beside it.

"Named in honor of you and now officially property of SuperNova Enterprises," Adrian winked at me.

"Seriously?" I said, as I sat down on the bench lining the side of the deck. It was so overwhelming. I would have access to the island the rest of my life.

"What's up with that island?" Johnny laughed, nodding in its direction as we sailed by.

"Long story," I laughed, as I wiped away a tear.

"Well, I have plenty of time to listen this week," Johnny smiled, sitting beside me and wrapping his arm around me.

Adrian looked down at his waterproof wrist watch. "We'll be reaching the docking point in about 30 minutes, so you guys might want to grab your stuff and meet here in about an hour. We'll have lunch and then you can boat the rest of the way there."

"Thanks Adrian, really, thank you guys so much," Johnny said, standing up again embracing him in a quick bro hug.

"On behalf of the Zhao's it's their pleasure," Adrian smiled.

Zhao's sweet smile flashed across my mind. I could never repay him for his kindness to me.

THIRTY-NINE

AN HOUR LATER, Johnny and I were on a small boat full of supplies for the week, gliding over the calm waters of the Pacific. In the distance I could see the top of my island slowly rise above the waterline.

"There it is!" I yelled above the purr of the engine, as he turned the wheel towards the island. I went over and stood by him wrapping my arms around his waist. "I want to go up, if it's ok with you," I said. "It's been so long."

"Sure," he smiled.

"I'll be back before you dock!" I exclaimed, reaching up and kissing him on the cheek.

"Ok," he laughed. "Be careful."

I went to the bow of the boat then turned around, blew him a kiss and shot into the warm ocean air. I looked below at Johnny who was blocking the sun with his hand as he watched me fly above the water. I scanned the vast ocean for any signs of other boats, but there was nothing except miles of empty ocean. A little to the north I could see the SuperNova anchored, awaiting our return at the end of the week and just to the south, my beautiful lush green and brown island popping out of the bright blue water.

I still couldn't believe it. "Claire Island," I repeated to myself, as I flew over. Everything looked the same way I had left it on the north side, but as I approached the treeline on the south beach something new peeked out from among the thick jungle brush. Just before the beach opened up a brown thatched roof, barely visible from the sky dotted a small clearing in the jungle. I landed on the south beach, then made my way up a narrow cleared path to investigate.

My heart skipped a beat as I neared the end of the path. There sat the cutest little cottage I had ever seen. Beside it was something that looked like a tall pole with a big fan on top blending in with the palm trees. It was so camouflaged I hadn't seen it from the sky.

I walked up the wooden steps and onto a small bamboo porch and inside. A bright coral colored couch and matching love seat along with a modest flat screen TV and fireplace filled the small living room area. Directly beside that was a pale yellow and brown kitchen with a small bamboo table and all the essentials needed for cooking. The two bedrooms in the back of the hut were tiny too, but somehow still managed to fit full size beds with space left over. Each bedroom had floor to ceiling windows and french doors that led to a long balcony that stretched the entire backside of the house. Squeezed in between was a full bathroom. It was just enough to be comfortable, yet go unnoticed to anyone passing by.

I quickly left the hut and shot back into the sky making sure I kept my promise to be back on the boat before Johnny docked it. I landed back on the bow just as he approached the island.

"You look really happy," he smiled as I squeezed in beside him and he pulled me close.

"It's just unreal," I said, as he leaned down and softly kissed me.

"I can't wait to finally see it all. Just tell me where to go Mrs. Angel."

I guided him around to the south side beach, where he docked the boat by my favorite sunbathing rock. "I thought you said the cave was on the north side?"

"We're not camping in the cave," I smiled and took his hand.

We walked up the tiny path to the hut. "Oh wow," Johnny said looking up at the tall fan thing that was spinning in the breeze. "It has a wind generator and everything."

"Is that what that is?" I asked, looking up at it.

"Yeah," he laughed, walking closer and knocking on its metal surface making a pinging noise. "How brilliant to make it look like a palm tree."

I grabbed his hand. "Come look inside!"

I bounced up the stairs and flung open the door. "Just

a minute!" Johnny said scooping me up and carrying me through the door. "If we're gonna do this, we're gonna do it right."

Later that evening, Johnny and I packed a picnic and walked to the west beach. I showed him the tree where I had carved our initials, then we laid out a blanket to watch the sunset.

"I can see now why you love this place so much. It's just beautiful," he sighed.

"I can't believe you're finally here with me. You don't know how many times I've dreamed of this moment and now you're actually here."

"I'll always be here, Claire."

I stared at him for a moment. I hoped that was true, especially with what I was fixing to lay on him, but now was as good of a time as any. "Johnny, I have something I need to tell you."

He squinted his eyes and smiled in amusement. "Oh no. That's never a good thing," he laughed, then grabbed my hand. "You know you can tell me anything."

I took a deep breath. "I know, but you better buckle your seat belt for this one."

Johnny's emerald eyes pierced my heart. "Shoot," he said simply.

I had been waiting for this moment and didn't even take a breath. "I'm part Alien," I said bluntly. "I mean…

what I mean is, I have a foreign DNA in my body. Alien as in, it doesn't exist here on earth, except in a very small percentage of humans."

I stopped and looked at Johnny who didn't seem bothered at all, so I continued, the words tumbling out. I told him about the Zhaos, the island, my new SuperNova family, and the origins of my super power. When I at last finished, Johnny gave me his cute little smirk I loved so much.

"You think I didn't know any of that?"

"What do you mean?" I asked, confused.

"Silva was Kearney's best friend, Claire. We spent a lot of late nights talking and just assumed this is what it would all come down to."

I was dumbfounded. "And you're ok with it? What about our kids? What if they are the same as me?"

"I want them to be the same as you Claire. You are amazing and I love you. All of you, whatever you are and the rest we'll figure out. We have the rest of our lives to figure it out, kids and all."

I placed my hand softly against his cheek. "I love you, Johnny."

That night, when Johnny was fast asleep, I slipped out of the hut and made my way to the moonlit beach. The waves splashed softly against my feet as I walked on the warm sand and looked at the millions of stars above. They were so brilliant and bright without the competition of the city lights. I had to go up.

I walked to the edge of my sunbathing rock and shot in the air as my favorite flying song *"Meet Me Half Way"* by Kenny Loggins began to play. I stopped at just 100 feet above the island, where I could still hear the waves and the tropical wind whistling through the palms.

I did a 360 and soaked in the moment. "You're the most blessed girl in the world, Claire," I whispered to myself as I thought about the last few years.

What if Alicia and I had not gone to the fairgrounds that warm summer night? I would have not met Johnny, which means I would have never got cut by the glass that infected me with the pink juice that gave me my superpower. I would have never joined the Air Force, met Zhao, or had any clue that I was a SuperNova. Just even thinking about it gave me chills. What I thought was a tragic event had turned into the best thing that could ever happen to me. I couldn't imagine my life any other way.

Out of the corner of my eye, a bright light caught my attention. From the east, a blue and yellow shooting star rumbled across the sky, temporarily lighting up the ocean below. My heart fluttered in appreciation. I had a super flying power, the world's most perfect husband, my family and friends, my SuperNova family...and unbeknownst to me, a new little life starting inside of me.

THE END

About the Author

Cynthia L. McDaniel is a Clarksville, Tennessee native, who resides in Northwest Indiana. When not writing, she enjoys spending time with her family, running, swimming in the ocean and vacations anywhere that involves a beach.

Super Nova is Cynthia's fourth and final novel in the Sky Walker series.

Cynthia loves to connect with her readers and other authors as well. You can find her on Goodreads, on Facebook @CynthiaLMcDanielauthor, on Instagram @cynthialmcdanielauthor, or TikTok @ cynthialmcdanielauthor.

Hi There!

Thank you so much for reading *Super Nova*, the fourth and final book in my Sky Walker Series! I hope you enjoyed it! I had the best time writing it. I don't know if other authors feel this way, but I had a hard time saying goodbye to Claire and all my characters in this saga. I've spent the last seven years of my life with them!

All four books in my Sky Walker Series are available on Amazon. If you would be so kind as to go there and leave a review, I would really appreciate it. Reviews help Indie authors like me tremendously!

I feel so honored that you would take the time to read my books and give me the opportunity to entertain you. Thank you again. I love to connect with my readers, so please feel free to reach out to me if you have any questions or would just like to chat!

XOXO,

Cynthia

www.ingramcontent.com/pod-product-compliance
Lightning Source LLC
Chambersburg PA
CBHW030548180626
46816CB00005B/1457